Hepu Muzz
How To Save Your Own Planet

Lilia Wakeman

Published by Green Pearl Press
www.greenpearlpress.com

Cover art inspired by a bas-relief from Angkor Wat
Cover art by Jill Cardinal
Cover design by Jane Canning
Interior design by S.E. Williams

Check out the map of the Cave at www.greenpearlpress.com!

ISBN: 13: 978-1480132696
10: 1480132691

Visit Lilia Wakeman on the Web! www.greenpearlpress.com

Printed in the United States of America

For all the dreamers

CHAPTER ONE

Muzz crouched by the window of a cramped observation room peering at the gloom that shrouded The Planet. Drifts of snow and soot outside caked its bleak terrain. She aimed her lantern through the darkness at the Cave's snow-choked mouth.

If only there was someplace to go, she thought. She pressed a hand to her forehead, shut her eyes, shook her head.

What do I feel? Not confused. Confused was what I felt in Month Eight when Hepu Dorne ridiculed me in front of all the Highers, she thought. That day she had said, "The sky is getting lighter."

"Impossible!" Hepu Dorne had chortled, his eyes sweeping the room. "Am I right, class?" Confused by the snickers around her, Muzz had lowered her eyes. She was glad not everyone had laughed.

Hepu Dorne had said, "Class, remind Muzz, why did wise Whitford bring us by rocket ship to The Planet?"

"For air and water and warmth inside the Cave," they answered in unison.

"And was there light?" he asked in an intimidating voice, staring straight at Muzz.

She joined in to avoid his wrath. "Nooooo, no light," they all replied.

"Then what was here for us?"

"The underground stream," they said.

Recalling how confused she had felt that day, Muzz tried to calm herself with a chant from Whitford's Wisdom: "...for **Whit**ford, **be**ing **wise**, knew **what** from **what**." *There's no doubt that Whitford was wise. When the earth lost its hold on life, he did understand and did know what to do,* Muzz told herself.

She loved the underground stream, its inviting flow along one side of the Cave's Great Hall. She appreciated the way it powered grow lights for the cultivation enclosures, and watered them season after artificial season just as Whitford planned.

It would be wrong to blame wise Whitford for our harsh life. What good fortune that he brought us here when the earth turned hot and dry. How kind he must have been!

Muzz shivered and took a banana leaf pouch she had sewn herself from the hem of her shawl.

She pulled out a card, yellow with age, that the pouch kept safe and dry. In the dimness, she could make out a dainty crimson bird perched on a green bough. The bird had a tuft of fluff on its head she had learned in Lessons was called a 'crest.'

In the background, light poured from the windows of a cabin tucked in a quilt of clean white snow. She remembered her father giving the card to her when she was small and saying he had found it in Book Storage. He had opened the card and read it to her.

"Wish you were here," it said. "Merry Christmas to all you dear ones. Love, Millie."

As she studied the card her eyes softened and she breathed more gently. She reread its message. She had heard about Christmas in Lessons. *But who is this Millie and whom was the message for?* When she asked her father recently, he shrugged and said he did not know.

Shadows flickered on the cramped walls and ceiling of the observation room. A pearl of water way up high began a long, slow trickle to a glistening stalagmite on the floor.

At Lessons, Hepu Dorne warned the Higher Form students against "weak thinking," which was forbidden. He told them to avoid fears, misgivings, longings, and *anything* that caused them. He put the observation window off limits for Muzz because of the ups and downs of her emotions. And yet she carried the card, peeked at it, and let herself wonder. And she sneaked to this window whenever she could to peer out at the dark, frozen world.

It was almost time to return to Lessons. She returned the card to its pouch, and slipped that back into the hiding place in her shawl. Then she turned her attention to chatter wafting from the Great Hall. It came from Lower Form children playing hopscotch on their break, or fetch with the yellow Lab pups. Their giggles were punctuated by deeper tones from her classmates in the Higher Form. The voices of the males among them, including her brother Chell, had begun to change.

Muzz heard muffled footsteps and turned to find the froosey forehead and bright hazel eyes of her best friend, Tendra, rising from the stairwell. To Muzz, Tendra looked appealing in a way she could not quite explain. Was it the special smoothness of her froose? Her eye-crinkling smile?

Tendra whispered, "What are you doing up here? You'd better come down before Hepu Dorne sees you're gone."

"Hepu Dorne, Hepu Dorne... I wish he'd — I don't know what."

Tendra eyed Muzz in a serious way. "He annoyed you much this morning, didn't he."

Is annoyance forbidden? Muzz thought. She shrugged. "No more than usual." She turned back to the window to avoid Tendra's gaze.

That morning, the Higher Form watched a film called *It Happened One Night* in which a 'woman,' as adult female humans had been called, ran off during her wedding ceremony without saying "I do" to the groom in order to marry someone else. The bride had dark eyes, fine plump cheeks, her frooseless face as pale and soft as a stone warn smooth by the underground stream. She made quite a stir rushing off with her bridal veil billowing behind her while a crowd of wedding guests milled around her father's rose garden in consternation. The garden was far more lavish than Muzz had ever imagined them to be.

After that scene, Hepu Dorne switched off the film to discuss with overblown amusement the woman's "fickle nature" and the depths of "human folly." He said it had been filmed in 1922 B.W. — Before Warming, but that even then the humans had displayed their unfortunate capacity for waste and greed: the man and woman in the film burned gallons of the fuel gasoline to move their thirsty auto through miles of lush, woodsy countryside. Though Muzz had been taught to dislike most humans, and though she tried to see them through disdainful eyes, she envied the sweetness of their freedom. The adventuresome young bride-to-be and the beauty of her world fed that envy.

Envy was acceptable, though Muzz was sure no one would choose to feel it. She cast her eyes down. *Not confusion, not mere annoyance, not even envy, but something new,* she told herself.

And at that moment neither the easy banter of the children down in the Great Hall nor the presence of her closest friend quelled her odd new feeling about Hepu Dorne and his deluge of rules and opinions.

Tendra began tickling Muzz from behind, and she whirled around with a cry.

Tendra cupped a hand over Muzz's mouth. "Shhhhh! We'll get caught. I mean, *you* will," she giggled.

Scowling, Muzz peeled Tendra's hand away. "Don't tell me Hepu Dorne didn't annoy *you.*"

"Not much. But then I'm not the first to turn thirteen." Tendra said this in a sing-song teasing tone.

Thirteen was the age of betrothal for every female in the Tribe, and Muzz's thirteenth birthday was just days away.

"Hoar ice and wilted greens, don't remind me!" Muzz chided. She had plenty more to say on the subject of betrothal, none of it respectful.

"Nice ursp," said Tendra.

—
3

Creative outbursts of that sort were called 'ursps' in the Hepunese dialect, and Muzz liked to make up her own.

"It was okay," Muzz shrugged, her tone still cranky.

"Hmmm," said Tendra.

The chime calling them back to Lessons cut their talk short. When Tendra tickled her again, Muzz fought off a smile.

"You shouldn't get so riled up," Tendra warned as they went downstairs. "You know where *that* leads. To weak thinking and—"

"If I didn't know you better I'd think you were part of the problem," said Muzz, tickling back.

The two rushed past a cave guard armed with a sharp spear and entered the Lesson Chamber just as the last chime sounded for afternoon classes. They sat on the rough rock floor in the third row on the right reserved for the three females in their thirteenth year — Muzz, Tendra, and Fluelle, who ignored their arrival.

"All right, my young Hepu friends," Hepu Dorne intoned with a distinct nasal twang. Like many adult males, his face looked hardened, his shoulders somewhat stooped. He eyed the class imperiously down the length of his nose. "Sit properly, pick up your boards, and let us continue reciting this week's segment of *Our Story*." Muzz and the thirty-five other Highers reached into their sacks and brought out slatted boards, the same boards used on Day Nine each week to wash their families' clothes in the underground stream.

Then they all adjusted the breeding beads they wore around their necks and folded their legs, females smoothing their silk wraparounds with care as their mothers bade them "to avoid distracting the young males." Muzz envied the easy silk jumpsuits of the males, a few shades darker than their froose. The wraparounds required too much attention to posture for her liking; so did tucking her legs to one side. Muzz tensed and pulled her shawl closer.

Hepu Dorne eyed the class severely from his stool and raised his director's baton. "Let's begin with what we have learned about 2013, D.W. so far," he ordered. "And *one*, and *two*, and *three*, and *four*, and *five!*" All of the Highers including Muzz began thrumming their boards in unison and chanting:

By **then** two **thous**and **twelve** had **come** and **gone**
with **hu**man**sens**ing **man**y a **fearful change**:
As **Alpine icecaps shrank**, torna**does**...

Muzz knew the segment by heart. By 2010, D.W. — During Warming — experts like Whitford were warning the humans that less than a decade remained to save the Earth from an irreversible spiral of damage. But some powerful leaders and others called their predictions jokes, lies, exaggerations. Worst of all were certain leaders of a tribe called the Ewesay.

In Lower, where they learned about the world Before Warming, the lesson segments had inspired Muzz. She marveled at the ways of humans, and sometimes secretly dreamed of joining them. But Higher Form segments were dismal, and knowing the end of the story made it painful to hear. So Muzz was not surprised when an eleventh yearling named Martrell who sat in the front row with the other two female elevens began yawning and twisting in her seat, or when the three male elevens across the aisle began acting the same.

"Hepu Martrell. Stop your incessant fidgeting at once!" cried Hepu Dorne. Martrell bit her lip.

"Tell me, my young friend, what is the matter? Can't you focus on what neeeeeeeeeds to be learned?" Everyone stiffened and a breathless silence filled the room. *This feeling I have burns,* thought Muzz.

She raised her hand and heard herself saying, "Why are we learning this?"

"*What* did you say?"

Muzz felt the burning surface to her velvet-like cheeks. She trembled at her impudence, but the fire inside spurred her onward.

"I — I want to know why we are learning this. What benefit is there for us, stranded forever on a planet so little like the earth, in learning these sorrowful details from the past?"

Hepu Dorne sucked in his breath and let the air flow slowly from his mouth. He looked almost ill. "We were harmed by the humans, our habitat destroyed. If it hadn't been for Whitford, we all would have died. We must never forget that." Hepu Dorne shook his finger. "We must observe the hideous humans and learn from their mistakes." He glowered at Muzz.

Muzz stared at Hepu Dorne. "Excuse my foolish question."

"Please," said Hepu Dorne. "Always use 'please' when you address me."

"Please," said Muzz. She clenched her teeth.

Hepu Dorne shot her a triumphant smile. "Questions are always welcome," he announced, "especially if they are *intelligent.* Isn't that right, my young Hepu friends?"

All the Highers replied in unison, "Yes, Hepu Dorne." Muzz mouthed the phrase without using her voice. *Anger,* she thought. *Anger is what I feel.*

Anger was forbidden.

Hepu Dorne raised his eyebrows and baton in one move, introduced a new verse about the worrisome plight of the Hepus.

Muzz knew it all by heart — how the Tribe had flourished deep in the Amazon Basin for eons untroubled by human affairs, and how wildfires had been unheard of in the rain forest until smoke, growing thicker each day, alerted them to approaching danger. The verse ended with the arrival of Dr. Whitford, the brave and gallant human who in his wisdom offered to take the Tribe "by metal bird" to Labrador on the first leg of a rescue mission. Whitford warned it would be cold where they were going, but promised furry, straw-colored beasts called Labrador Retrievers to entertain them and keep them warm. After careful thought the Hepu leaders — the Beacons — accepted Whitford's offer.

Sitting there Muzz wondered what Hepu Dorne would tell her parents, what else he would do, and where her forbidden anger might lead.

Finally the lines in praise of Whitford signaled the end of the verse: "...for **Whit**ford **in** his **wis**dom **un**der**stood**." Hepu Dorne sounded a chime, and the Highers rushed for their break.

Tendra grabbed Muzz's hand. "Hurry," she whispered, pulling Muzz toward the door.

"Not so fast, Hepu Muzz," called Hepu Dorne, "I need to speak with you. Alone."

Tendra sighed and left the chamber.

Muzz crossed to the instructor's platform. Tall for her age, she saw that with no platform she and Hepu Dorne would have stood eye to eye.

Looking down at her with his arms folded, he had a grim twist to his mouth. "Hepu Muzz, what is happening to you? Lately you have undergone some troublesome change."

He pushed his face in close and made his eyes unusually large.

Muzz gulped. "I'm not sure, sir. I AM different, but it isn't easy to explain or think about because—"

"Your reaction to the film this morning? You seemed to side with the *humans*, deliberately missing the point of our lesson. Can you explain that?"

Muzz pictured the young man and woman fleeing injustice, growing closer till they knew they did not want to part. She longed for some kind of chance in her life that involved a mysterious stranger. But a wall of darkness filled Hepu Dorne's eyes.

"No, sir. I cannot."

Hepu Dorne frowned in a way that could only be called menacing. He seemed to be staring at her breeding beads. She had to fight the urge to cover the beads with her hand.

"Well let me tell you, my young Hepu friend, I will not tolerate insolent behavior. Your parents will hear of this and, I am sure, act appropriately. In the meantime and for all your remaining time here, you will obey my instructions and accept my ideas and, whenever you cannot agree, keep mercifully still."

"As you say, sir," Muzz replied.

"There is something else. You turn thirteen in a few days. I am sure you are aware that I have a large say in the matter of your betrothal.

"Every female, betrothed at thirteen to a sixteenth-year male, *will marry him* exactly five years later on her eighteenth birthday. It is essential to the preservation of the Tribe that you agree to marry at the appropriate time whomever the Beacons and I choose for you. Our decision will be in the best interests of the Tribe. Those interests should not differ in the slightest from your own."

Muzz held back angry words. She conjured the film's lovely rose garden, imagined pressing her face in a cluster of blooms and breathing their spicy smell.

"Thank you, sir," she managed to say. "May I go?"

"One last thing." Hepu Dorne jabbed his finger into her shoulder. "For Whitford's sake, learn what from what!"

"Oh, I will, sir. I certainly will," she said, edging toward the door.

CHAPTER TWO

A chime sounded the end of the afternoon break, and Muzz slipped into her space on the floor. Her shoulder still hurt where Hepu Dorne had poked it, and she still felt the burning inside. She sat looking down at her hands, but whenever Hepu Dorne had his back turned, she could see from the corner of her eye almost everyone, including Tendra and her brother Chell, sneaking peeks at her.

Chell sat in the front row on the opposite side of the room with Jerith and Drent, the other two sixteenth yearling males who helped him oversee the class.

Muzz wanted to ask Chell, at least, to please ignore her. She wondered what he was thinking when he turned her way and what he would tell their parents. He often took her side in disputes, but sometimes his treachery surprised her.

Muzz considered the changes he was going through. He had always had their father's black scalp-hair, so different from hers or their mother's chestnut brown. At sixteen he was developing the firm jaw and piercing blue eyes of their father. Ebony face hair like his had begun to jut through the beige froose on Chell's cheeks and chin. *Is he starting to take on Father's sternness too?*

Something odd had happened to their whole family, especially to their father. She recalled how gentle he acted when he gave her the card with the red bird on it.

She was small then, and he lifted her onto a grottoette table, pulled the card from his jumpsuit pocket. When he showed her the picture and read the message to her, his voice sounded soothing as oatcakes fresh from the oven. He gave her a gentle squeeze, and asked, "Want to come with me and visit—?" But someone — maybe her mother — whisked her away.

That was her earliest memory. *Why has he changed? Nowadays he hardly ever smiles, and neither does Mother. Nowadays his voice isn't soothing. Nowadays they both seem grim.* Muzz had no idea why, and they never talked about it.

Finally the last chime of Lessons sounded and she grabbed her school sack, tried to hurry out. She had chores in the Tropical Cultivation Enclosure, and wanted to work alone, think. Luckily Chell left in the opposite direction with his best friend Jerith without even a glance at her. But Tendra was waiting in a nook at the far side of the Great Hall, and tried to drag Muzz in.

When she resisted, Tendra began walking beside her clutching her arm. "Tell me what happened with Hepu Dorne or I may have to torment you," she said cheerily.

"I'm in a horrible mood," Muzz replied. "I want to be alone." When Tendra persisted, Muzz sighed. "Okay, but you'll have to come with me to Tropical."

A drubbed up orange ball rolled across their path. One of the caveball teams had kicked it out of bounds, and Muzz stopped, scooped it up. She turned and saw sixteenth yearling Drent charging over. He slowed just long enough to grab it and rush back to his game.

"He's so rude," she whispered. Tendra rolled her eyes and nodded.

They left the Great Hall, heading along a tunnel just wide enough for two. Twelve tunnels in all branched from the Great Hall like spokes of a huge, wobbly wheel. Parts of the tunnels, hacked by early settlers, had a chiseled look, especially the grottoettes — rooms carved out for individual families, and containing sleeping ledges and dining tables. In other parts of the tunnels that were etched by nature over time, stalagmites and stalactites sprang from the floors and ceilings. This part was one of the ancient originals, and flickering lamps made the walls seem to slither and dance as the two females passed through.

Near the end the tunnel gradually rose higher, as if climbing an underground hill, and its walls took on the chiseled look. This section, hewn by Whitford's crew with pickaxe and shovel, led to a huge windowless hothouse on the surface of The Planet — the vast, steamy Tropical Cultivation Chamber — one of six chambers in all, each set up to grow certain crops, such as nuts, oats and quinoa, apples and pears, leafy vegetables, root vegetables, and so on. There was even a chamber devoted solely to silk production with mulberry trees and silk worms that produced all the yarn for knitting and weaving cloth that the Hepus required.

Inside 'Tropical,' as it was called, many rows of equatorial fruit trees basked under grow lights — the closest thing to sunlight The Planet had to offer, and the strongest light the two young females had ever seen. Emerging from the dim tunnel, they squinted at first.

Muzz had a fleeting urge to slip into the foliage and disappear, but she kept pace with Tendra. Passing the piva palms and breadfruits tended by Drent's cousin Jeeklo, they soon reached the center of Tropical where plantains sent up glistening fronds that formed a dense thicket. Beyond it, citrus trees soaked up the artificial light — oranges, lemons, tangerines, grapefruits. Muzz took care of plantains and their banana cousins, and row upon row of graceful, sturdy avocados. Citrus was Martrell's territory.

Muzz checked around, motioned to Tendra to follow, and crept deep into the plantains where they dropped to the carpet of soil and sat cross-legged, facing each other.

Muzz leaned close and told how Hepu Dorne had scolded and lectured her. By the time she finished, her eyes were brimming with tears. She said, "I'm angry." Her voice seemed to echo through the stillness, and Tendra gasped at the forbidden word.

"You're much pitiable," said Tendra, grasping her hands in a firm, kind way. "And he wants *you* to learn what from what? What a cockroach!"

"What a wasp," Muzz sniffed, wiping her eyes. Cockroaches, wasps, and other intruders in their world — hitchhikers on the spacecraft to The Planet — were captured and banished in a sealed-off place dubbed 'the Hole' full of pale weeds and stunted fungi. There they had to fend for themselves.

An image of Hepu Dorne pleading for mercy as he was shoved through the Hole door cheered Muzz some.

Tendra held her at arms length and looked at her. "Hepu Dorne is not what angers you most, is he. I mean, isn't this more about being betrothed?"

Muzz nodded and more tears tried to surface.

Tendra solemnly shook her head. "I don't get it, Muzz. What do you have against Jerith? He's kind and intelligent." She sighed and gazed into space. "Of course, I prefer your brother Chell. I'm hoping it'll be you and Jerith, me and Chell. Best friends with best friends, together forever."

Muzz grimaced. "Why should you have to hope? Chell prefers you. Why can't you simply *choose* each other? Why should our lives be so freezing controlled? There are two males on this whole frigid planet I'm allowed to marry!" She folded her arms. "And why should I have to get married at all?"

Tendra's jaw dropped. "You're questioning the productive life in our warm, safe Cave?"

"What's 'warm and safe' about every thirteen-year-old female being forced just five years later to marry whatever sixteen-year-old male a bunch of old codgers chose for her? I wish I could be that spunky human bride in the film even if she had no froose. I'd run off and shock them all."

Tendra looked shocked herself, which only made Muzz more insistent. "If I accept betrothal, I'll do it only because I must."

Tendra's threw up her hands. "'If?' You mean you might refuse? Acceptance is only a formality. Everyone accepts."

Muzz hunkered down and did not reply, and Tendra dropped limp hands to her sides. "Please don't refuse, Muzzy. It scares me to think what might happen."

They were facing at each other, not talking, when a nearby frond rustled. "Someone's here," hissed Tendra.

She held a finger to her lips and crawled noiselessly out, stood up, looked all around, gave an exaggerated shrug.

Muzz heard a thud behind her and jumped up. "Who's there?"

She riffled through rows of plants, peering into shadows, lifting long fronds. "What if that was Hepu Dorne? What if he followed us?"

Tendra covered her mouth to muffle a moan.

"We'd better get to work," Muzz whispered.

Tendra nodded, crinkled her nose. "I have three Lab runs today."

"Hail storms!" said Muzz. Everyone's least favorite chore was cleaning up Lab poop, but they all had to do it now and then. It went into a large sealed bin to be picked up once a week, processed for fertilizer.

"Nothing can be wasted in the Cave," Tendra said airily. It was one of the Ten Edicts they were made to memorize on their fingers and thumbs in Lower, and one of the few things she allowed herself to mock. "Nothing."

"Except our lives, except our lives," Muzz quipped.

Tendra cast Muzz a piercing stare. "Listen. Before you go home, stop by old Mrs. Whitford's. Sometimes I think *she* must know what from what about as well as Whitford did. See what *she* thinks you should do."

"Maybe..." Muzz replied. It was true that Mrs. Whitford, the only human still among them, might understand. *But is there really any way she can help?*

Tendra smiled. "She says she enjoys your 'little oddities,' remember? I think she really likes you, and she's much knowledgeable and wise."

"Hah! My oddities. Yeah, well... maybe before I go home to see what kind of trouble I'm in."

"Good," said Tendra. Pulling Muzz to her feet, she aimed her toward her tool shed and gave her a nudge.

Muzz put on a tattered space suit that some First Settler had worn on the way to The Planet. She pictured Mrs. Whitford sixty years younger wearing such a suit while speeding bravely through space with her revered husband and others. Word had it that she had overseen Hepus as they slept in suspended animation on the journey. Somehow in her nineties she still seemed youthful, strong, and daring. *Will Mrs. Whitford — the last living human on The Planet — find some way to sympathize with a thirteenth yearling female accused of weak thinking?*

Muzz climbed a stepladder and started pruning the brownish lower leaves of plantain trees and stacking them by the path. They would be dried and cured for mats, baskets, rugs, the soles of slippers and shoes. Nothing could be wasted.

Nothing could be picked or eaten by the Highers who tended the crops either. Their job was to cultivate fruit, period. So when she spotted a ripe cluster of reddish-brown plantains on the tallest stalk, Muzz knew she should report a ripening at once.

But instead of going for her clipboard to jot that down, she reached up, grabbed the thick stem of the cluster with one hand, slit it with the other. It thudded to the ground.

"Hot foots galore! Why did I do that?" Her mind raced. *I have to destroy the evidence. I'll eat every last one even though they're raw.*

She dragged the plantains into a dense thicket, slumped, pealed one, gobbled it, then another. The raw fruit was pulpy and tough to swallow. *What about the peels?* Someone would be sure to notice coarse, red peals in the mulch pile. *Am I the first food thief ever on The Planet? What will happen if I'm caught?* One thing was certain: There would be consequences.

Halfway through the third plantain her stomach started aching, but she crammed the rest of it into her mouth, chewed ferociously, managed to get it down. Then she started rocking back and forth, moaning. "Oooooh, oooooh. I'll never eat them all."

She lugged the rest to her shed where she planned to hide them under an old Lab hair cushion and eat a few each day. She would smuggle the peels to the rubbish bin in the main kitchen.

Muzz felt relieved. *If I'm not caught, the evidence will vanish in six or seven days.*

As she nudged the telltale fruit under a cushion with her foot, the dust she raised made her splutter. The door to the shed darkened with a tall figure lit from behind.

"What are you doing?" a deep voice asked.

"Hep— Hepu Dorne?"

The figure chuckled, stepped into the light. Muzz saw the pleasant, angular features and mahogany scalp-hair of her brother's best friend. "Jerith! Thank Whitford it's you."

Jerith, somewhat taller than Muzz, folded his arms and gazed at her with a mixed expression — friendly, stern, confused. "What are you up to?"

"I— I hacked off this bunch of plantains."

"And you did that because...?"

"By accident, sort of."

"Hmmm... 'Sort of?' Let me have a closer look."

Reluctantly Muzz lifted the cushion.

Jerith examined her handiwork. "So you're hiding it," he said. He studied the bunch for what seemed to Muzz a long time. "Three are missing."

"I— ate them." Jerith stared from her to the plantains and back. Then he clutched his middle, started to laugh. Muzz had to smile.

He flipped the bunch in question over, dusted it off. "Funny One, you never change. You've been a scrapper since you turned two."

"You remember that?"

"Sure. I was five then, and I played with your brother much." Jerith glanced around. "I have a better plan."

"What?"

"Before I tell you, I want to say one thing." He paused. "I — Chell and I — followed you and Tendra here. I don't feel right about it, but we eavesdropped."

"Blighted turnips! We thought someone was— What did you hear?"

"Everything."

"What do you mean 'Everything?'"

Jerith idly brushed more dust from the fruit. "I know you hate Hepu Dorne," he said with one swipe, "I know you don't want to be betrothed," he said with another, "Not even to me." He waited.

"I'm sorry" was all Muzz could say.

"Me, too." There was a heavy silence before Jerith roused himself. "Maybe that puny despot is going to give you to Drent anyway. He knows I care for you. It would be just like him to— "

"This is not about you," said Muzz. She searched for the right words. "It's about being... given. To anyone anytime." She scrunched up her face. "I'm not a thing to be passed from one owner to the next."

"Of course not. No one should be. But life in the Cave makes us... we struggle much."

"That's no excuse. Why should life be so full of rules?"

Jerith shrugged, his eyes filled with sadness. "Let's not discuss this anymore, okay? I just had to confess. And warn you."

"Warn me?"

"Chell is crunching icicles over your threat to disobey."

Muzz felt her eyes go wide.

"He wants a good assignment after graduation — a respectable Calling as an engineer. His grades are good enough. He's afraid you'll hurt his chances."

"Why should he be judged by what I do?"

"I don't know, but I'm sure he's right. Whitford knows what could happen to him." Muzz felt her face tighten.

"Enough said," Jerith told her. "Help me with these, will you?" He took out his knife, trimmed the three stumps of the missing plantains.

She gasped at his boldness.

Jerith shrugged. "I'm a veteran Harvester. Sometimes there are bad ones and I have to cut them off."

She relaxed.

"In fact, here's another, Funny One," he said, slicing.

"I can't eat any more and you know it."

Jerith's eyes twinkled. "It's for Mrs. Whitford. Tendra's right. Go see her. She has lived through much in many places. If anyone in this dank hole can understand you, she can."

Jerith gave Muzz a serious look, pocketed the plantain peels. "If I write this up right, no one will suspect." Then he broke into a grin. "Be sure to eat your supper tonight, or you'll arouse suspicion."

When she shuddered, he chuckled softly.

After he left, she changed into her silk wraparound, stashed Mrs. Whitford's plantain in her school sack, started for the tunnel.

CHAPTER THREE

Mrs. Whitford's was the last grottoette before the Cave's hot stream surged through a thick pipe onto the frostbitten surface of The Planet. From the Great Hall, Muzz followed the main tunnel downward beside the stream as it sang with a soothing gurgle. She breathed deeply of the cooler air — less humid than Tropical's — and arrived at Mrs. Whitford's in a better mood. She rang a bell hanging by the entrance.

"Just a moment," cried a surprisingly vigorous voice. The door opened.

There stood a tall, slender woman with pure white hair, round wire glasses, radically wrinkled skin, and clear hazel eyes.

Mrs. Whitford lit up when she saw Muzz. "Why, Muzzy, come in." She opened her arms to Muzz, who received her hug with only slight misgivings about the furless skin that disappeared into the sleeves of her worn silk cardigan.

Mrs. Whitford led her to a bench, where Muzz sat looking around with interest. Mrs. Whitford had a pale blue comforter filled with the feathers of large earth birds called geese. Once when Muzz was small, Mrs. Whitford let her run her hand over its gleaming silver-blue cover again and again to hear a soft whistling sound.

"That's because the cover's made of taffeta," Mrs. Whitford told her. Muzz longed to have a taffeta cover of her own.

Mrs. Whitford also had an ornate yellow teapot made of something called 'china,' though Muzz could not see how a teapot could be made from what she knew had been a powerful human tribe.

Then there was the painting on the rocky wall above Mrs. Whitford's sleeping ledge. It showed a woman in a long white garment and a man in black with an oddly tall, black hat. They were standing among rounded things Mrs. Whitford called 'umbrellas' and flowers and windblown flags, gazing over a wide expanse of water deep enough to look blue. A dark boat with three sails was gliding by. An older man with white chin hair sat watching the man and woman, and the boat. A closer look revealed another woman under one of the umbrellas, also watching.

Once in Lower, their class made paper sailboats and floated them in the underground stream. They blew hard to propel the boats, creating gentler wind than the kind outside the Cave. Muzz tried to imagine boats sturdy enough for passengers, a stretch of water deep enough for real boats to sail.

Muzz had seen enough films and photos in Book Storage to identify earthly oceans, gardens, even flags. She marveled at the dazzling colors in the sky, the clear reflections in the water. *Earth had so much light!* she thought.

Mrs. Whitford drew up her chair and sat facing Muzz. "What brings you here?"

Muzz took the plantain from her pocket and held it out.

Mrs. Whitford raised her brows. "To bring me this?"

"More to talk with you."

"It's been a very long time."

Though 'very' was not a Hepunese word, Muzz more or less knew what it meant. "I'm afraid I'm in *very* much trouble."

Mrs. Whitford nodded. "Hepu Dorne came to see me today."

"Was I the reason?"

"The main one." She cast Muzz a pensive glance, took up her knitting. Muzz felt sorry that the damp air and walls of the Cave chapped Mrs. Whitford's skin. She was forever knitting leggings and cardigans from silk yarn for protection.

"Hepu Dorne thinks I don't appreciate Lessons, and says I must learn what from what."

"I would like to hear what *you* think, dear."

"Mostly, I don't want to be betrothed."

15

"Mostly?" She dropped the knitting to her lap. "It was a mistake to space you and Chell the way we did. Now there are only two sixteenth yearling males you can possibly marry. Only two instead of three with the right breeding beads! Is that the problem?"

"The problem is I'm" — her voice fell almost to a whisper— "angry."

Mrs. Whitford closed her eyes and kept them that way. "Can you say why?"

"I don't want to be given away like a Lab hair mattress or a — a—"

"An ear of corn?" Mrs. Whitford's eyes flashed open.

"Yes. And there's more."

"Go on." Mrs. Whitford's voice, her face, her whole self seemed sympathetic.

"The Cave's a dark, unhappy place," said Muzz.

Mrs. Whitford nodded and took up her handiwork again. During the brief silence that followed, the grottoette began rattling and shaking, and an echo rumbled through the tunnel outside. For the few seconds it lasted, Muzz sat absolutely still and Mrs. Whitford put down her work, listened, looked around until it was over. "Another tremblor," she said, and resumed knitting with ferocious speed.

Usually harmless, tremblors like that came often enough so that Muzz, too, mostly ignored them.

"A dark, unhappy place," she repeated.

"And Hepu Dorne and the other adults make everything worse. I *hate* our Lessons; I *hate* the rules. All of them!" Saying this made Muzz feel somewhat better.

Mrs. Whitford dropped her knitting to her lap. "You're filling me with doubts. It *is* a cold, dark place. Our lives are *riddled* with rules. Sometimes I wonder if I — I should say 'we' — were right to bring you here."

Muzz felt shocked. "You question Whitford in all his wisdom?"

Mrs. Whitford shook her head. "Sometimes I think The Planet is way too unforgiving. This is so much harder than anyone expected."

"It is?"

Mrs. Whitford nodded, gazed wistfully into her painting.

"Is that a picture of you and Whitford in your youth?"

"Goodness no! It's a painting by the famous artist Claude Monet — a copy of it. He painted it at a place in France called Sainte-Adresse." She smiled wanly. "Mr. Whitford and I honeymooned there."

"You did?"

"We were very lucky."

"Because Whitford was a great scientist?"

"Because we lived in such a fragile, lovely world."

"That *was* lucky."

Mrs. Whitford's eyes through her spectacles looked weary. She threw out her arms. "Come here, Muzz. You need another hug."

She folded Muzz in a long, tender hug. Muzz could feel how surprisingly strong she still was. Afterward, holding Muzz at arms' length and searching her eyes, the old woman exclaimed, "My poor child! I have so little comfort to offer. You see," here she seemed to choose her words carefully, "there can be very few choices of any kind here. The Planet itself is so harsh. And remember how the humans' choices ruined what they had? Too many choices — especially in a place like this — can be dangerous."

"But humans were not all bad. *You* are human."

"Good? Bad? In the end it hardly mattered. Let's just say that rules for living are essential. That said, I don't think Hepu Dorne or the others use their best judgment in explaining the rules or carrying them out. I'll ask Dorne to soften his ways."

Muzz felt grateful for what Mrs. Whitford said. She decided to try harder to obey. She would accept betrothal, and do all she could to follow the path that the Tribe laid out for her. She told Mrs. Whitford so.

Mrs. Whitford took Muzz's froosey hands in her sturdy, frooseless ones and squeezed. "Trust that it's for the best. I can't change things here. I doubt anyone can. But you'll always have my sympathy and love. And don't forget your dreams. You're a powerful dreamer, and you'll always have that. I wish I could offer more!"

Why does she think that about me? With that Muzz went home for supper.

Each Hepu family had two parents and two children, a boy and a girl. 'Home' in the Cave meant a grottoette for four hacked with pickaxe and shovel into the wall of a residential tunnel. Inside each grottoette (about the size of a small bedroom) an electric lantern hung over a low table — a slab of rock carved higher than the floor. And in one wall two narrow bunks were hollowed from the rock, one for each child. A wider sleeping ledge for the adults was dug in the opposite wall. And for each family that 'fed' a Lab, which most families did, a padded dog pillow filled with the Lab's own hair, clean and covered in coarse silk, lay by the door.

To reach home from the Great Hall, Muzz followed her family's residential tunnel past a honeycomb of grottoettes, a communal kitchen, and a small lounge. Activity buzzed as families waited for their adult females to carry savory pots of stew from the kitchen for supper. On her way, Muzz saw Hepus waiting and chatting, or eating together around their low rock tables seated on Lab hair cushions of their own. Everyone knew her and some called out greetings. She wondered if even one among them had missed the news of her clash with Hepu Dorne.

When she entered her family chamber, she knew *they* had heard. Her father and brother Chell, seated at the table, ignored her. Her mother shot her a furtive glance while stirring the stew.

Only her enormous Lab Emily seemed glad to see her, yelping, leaping, wagging her entire body, not just her tail.

"Not now, Em. Go lie down," said Muzz. Emily slunk off, flopped on her pillow.

"When are you going to train that animal?"

"I keep trying, Father... Hello, everyone. Sorry I'm late."

There was silence as Muzz set her sack on her bunk and joined the family.

"Praise Whitford," her mother said with a tight smile, "the food is still warm." She ladled some stew into the bowls and handed them to Muzz who served first her father, then Chell, then her mother and herself.

In unison, they raised their spoons, voiced "Thanks to Whitford," and started to eat.

Still stuffed from the plantain debacle, Muzz dug her spoon into the stew and bravely took a bite. But her father put down his spoon, stared at her, and her spirit shrank. *Will my promise to Mrs. Whitford placate him?*

"I went to visit Mrs. Whi—," she began.

"Quiet!" Her father's tone was fearsome. "Your mother and I were called from work today by Hepu Dorne. Do you know why?"

" He told me he—"

"He says you've been disobedient and impudent, riling yourself at the observation window again, challenging his ideas and methods."

"Yes, well, I—"

Her father struck the table with his fist and Emily raced to the door barking.

"It's all right, girl." Muzz led her back to her cushion.

Her mother reached over and touched her father's arm. "Softly, please, Fentish." She gestured toward the door.

Her father scowled, but lowered his voice. "You've brought shame upon our family. That must stop. Do you understand?"

"I do, but I—"

"May I speak?" asked Chell. Muzz clenched her fists behind her back. *When do I get a chance?*

"Go ahead, son," said her father.

Chell turned to Muzz. "I have heard," he said with a knowing expression, "that you don't want to be betrothed."

Her mother's eyes bulged and she sucked in air. Her father shot her an intimidating stare and leaned forward. "Is that right?"

Muzz froze.

"I heard that." Chell set his jaw, frowned at Muzz. *Why couldn't he speak to me alone the way Jerith did?*

"And I hope, Father, that you'll make her accept betrothal to anyone the Beacons choose. Even if they choose a Lab!" Their father eyed her through narrow slits.

Chell turned to him. "I'm receiving my Calling soon, and it won't be any good unless the whole family's behind me."

"Muzz, did Chell hear right?" her mother asked.

"It's true that I find betrothal... difficult. But I've been to see Mrs. Whitford and we talked. I *want* to be focused and compliant. And I don't want to do anything to hurt your chances, Chell."

"What are your reasons, Muzz?" her mother wanted to know.

"For Whitford's sake," said her father, "never mind her so-called 'reasons.' We'll hear no more of this." He started eating his stew, and when no one followed his lead, glared around the table until they did. Everyone finished supper in silence.

That night Muzz dreamt about a world with sunlit streets, bustling throngs of humans. In the dream she was frooseless, which did not matter since it was a warm summer day. She wore a long lavender frock of some unusual material — certainly not the silk everything was made of in the Cave — and her scalp hair tossed on her shoulders in a gentle breeze. She and some friend with bright hazel eyes who was wearing pastel pink stood in a crowd watching a festive parade. Everyone in the bands and floats that passed had rosy cheeks and a joyful face.

Toward the end of the dream, some musicians marched past and a handsome one playing a clarinet waved in Muzz's direction.

The dream was so vivid it felt real. She woke up elated at first, but soon the pitch-black grottoette and the sounds of her sleeping family brought her back to the harsh reality of the Cave. She lay shivering in her bed. *Maybe Mrs. Whitford knows a powerful dreamer when she sees one,* she thought, *but what good are dreams that fill me with longing and regret?*

The following afternoon Muzz finished her work in Tropical early, arrived at the family grottoette just as her mother was returning from the looms, where she went a few afternoons each week to weave, knit, mend, or sew their garments. The others were not yet due home.

Muzz tried to make her "Hi, Mother" sound casual.

Her mother sat at their table and patted the seat next to her. "Oh, Muzz, I'm glad we're here alone. Come. Talk with me." She could see some softness in her mother's eyes, and hear kindness in her voice.

"You started to say something about Mrs. Whitford last night."

"I went to ask her a few things."

"About betrothal?"

"That, and about the trouble I was in." There was a silence, and Muzz knew her mother was waiting for more. *So hard to talk about.*

"I love you much, Muzz, and always will. I hope you know that.

"I love you too, Mother."

"And if I can help, I want to. It's just that..."

Just that you're a powerless female? Muzz clutched her beads and raced through ways to dodge this difficult subject. One popped up. "I've been wondering..."

"Yes?"

"About my beads."

"What about them?"

Muzz unclasped her necklace and set it on the table. "Why do I have a bead that Chell doesn't have? Shouldn't we have the same ones? We're brother and sister." She pointed at the bead that genuinely confused her.

"You mean the clear bead?"

Muzz nodded. "Why doesn't Chell have that one?"

"Good question." Her mother sounded pleased to be able to help her with something.

"That's a special bead. It passes from female to female in our family, which is why only you and I have it. If your grandmother were still with us, she would wear it too."

Muzz wanted to know more about this grandmother, who she knew had died of cave fever when she was small, but her father arrived home and the conversation abruptly ended.

The two females jumped up and started neatening the grottoette while her father, after a hasty greeting, sat on a cushion at the stone table reading his daily news bulletin *The Cavern Gazette*. In minutes, their grottoette chores done, they set out together for the communal kitchen a few doors down to prepare supper with the other females.

That night Muzz had another dream, a peculiar one in which she knelt before the Beacons with her head down. They were dressed in their ceremonial robes and hats, and their voices as they lectured her conveyed deep displeasure. The room they were in was not at all like the Great Hall where her betrothal was to take place. In fact, it was a small, dark, cramped room that made her breathless, almost claustrophobic. Though they spoke to her in loud, angry voices, everything sounded garbled. Finally, to hear them better, she glanced up. But their faces were missing! Between the tops of their robes and their hats was nothing by empty space. That frightened her so much that she woke up, unable to fall asleep again for a long time. *Was that a powerful dream, the kind Mrs. Whitford had in mind?* she asked herself. *If so, I'd rather have weak ones, or none at all.*

CHAPTER FOUR

On her thirteenth birthday Muzz awoke with a knot in the pit of her stomach. The Beacons and Hepu Dorne had met and chosen. Drent or Jerith? Jerith or Drent? Only they knew. *Jerith is much nicer than Drent,* she told herself, *so I can't help but hope for him. But why should those dusty old males have so much power over us?*

On betrothal days both forms finished Lessons early, and everyone in the Cave met in the Great Hall for the ceremony. By lightdown the couple's fate was sealed.

Muzz did not have to attend Lessons. This was like an extra Day One in the week for her. She could eat, bathe, and dress at a leisurely pace. There the similarities ended.

Instead of strolling to Book Storage for a chat with old Hepu Marfone about stories the two of them liked, she had to style her chestnut scalp hair into a smooth twist, and fasten it with a silver clasp passed down to her by her mother. Then she would wait for her mother to bring her a 'surprise' silk wraparound woven and sewn for the occasion. Once dressed, she would walk between her parents to the Great Hall to be offered.

She lay staring at the bumpy ceiling of their grottoette until Em jumped on top of her and stuck a cold nose in her face. Muzz sat up and sent her pup rolling to the floor, and then slipped down beside her. She began scratching her behind her soft, silky ears.

"Oh, Em, what am I going to do? I don't want to be offered."

Emily cocked her head at Muzz.

"No one understands." When Em wagged her tail furiously, Muzz shook a finger at her. "No one's going to give *you* away."

All this talk was Em's idea of a game. She nuzzled Muzz's neck. "Stop it! Your nose is a chunk of ice!" Muzz pushed the dog away with a sassy grin, and started a romp that ended abruptly when she recalled what day it was.

Her mother had set out a nice breakfast: steamed oats with nut milk and a glass of cabbage juice. To one side Muzz found two coarse silk towels her mother must have made especially for the occasion. Two was symbolic, Muzz knew: one for her, one for her mystery future husband.

She checked herself in the mirror. "I'd better not think, and just get on with my morning." Em leapt for her leash, and they left for the closest Lab run.

An hour later Muzz sat alone in the Cave's drying chamber since nothing dried properly anywhere else. Laundry hung all around while a ceiling vent whirred humid air to the surface of The Planet. *If only it could take my jittery mood with it.* When the last Lesson bell rang, she returned to the grottoette with her scalp hair styled, and waited demurely in her robe at the family table.

"Why, you look perfect!" her mother exclaimed when she arrived. "Fentish, doesn't she look lovely?"

"Just so she *acts* lovely. No shenanigans, my *dear* Hepu daughter," her father told her, a trace of threat in his voice.

Her mother sighed softly. "Here, Muzz. This is for you." She held up a small package wrapped in a glossy plantain leaf.

Inside was an exquisite silk wraparound. In one direction it looked green, in another, pale blue.

"Oh, thank you, it's beautiful! What a lot of work it must have been to make this for me, Mother!"

Her mother smiled shyly, but before she could reply, her father said, "Hurry up with that wraparound." He began to frown and pace around.

As they approached the Great Hall, Muzz could hear a melee of voices, pipes, drums, and melodic gongs, the yipping of Labs. She felt she needed Emily, but only Labs from near the Great Hall were allowed in, and only to stop their whining. Her parents at her sides each held one of her hands, something neither had done since she was small. As they entered together she saw the Three Beacons seated on their platform in black robes and towering ceremonial hats with Mrs. Whitford at one side in her seat of honor — a stark upright wooden chair. Young males and females from Lower and Higher stood at attention facing each other, the music ensemble was tuning up, and the rest of the Tribe milled in an agitated, shapeless mass.

"They're here!" someone shouted.

A hush fell on the hall, an aisle formed down the center and, when the ponderous traditional song that was played just three times each year began, Muzz and her parents started their ceremonial march to the platform.

She felt her heart pounding.

She searched the mob of elderly 'Witherers,' as retired Hepus were called, who were cramming the tunnel exits. Somewhere in there stood her paternal grandparents. She had only ever known her father's parents and had hardly set eyes on them since they retired. Her mother's parents had died young.

Next she noticed Chell in the front row of the Highers flanked by Drent and Jerith, and recalled Jerith's half-spoken wish that he would be the Beacons' choice. She noticed how brightly his eyes shown. Surely along with hoping, he was enjoying the music. He played keyboards and always wrote "musician" at the top of his Calling wish list. Muzz felt a faint quiver of fear for him and for herself.

How weak and numb my body feels, as if it's not really mine.

"I'm nervous," she whispered to her parents.

"You have only one word to speak, and that is 'yes,'" said her mother.

Her father gave her arm a sharp squeeze and tugged her forward. "Don't you dare disgrace us."

A surge of cheering voices filled the hall, and in no time she and her parents were standing directly below the Beacons. The music stopped, and the ceremony Muzz had seen so many times for others began for her.

As the Three Beacons stood, everyone cried in one voice, "Hail, Beacons of Light!" With stiff smiles, all three nodded ever so slightly to avoid toppling their hats.

"We offer this thirteenth yearling to her rightful mate," her parents said in unison. They whisked Muzz one last step forward, dropped her hands, and stepped back. Her knees trembled and her breath came fast. A great roar overtook the hall, and the ensemble broke into music again.

Half-formed thoughts careened through her head as the Third Beacon smiled down at her, and reached for odoriferous garlands of daisies held by the other two. The least stern of the Beacons, he stepped down and circled her neck with one garland. As the drums rolled to a crescendo, he walked sedately with the other garland toward the males in the Higher Form.

Muzz felt so dizzy that standing straight took all of her strength.

The crowd parted and the drums reverberated as the Third Beacon stopped in front of the three sixteenth yearling males, and hung the other garland on Drent's neck. A huge roar rose from the crowd.

Chell turned with a broad smile and shook his hand.

Jerith stared straight ahead with only the slightest falter. Muzz felt a wave of sorrow for him. Then there it was — the burning again.

Drent's parents rushed forward, grasped their son's hands, deposited him next to Muzz. She felt him there without turning to look.

"We accept this thirteenth yearling female who has been offered," Drent's parents repeated in unison. All that was left now were the final questions.

The First Beacon stood over them and held their hands a few inches apart. Up close, Muzz was stunned by the asymmetry of the Beacon's face, the way his left eye blinked while his right eye stared at her. It was as if she were seeing two faces in one, neither of them all that friendly.

Muzz had not looked at Drent, and could tell he was not looking at her. *Is his mind here or playing caveball? That's easy,* she thought, and bit her lip to suppress a smirk. The Beacon turned to Drent. "Do you accept this female that the Tribe has chosen for you?" Drent's "Yes" rang out.

The Beacon turned back to Muzz, his left eye still blinking. "And do you accept your place as his female?"

Muzz hesitated, feeling the crowd's anticipation press against her, but something more intense inside. And in that moment the burning welled into a fury. "No," she said evenly.

When the First Beacon's staring right eye pierced her with disbelief, her fury found its voice.

"No, no, no!" she shouted.

She whirled from the platform. Later she recalled with satisfaction the shock on the First Beacon's lopsided face. But in the furor of the moment, all she thought of was dodging the hands trying to grab her as she ran.

She barely heard her parents' cries or Hepu Dorne's voice boom "After her!" and blindly ran toward the entrance to a tunnel, dodging one, two, three yellow Labs who trotted up with big canine smiles, and then sidestepping a guard. She took the tunnel and, at a sharp turn, nearly slammed into a wall. A stalagmite caught her hem and tore it. Looking back though, she could tell she had a good lead. There was no one in sight. Her numbness from the morning gone, Muzz understood without really having words for it that her life would never be the same.

She raced down the closest tunnel, and did not realize it was the Forbidden Tunnel until she reached a door she had never seen before. The sign on it read 'Science Lab'; it was locked. She stopped to catch her breath, listen, and think.

She could hear far-off voices calling and Labs barking. *I don't have time to feel sorry for disappointing anyone.*

She tiptoed past an office with bright, cold lighting of some kind. It was empty, but with no place to hide. The other doors were locked. *Freeze me, what'll I do?*

Some voices seemed to be getting closer. She sprinted to a large room at the tunnel's end, the only one left. From the entrance she saw a wardrobe against the far wall with its door slightly ajar, ran to it, yanked the door open. It was full of Beacon ceremonial robes! She spotted a thin slice of space way at the back and slipped in, setting the wardrobe door slightly ajar as she went. When she looked up at the robes, she saw Beacon hats attached at the top of each one. *Oh, wow! That's just how the faceless Beacons looked in my dream. How creepy! 'Powerful dreamer.' This must be what Mrs. Whitford meant. But it's too odd.* The voices grew louder until a Hepu walked right into the room! Muzz held perfectly still, breathed as softly as possible.

"I told them to check her shed. We'll find our runaway soon, and when we do..." This was the gravelly voice of the Second Beacon. She could just make out his feet, and also part of the doorway beyond. More Hepus shuffled in.

The nasal voice of Hepu Dorne replied. "I wouldn't be so sure. That one is twisted. I knew she was capable of something like this. She's the only one in her generation with the clear bead."

Mother never said what it was for.

Another voice boomed, "Then why didn't you warn us?"

"I tried, Father. Yesterday when you didn't have time for me." It pleased Muzz to hear Hepu Dorne get scolded. His father was the First Beacon.

Some feet that had been pacing stopped. "I'm feeling sorry for the child. That dunce Drent is a much poor match for her. He wants to join the *cave guards*!" This was the Third Beacon speaking, and Muzz silently thanked him for taking her side.

"That's an honorable profession."

"They're a squad of somnolent spuds, and you know it, Dorne. He's no good for her."

"Not so. I chose him for her because he's stable and reliable."

"And unremittingly dull!" The Third Beacon sounded cross.

"Ha! Trying to curb her so-called talents, were you, son? If you ask me, she's a ringer for that grandmother of hers. I say she deserves the same fate."

"But no one knows *what* happened to that female, Father. You know that. She just disappeared."

"Hmmm." Muzz wondered if the First Beacon was agreeing or not.

There was a silence, and then the sound of more steps. The boots of two cave guards entered the room, and their heels clicked.

"So! Have you found the rapscallion?"

"Not a trace of her in Tropical, sir."

"Unacceptable!"

"Request permission to search other enclosures."

"Search every inch of the Cave if you have to. There's no way she can hide from us for long."

"Yes, *sir*!" The guards clicked their heels, and left.

The Third Beacon's shoes followed them to the door, turned back. "We need to tread lightly here. Betrothal is a dicey affair at best. When we find the child, we should be firm, but not cruel."

The First Beacon groaned.

The Second Beacon piped up, "There's no need to decide how to treat her now. Let's concentrate on finding her." He chuckled. "Apparently that may take a while."

Another groan.

"Relax, Father." A grunt was the only reply.

The Third Beacon said, "Yes, for Whitford's sake, let's all relax. We'll meet again when they find the child."

"My thought precisely," said the Second. The First Beacon muttered again, and pretty soon the Second and Third Beacons left.

When Hepu Dorne and his father were alone, his father pounded something and sat down. "Dorne, get out there and reconvene Lessons. We should treat the rest of this day like any other. No festivities and no special foods. Toss them if you have to. No! On second thought, have them sent here."

Hepu Dorne snickered. "Marvelous! They shouldn't go to waste. We can have a little party. I'll see to it at once."

Hepu Dorne crossed to the door, and turned. "May I speak, Father?"

"Make it quick."

"Muzz has challenged my authority and, indirectly, yours."

A grunt.

"It's that clear bead of hers."

The First Beacon made a hissing sound. "Hard to disagree."

There was a pause while Hepu Dorne paced. "At least her mother's meek enough, but... "

"But what? Out with it."

Hepu Dorne stopped. "But I don't care what the others say, we need to set an example with her. She has refused Drent, and she should be culled."

"That goes without saying."

"Also, Father, there are two more betrothals coming up. Contrary to the Third Beacons' mamby-pamby theory about "poor" matches, I do *not* think we need to coddle anyone. We should treat those betrothals *as we see fit*, and force the Highers to adapt."

The First Beacon broke into a harsh laugh. "You know how to treat insubordination, Dorne. Lay it on them. You have my full support."

Hepu Dorne left the room.

Muzz stayed hidden as the First Beacon cussed and puttered for a while. Once he stopped and pounded his fist on the table, mumbling, "Get her! Get her!" in a most terrifying way. Then he left without closing the door. Muzz heard voices in the tunnel and waited, scared for a while, but eventually calmer, even dozing briefly. She awoke to a curious snippet of conversation.

"...had problems with that last batch. One of 'em was a biter. So was the mother. We nearly had to put her down."

"What was Whitford thinking when he—"

A door clicked shut and she heard no more.

Hungry, aching, frightened and confused by what she had heard, Muzz stayed put until lightdown fretting and planning. Much later someone opened the door, made a jingling sound, pulled the door shut. She heard retreating footsteps, then nothing.

Finally she edged from her hiding place. She spotted a set of keys on the hook inside the door, took them, and tiptoed out. At the Science Lab, on impulse, she tried the keys, found one that unlocked it.

She went in. Lights switched on automatically and startled her, so she dashed back out, but soon returned.

It was a large room with three high white tables strewn with strange instruments. Each table had its own high stool. She was standing there blinking and considering what to do when a tremulous squeal erupted from a box in the far corner. A blanket covered the box, and when she lifted it she found a newborn Lab in a nest of dried leaves. It trembled and whimpered soulfully, so of course she picked it up.

"You cute little thing. You're crying! What are you doing here?"

The puppy wiggled with pure joy when she rubbed its soft belly. A sign on the box read, "# 3 (EBB) Deliver Week 10."

"Poor nameless puppy!"

The pup had only a bottle wired to the side of the box to drink from. Muzz wanted to abduct the cute little thing, but given her situation merely kissed it and set it back among the leaves, where it rested on its haunches and squealed some more.

"I'm much sorry to leave you," she told it, "but I'm on the run."

After a quick peek at various kinds of plant life under refrigeration, there was nothing more to see. Muzz left, locked the door, and pocketed the keys. Then, keeping to the lantern-less side of the tunnel, she snuck back the way she had come.

When she was almost out, she passed a door marked 'Impregnation.' *Mother must have gone there first for Chell, and again for me,* she thought, recalling what she had learned about Hepu babies. The process of attaching a fertilized egg to the mother's womb took place twice, once for each male child, and once for each female.

CHAPTER FIVE

The cave guards habitually snoozed on night duty, and the guard for the Forbidden Tunnel was no exception, not even with a runaway at large. Propped against the rough-hewn wall, he was snoring peacefully when Muzz slipped past him and headed toward Tropical — *her* world.

By the time she reached her shed, the quiet was gnawing at her. Not even the slightest echo, muffled voice or footstep had floated her way. *Are they secretly watching me? Are they on the sidelines ready to pounce?*

In a play she had read by a human named William, some soldiers disguised themselves as trees. *Maybe I can disguise myself somehow.*

She took off her wraparound, tugged the silver clasp from her hair, undid her beads, pausing just long enough to examine her clear bead. She shrugged at it, hid everything under a Lab hair cushion and put on a worn gray space suit from the heap thinking, *I'll blend with the shadows.* She grabbed a length of cord and a short knife, crept to the densest part of the plantain grove. Slicing three fronds from a bushy plant and stepping into the gap that made, she eased herself into the thicket. Next she secured the leaves to the back of her head using the cord like a headband. She could not see out. *Can anyone see in?*

"Youch!" The leaves dug into her neck, her knees ached, and her ankles itched. She found a way to lean on a neighboring plantain, which gave her a moment to ask some questions she had been avoiding: *Why in icebergs did I do the opposite of what I promised? What will Father and Mother do if I'm caught? Was Jerith much disappointed to lose me? Is Tendra still my best friend? What's the big deal with my clear bead? Can the less stern Third Beacon convince the others not to cull me?* The word 'cull' sent a shiver up her spine.

Later distant voices startled her. She had been asleep, slumping, and straightened up fast.

"Muzz! Hepu Muzz!" a male voice called.

Not twangy, so not Hepu Dorne, she thought.

"No sign of her. I'll check over there."

Leaves thrashed nearby, footsteps came closer. She held as still as a statue and breathed in a soft, even rhythm.

Someone was searching plant by plant. A hand moved one of her camouflage leaves and the headband squeezed her forehead. "Muzz?" someone whispered. "I know you're there. It's Jerith. I can hardly see you, just a little of your suit."

Muzz held her breath and Jerith moved on. "Stay put. I'll come back later and tell you what's happening." Jerith waited. "If you can hear me, move something."

Muzz gave the branches an infinitesimal rustle.

Jerith moved on, calling, "No sign of her over here."

The search party combed Tropical for a long time. Twice she had to stifle sneezes and once she almost fell on her face, so she badly wanted everyone to leave. Finally they met up near her tool shed.

Muzz had all she could do to keep from getting up to gawk at them. She wanted to know who the others were, and whether they had nets or ropes to catch her with.

"Let's write her a note," someone suggested.

"And say what?" That sounded like Jerith.

"She needs to know there's going to be a trial." That sounded like Chell talking.

"She'll never surface if she hears *that*!"

"If you knew my sister the way I do, you wouldn't be so sure."

After more bickering, the search party left without writing anything.

"What in froose is a trial?" Muzz staggered out rubbing her legs to get her circulation going. "It's something unpleasant, for sure, but what?" From what she had overheard, it involved the Beacons. *Should I stop hiding? If I do what will happen to me? And what am I going to eat?* No answers came. She crawled back into the plantains and fell into a fitful sleep.

"Muzz, wake up!" She bolted upright with a squeal.

"Shhh! Calm yourself. Come out." When she did, Jerith handed her a bowl of yam stew, still warm. "You must be famished."

While she ate, he crouched and said, "Listen. Drent's family has gone avalanche. Not Drent; he's either too cool or too dense to get riled up. But his parents want blood."

"Mine?"

Jerith's nod was so matter-of-fact that it sent a pang through her, though she kept on eating.

"They're taking the she's-shamed-our-family stance. Brutish. They want you culled from the Tribe."

There was that horrid word again. Hearing it, Muzz could barely breathe, let alone ask intelligent questions. But she could chew.

"Of course, your friends won't let that happen."

"Who are my friends?"

"Me, of course. And Tendra. Also many of the other Highers, though they're afraid to say so."

"And my parents? Chell?

"They sure as shivers don't want you culled."

"Do you think Drent's parents will be allowed to take my blood with that trial thing?"

Jerith eyeballed her closely. "You don't know what a trial is, do you." He searched her face. "Of course you don't. You were too young for the last one — the only other one I've seen." He paused, thinking. "There was a trial when I was a fifth yearling and you had only two years." He paused so long that Muzz wanted to shake him.

"Someone — a female, an older female, I think — was in trouble for... something. He shook his head. "This is really helpful, isn't it."

Muzz ignored his sarcasm. "Could it have been my grandmother?"

"Maybe."

"Because I overheard the Beacons badmouthing her."

Jerith's eyes bulged. "You were eavesdropping on the *Beacons*?"

Muzz nodded. "I went down the Forbidden Tunnel—"

His jaw dropped.

"—by mistake..."

He grimaced.

"—and I had to hide in a wardrobe, and—"

"Whitford's wisdom! You're scaring me frozen."

"Okay, I'll skip it. Tell me more about the trial."

"Right, let's see. Mrs. Whitford and her husband — or someone — tried to defend... whoever it was."

"Whitford himself?"

"Weird! I guess so. He seemed so entirely... human that I've never thought of him as *that* Whitford. Just an ordinary person, really."

"How odd. But what was the trial like?"

"A lot of questions, speeches. The Beacons took charge, of course."

"How did it end?"

"I don't know."

"Was the outcome kept from you?"

Jerith shook his head. "Maybe."

Something about the way Jerith said this and the look on his face made Muzz uneasy. "Maybe I should stop hiding. Turn myself in."

"Maybe... So do it."

"On second thought, no."

"Why 'no?'"

"The Cave is full of thickets, shadows, nooks. Let them try and find me. They deserve this game of hide and seek."

Emboldened by her own words, Muzz thought of William's play again. "I need another disguise. To get around unnoticed. I want to attend my trial."

Jerith closed his eyes and shook his head slowly from side to side. "You are im*poss*ible. If you do, they're sure to catch you."

"Not as a Witherer. Witherers are so out of it that they hardly notice each other. If I dress like my grandfather, say, who'll even take a second look at me?"

Fear seeped into Jerith's eyes. He kicked a little clump of soil, and spread the crumbled dirt around with his foot. "There's no stopping you, is there" was all he said.

Muzz shrugged with what she hoped was an appealing smile. "Hide and seek... I'll need a real Witherer stocking cap to hide my scalp hair."

He sighed, nodded gravely. "I think I can get you one of my maternal grandfather's. I have an old, worn jumpsuit too. It won't be missed." He glanced around nervously. "Listen. I'm supposed to check for you whenever I come through with the harvest cart. But that doesn't mean no one else will be looking for you. Everyone's on the alert. The only reason you weren't caught in the Forbidden Tunnel was that no one thought you'd dare go there. So get what you need out of your shed and hide really well. I'll bring the stuff you want late tonight."

Later that night, it was Tendra, not Jerith, who came looking for Muzz, who was dozing on a nest of rumpled space suits in the plantain grove, and woke with a sharp cry when Tendra touched her.

"Jerith warned me about that," Tendra whispered. "If you're going to be a fugitive, you'll have to stop shrieking every time your sleep's disturbed."

Muzz tugged at her scalp hair and rubbed her eyes. "Where's Jerith? Is he iced with me?"

"No, no. He's under surveillance."

"Aren't you?"

Tendra frowned and looked around. She unrolled a bundle containing a tattered jumpsuit, an old knit cap, a steamed plantain, and a handful of hazel nuts. As she watched Muzz down the plantain and start in on the hazel nuts, her mouth trembled.

"Listen, Muzz, you're my best friend. I'm worried much about this. I still don't get what's so wrong with Drent that you need to throw away every good thing in life over him. You've put yourself *and* your family *and* friends in serious danger. The Highers are mute with fear, your father's a seething sleet storm, and Chell says his Calling just washed downstream. As to Drent's parents—"

"Freeze them! Freeze everyone! We need more freedom in this pit. If you don't get that, how can I expect anyone to?" Muzz chomped a hazel nut and scowled.

They stared at each other. Tendra slowly shook her head. "Fine, do what you have to do. Put this stuff on. Come and watch your trial. But for Whitford's sake, puuuhlease don't get caught! It starts two hours before lightdown — which is soon — in the Great Hall."

She grabbed the jumpsuit. "Here. Quick. Put this on and I'll tuck in your scalp hair. And look, I brought glasses, and scissors to make authentic little nicks in your froose."

Muzz's hands darted to her face. "Nicks?"

"To make you look old. It's Jerith's idea, and a good one. Come on. Hurry. I can't be late for your trial."

Muzz sagged in an ill-lit corner of the Great Hall, arms folded, back bent. So far no one had taken the slightest notice of her.

She could tell Jerith was scanning the knots of Witherers by the exits, and felt glad when he gave up without spotting her.

Nearby a handful of elderly Hepus hunched together.

"Why in blizzards can't they catch that little recusant?" one asked.

"It's only a matter of time," said another. His voice sounded gruff, annoyed. A look at his beads said he was Drent's maternal great uncle.

Oh no! What about my *breeding beads?* As casually as possible, Muzz turned her collar up to make hers hard to see, folded her arms, and checked her posture. Thankfully, no one seemed the least bit interested in her. *Are all Witherers* this *invisible?*

"Look who's here," another Witherer hissed, and Muzz saw her own paternal grandparents arrive. She had not seen them up close for over a year. *How decrepit they've grown, poor things.*

Her grandmother gave her grandfather a pat on the arm, and he answered with a squeeze. *They mustn't notice me*, she thought.

The scene in the hall is eerily similar to my betrothal — minus the band and goodies, of course. The Lowers and Highers faced each other, Hepu Dorne looked severe, Jerith, Chell and Drent stared straight ahead, Tendra was trying not to look for her, Mrs. Whitford sat at the side of the stage on her special seat. Muzz could not find her parents, or Drent's, and was still searching when a single drummer began a sharp drum roll. Silence fell on the crowd, and she could feel the tension mount.

The drum roll built to a crescendo as the Three Beacons took center stage, and the crowd hailed the Beacons in the usual way.

The Second and Third Beacons sat down, but the First Beacon stayed standing, scanning the crowd. His thin smile and wandering gaze made her sure he was searching for her. He let the drummer go for a long moment before raising his hand for silence.

"Bring on the guards!" Cave guards fanned out, flanked every door in the hall.

At this show of force, Muzz had to concentrate in order not to bolt. One guard was stationed just steps away. Slowly, she reached up and readjusted her collar till none of the beads on her necklace showed.

The First Beacon still scanned the audience, seemed to enjoy the silence.

"If anyone knows the whereabouts of Hepu Muzz, I command you to come forward."

A rustle went through the crowd. From the corner of her eye, Muzz saw the guard looking around; his gaze glided past her. Then suspenseful silence filled the hall. She held perfectly still.

"So be it. This trial shall proceed without her," said the First Beacon. "There is no need to establish guilt. You all witnessed Muzz betray the trust of the Tribe at her betrothal, you all heard her cry 'No,' and you all saw her leave young Drent mateless before the Beacons. Her rebellion cannot be tolerated. All we need do now is decide what's to be done with her. Will the aggrieved family please come forward."

Drent's parents came down the center aisle to stand before the First Beacon. His mother had her head down and her hands folded, but his father stood tall, peered scornfully around. "Explain your grievance," the First Beacon told him. "Loud and clear."

"Your honor, Drent's mother and I come before you because our son was rejected, his hopes for the future dashed, our family insulted. When Muzz is captured, we want her punishment to reflect the severity of her crime: we ask that when she is caught, she be culled from the Tribe."

Hepus exchanged frightened glances and chatter rattled the hall.

Muzz's grandmother was standing close enough for Muzz to hear her gasp. Her grandfather squeezed her hand, maybe to calm her, maybe to quiet her, or both.

The First Beacon waited for silence. "You have spoken well," he replied. "Step back, and we shall hear from the wrongdoer's parents. Come forward and state your defense."

As they came down the aisle, Muzz noted her mother's red eyes and her father's cold scowl.

Her father began, "Your honor, our daughter has disobeyed us and cast dishonor on the Tribe. Full of disappointment and dismay, we apologize for her actions. We can see no honorable way to defend her, and do not plead for clemency on her behalf."

At this Muzz saw her mother's chest heaving. *Mother disagrees, but she's afraid to speak.* Her father went on, "We won't resist the will of the Tribe. And," here her father raised his hand ominously, "*if* she's allowed to live, let it be somewhere other than with us."

A ruckus erupted and, when it died down, the First Beacon replied, "You're right to favor the good of the Tribe over the wrongdoer. I hope that in due time Drent's family will accept your apology. Now, before we sentence Muzz, does anyone else wish to speak?"

Silence. Then Hepu Dorne came forward. "I do." He exchanged a glance with his father, the First Beacon, that made Muzz cold inside.

A Witherer whispered, "Look how much alike they are."

"Father and son," someone shot back.

Someone else shushed them.

"Your honor," Hepu Dorne began, "I have something to add to this portrait of Hepu Muzz. She has been a terror in the classroom lately — disruptive and disobedient. If she is allowed to live, I want her barred from returning."

"We shall take your comments into account," said the First Beacon. He scanned the crowd. "Anyone else?"

Silence. *Won't anyone speak for me?*

"Then we shall retire to confer." The First Beacon turned to the other two. "Ready?"

"Wait! I have something say." Mrs. Whitford rose, white-haired but sturdy.

There was more chatter, and the First Beacon glowered at her. Mrs. Whitford stood her ground.

"To avoid a rush to judgment, I want to defend Muzz by dabbing some color onto the drab portrait you've painted of her. I've observed her closely for many years and appreciate how thoughtful of others she can be — back when I broke my wrist, for example. Muzz cleaned my grottoette and fetched my meals until I could do it myself. I've also found her in Book Storage many times. She reads, shows curiosity, and can talk intelligently. In fact, if the rules allowed it, I think she could handle a Calling of her own, and—"

"If Hepu Muzz is so responsible, where is she now?" the First Beacon demanded. "And why should we be lenient with *dis*appearing females?"

He stared at Mrs. Whitford, who boldly returned his gaze. She was about to speak again, but stopped herself, sat down.

Their interchange piqued Muzz's interest. *Are they talking about my grandmother?* She filed away the "disappearing females" phrase.

"Your Honor? I have something to say." All eyes turned to Chell.

"Sir— Your Honor. My sister is special."

The First Beacon chuckled. "Oh, she's special, all right." He looked around and laughter rang out.

"No, special in a *good* way, Sir." Even as he said that, Chell seemed unsure.

"Explain yourself."

Chell took a deep breath. "I've been close to Muzz her whole life, as you know. Of course a younger sibling can be a pest."

"I can imagine," said the Beacon, pulling for more laughter.

"But Muzz can also be lively and fun. She tells exciting stories, makes up interesting games, and used to earn good grades until her problem began."

"What sort of problem?"

"Muzz thought the sky was getting lighter."

Derisive laughter burst out around the hall, and the First Beacon shook his head.

"We've seen *that* symptom before! A classic case of weak thinking. Did you explain that to her?"

Hepu Dorne called out, "I did, and I forbade her to go to the observation window, but she went anyway."

The Beacon cast a triumphant grin at Chell, who looked crestfallen. "Anything to add?" Chell shook his head.

"Then it's time for deliberation."

All three Beacons exited through a door behind the platform.

Muzz thought, *How rigid, snide, and dangerous the First Beacon is.*

Her grandmother turned to her grandfather. "Did you catch that remark about disappearing females?" she whispered.

Her grandfather put a finger to his lips, and her grandmother pursed hers, went quiet.

Muzz thought again about the power of that phrase. *Mrs. Whitford acted as if she had been scolded. But why?*

When the Three Beacons returned, it was the Third who spoke and the others who sat.

He came to the front of the platform, signaled silence, cleared his throat, gazed around the hall.

"The Beacons have decided," he said, and as he spoke, the guards lifted their weapons in unison in what was, for Muzz, a terrifying gesture.

"Due to Muzz's tender age and Mrs. Whitford's praise, when she is found she shall not be culled."

Drent's father stomped his foot, and a murmur crossed the crowd.

"However," the Third Beacon said, and more loudly, "however!"

He waited for complete silence. "When Muzz is found, and we have no doubt that she will be, she shall be banished to the Tropical Cultivation Enclosure for hard labor. Let her shed be her new home. Let her eat and sleep *alone* — without visitors, games, or books — eating only a portion of what she grows. She'll have twenty days to rethink betrothal and accept Drent as her life partner. After that she'll be banished for life."

The First Beacon rose. "Everyone hear this: If Muzz knows what's good for her, she'll go to her shed without being forced. Anyone who sees her should tell her so. Now, return to your grottoettes. Complete your normal evening routine. Praise Whitford."

"Praise Whitford!" was the crowd's response.

The First Beacon nodded. "You're all dismissed."

Muzz saw Tendra, Chell and Jerith exchange looks. Drent's parents grabbed him and left in a huff; Hepu Dorne looked peeved. Muzz lost her parents in the crowd. Her grandmother hugged her grandfather. "'Praise Whitford' is right!" she whispered.

CHAPTER SIX

The crowd drained from the hall in subdued silence. Muzz's sentence — somewhere between a slap in the face and a knockout — seemed to have left them as stunned and confused as she was. But there would be time to make sense of it; she needed to leave with everyone else.

She noticed her grandparents hobbling past the guards, and followed the two of them to their grottoette, darted through their grottoette door. She felt rather than saw the shabbiness of their quarters. *How sad,* she thought.

"Oh, no! Not again. Gronthor, this is not your grottoette. Go home." Her grandmother rushed toward her.

"Grandma, it's me. Muzz."

Her grandfather pushed himself up from his cushion; they both stood staring, slack-mouthed.

"Whitford be praised, Trontal! It *is* Muzz!" her grandmother exclaimed. "Dear Muzz!" She threw her arms around Muzz and kissed her.

"Quiet down, or we'll have the whole patrol unit in here." Though her grandfather scolded, his eyes danced behind his thick spectacles the way they always did when something pleased him.

"You look awful," her grandmother snapped. "How'd you get here? What happened to your froose? And your clothes?"

"I'm in disguise for my trial. Don't worry, no one spotted me." Muzz surprised herself by adding, "I came to ask you something."

"Trontal, lock the door. Muzz, we've been crazy with worry. Are you all in one piece? Are you starving?"

"No, Grandma. I'm fine. Some of the Highers bring me food."

"Thank Whitford! Where have you been hiding?"

"Well, I—"

"She'd better not to say," her grandfather cautioned. "What we don't know no one can force out of us."

"This isn't a spy game, Trontal."

"Of course not. It's more serious."

Her grandmother swatted at him, but said, "I guess he's right." Tears welled in her eyes. "A year and four months since we've seen you up close! We're treated like ghosts."

"Like the dead," said her grandfather.

Her grandmother tugged on Muzz's jumpsuit. "Come. Sit." Muzz sat on a Lab hair cushion. "See how you've grown. And how pretty you are. Look, Tront, even disguised as an old man, she's a beauty. What gorgeous eyes! Almond shaped and green like her—"

"No one else has green eyes," her grandfather interjected.

Her grandmother slapped her own forehead. "Of course! What was I thinking?"

"Sit down, Fernza. Quit suffocating the child."

"Sit down yourself, you old froose bag. All right, let's calm down." Her grandmother smoothed the air as if it were a wrinkled blanket and they both eased onto cushions. "So tell us everything. First off, what's so wrong with Drent?"

Muzz looked from one grandparent to the other. How could she explain to a dutifully married couple who had bickered most of their lives? "It's not Drent. It's betrothal and all the other rules I despise."

Her grandfather's mouth twisted down at the corners. "Despise! That word is much strong. Too strong for your own good."

Her grandmother turned to him. "Let her speak. She doesn't like the rules. Who likes the rules?" *These two are the same as they ever were. How I love them,* Muzz thought.

"Now, Fernza, watch your tongue."

"If I had to do it again, I might refuse to marry a wasp like you."

"*You're* the one with the stinger, Fernza! Let her explain." He raised his bushy brows expectantly.

"Well, for one, rather than marry in five years and spend my time cooking, spinning silk, and stuffing Lab hair cushions, I'd like my own Calling."

"What kind of a Calling?" her grandmother asked.

"I'd like to apprentice with Hepu Marfone in Book Storage."

"You want to be *Bookwatcher*?"

"What's wrong with that?" her grandfather asked. "It was one of the jobs on *my* wish list."

"Poor Grandpa! Instead they gave you fix-it duty? No one even cared what you wanted to do."

Her grandfather sighed, stared into space. "Marfone isn't bad at what he does. He stirred up excitement by proposing that we name the Labs after famous authors. But *I* would've made the authors' names *mean* something." He shrugged. "Oh, well. The will of the Tribe..."

"I think Highers should have choices, both males *and* females. Maybe even invent new jobs."

"*New* jobs?" Her grandmother's mouth became a large O.

Her grandfather stood up, and began shuffling around. "No, no," he said. "That was much fun for the humans. But look where *they* ended up."

There was a loud knock on the door that made him jump.

"Who's there?" cried her grandmother.

"Cave guards doing rounds. Open up!"

Muzz's grandmother pointed at her and hissed, "You're Gronthor!" Muzz felt her heart begin to thump. Her grandfather cracked the door.

A guard stuck his head in. Two others stood behind him. He peered at his clipboard in the sparse evening light. "Fernza and Trontal?"

"Correct," said her grandfather. It was all Muzz could do not to bound away.

"Who's that?" The guard pointed.

"Our neighbor Gronthor," said her grandmother.

The guard leaned in and inspected Gronthor. "I saw you a couple of doors down, didn't I?"

"He can't hear you," said her grandmother.

Muzz stared at her foot and scratched her jaw.

The guard stepped in and looked around. He pointed at Muzz. "Make sure the old guy gets home soon. There's a curfew tonight, you know."

He turned to her grandfather. "Hepu Muzz is your grandchild, is she not?"

"Correct."

He jotted a note on his clipboard.

"If she contacts you for any reason, or shows up here, report it to the authorities at once."

"Yes, sir!"

"All of you off to bed," said the guard. "Now."

"Right away," said her grandfather.

The guards shouldered their weapons, and left.

When they started banging on the next grottoette door, her grandfather locked up, turned, and let his breath out slowly. "That was way too close."

"Good work, Gronthor," her grandmother whispered. "You'd better sleep here, old fellow."

It took a few minutes for Muzz to calm down. She slept in her disguise. With her grandparents snoring like engines, she had strange dreams of broken machines and twisted tunnels. Each time she woke with a start, which she did often that night, the dream would fade.

Near morning, however, one dream seared itself to her memory. In it she was walking through an unknown part of the Cave when she came upon a large circular stone propped against the wall. She rolled it aside and found a low door. Inside she was astonished to see a small, curved tunnel and a cavern at the far end with walls that glistened faintly. *A secret cavern cut off from the rest of the Cave?* She crawled in.

But the farther she went, the longer the tunnel seemed to grow. Perplexed and exhausted she lay on the rocky floor gasping, "I give up, I give up." Then she heard a loud 'whoosh!' and the tunnel snapped like a rubber band. The cavern entrance was right in front of her!

She went in and, yes, it was a huge space with an arched dome as high or higher than the Great Hall's. She heard water someplace nearby. Shimmering colored glass lanterns lined the walls. In one corner a whole slew of Lab puppies tumbled and played together.

It was while she was petting the puppies that small winged creatures in luminous shades of blue and green came darting and swooping in fancy loops high up in the dome.

A single glowing creature perched on her pointer finger and she drew her hand down to examine it. Each wing had a black dot almost like an eye.

"That's a butterfly," a voice behind her whispered. Startled, she turned to find a human — a woman — standing over her, tall and pale with gentle eyes above elegantly sculpted cheeks, and silver hair swept up and fastened with a beaded clasp. The expression on her face looked serene and kind.

Questions flooded Muzz's mind. "What place is—? Will you—? Can I—?" She saw that the woman wore breeding beads, including the clear bead, and pointed at it in bewilderment.

Then the butterfly on the tip of her finger sailed soundlessly into the clear bead. The woman held the bead in both hands and nodded at Muzz.

"Who are you?"

"You came with a question. Ask, ask," the woman intoned.

Then Muzz awoke, and found her grandmother bent over her. She blinked, lost in the floating feeling the best dreams leave behind.

"Oh, Grandma, I had an extraordinary dream."

"Not surprising from the extraordinary noises you were making. But we have to get you out of here. You're going back to your shed now, aren't you?"

Muzz sighed, frowned, nodded. "I guess so. In my disguise."

"Good. If they don't catch you, it'll be better for all of us. Less fuss. C'mon."

"Before I go, please tell me why at my trial the Beacons brought up 'disappearing females'?"

"What's that she's asking?" Her grandfather leaned over the mound of her grandmother's body to peer at Muzz.

"She says the Beacons mentioned 'disappearing females' at the trial. Did you hear that?"

Her grandparents exchanged a look, and shook their heads.

"But you *must* remember. You spoke about it."

"I don't," her grandfather shrugged.

"Me neither," said her grandmother.

They always tell me the truth. Are their memories going? Muzz asked inside. "Never mind," she told them. "Maybe I'm imagining things."

Her grandfather winked at her. "You always had quite an imagination."

Her grandmother made her oat bread with apple jam and a mug of chamomile tea. While she ate, they kept one ear on the door.

"No one's up yet," said her grandfather.

Her grandmother handed her a worn basket with a broken handle. "Some mornings much early, Gronthor collects wilted produce and brings it to our kitchen. He uses a basket like this."

Her grandfather examined her head to toe. "You look convincing. I doubt they'll stop you."

Her grandmother tucked a handful of oatcakes into her jumpsuit pocket. "Be safe," she told Muzz.

Both of them hugged and kissed her, and she kissed back hard. *It could be years before I see them again, or never.*

After that, bent slightly and hands in pockets, Muzz and her grandfather strode together toward the entrance to the Great Hall, where a drowsy guard waved her on. Muzz slipped through the Great Hall to her own tunnel, and hobbled away.

CHAPTER SEVEN

She made it to Tropical without a hitch. When she spied her shed, she wanted to dash to it, but she hobbled every last step. What she saw inside made her eyes snap shut. Windowless, stuffy, crammed with tools and supplies, the shed would be a tough place to call home.

At her real home, her parents and Chell would be rolling out of bed for morning oatcakes. *Are they missing me?* Her classmates in Higher would be praising the antics of their pets in the Lab runs. *Are they missing me? And who will feed Emily? Brush her? Pet her?*

But Muzz knew enough not to dwell on all that. "I'll clean you. I'll change you. I'll learn to like you," she announced to her shed as she entered.

After yanking off the Witherer's cap and letting her scalp hair tumble to her shoulders, she heaped some space suits over the Gronthor disguise, and set to work.

Half an hour later she had swept and scrubbed the shed, cleared a space on her rustic worktable, stowed her tools and seeds, scoured her sink, opened a patch of floor where she could sleep. Trouble was, she had no Lab hair mattress, no bench to sit on, no stew for the table, no pup to warm her feet, not one story book to open after lightdown, no lamp to read by if she did. Battling self-pity, she set about tending her plantains and avocados.

Muzz fell asleep under an avocado tree and woke up confused. *How much time has passed? Is it still the same day?*

She could hardly grasp why, in a patch of tropical plants she had tended so long, she felt so disoriented. She spied Martrell walking down the far side of the enclosure, and rushed over to get her attention. But Martrell fixed her face in a blank stare, trudged toward Citrus in silence.

Muzz turned away with burning cheeks. *What if no one ever speaks to me again? What if I sigh, sniff, pout and fidget forever while I'm hoeing and pruning trees? How long can I stand a forever like this?*

She picked up a shrunken avocado that must have dropped weeks before, and tossed it from one hand to the other. *If only Em was here,* she thought, *what fun we could have playing avocado fetch.* She knew Em would have liked sniffing and digging in the enclosure. *She might even start to prefer plantains to Lab food.*

If only I could smuggle a few fat volumes from Book Storage for entertainment. I would make them last forever by slow reading. I'd forget the beginning by the end and start all over. She wondered how to get hold of some good books.

A brainstorm sent her to the shed for her harvest report pad and writing stick. "Hi, Jerith," she wrote. "If I'm asleep when you come through, please wake me up. I need to talk."

She set the note by the central path where Jerith would spot it on his harvest rounds. Then she felt good enough to start hunting down food for her first meal — two softish plantains, and an extra-ripe avocado. The raw plantains tasted dry and mealy, of course, not at all like the ones her mother simmered in walnut oil. But the avocado's smooth texture was delicious. *This is not so bad. I'll eat these and ration the oatcakes Grandma gave me.* Encouraged, she lay down to nap until Jerith arrived.

A twig breaking underfoot woke her. She jumped to her feet, and called "Jerith?"

But it was only Martrell retracing her steps — *Martrell the silent, Martrell the stuck-up.*

It took Muzz a few days to comprehend that everyone was ignoring her, and even Jerith might never come again. After the second day, she retrieved her note, ripped it up. By the third, she was glad she had. Because when she heard the familiar creaking of Jerith's cart, she wanted to shriek for joy. But instead of Jerith, a gruff cave guard — tall, broad-shouldered, with a mechanical gait and one of the detestable shiny helmets — marched up pushing the harvest cart.

When he drew near, she saw it was Framp's cousin Ninskor, and crouched behind some big plants. But he spotted her and came to a rattling halt.

When Muzz stayed low, pretending to search for weeds, he cleared his throat loudly.

"Everyone knows you're here, Muzz, and there's something I've been told to ask you."

She stood up, but stayed put.

"Do you realize you've been banished, ha ha ha? That means you can't go home again. Not ever, ha ha ha. You won't see your family, your friends, or even your Lab. You're stuck here weeding and snipping dead leaves and branches, eating only a bit of what you grow until you change... or else."

"Or else what, Sir?"

"Or else suffer, foolish female. The Beacons have given you twenty days to change your mind."

"How many days are left?"

"Seventeen."

Frosty toenails! I lost a whole day, she told herself. After Ninskor left, she used her clippers to dig three notches into her worktable. Since lightdown never happened in Tropical, she would make a notch each time she heard Martrell coming. *But I promise not to call to her again no matter how lonesome I feel.*

The day she scratched her fifth notch, a tremblor rattled Tropical, swaying the grow lights in the beams, and toppling her pitchfork and spade. She thought to make a longer notch each time there was a tremblor. On the morning of notch ten, Muzz awoke incredibly hungry. *Could more than one day have passed since I last ate? What if Martrell came down with cave fever or ditched her chores, and threw off my sense of time? Or what if I slept right through her rounds?*

There was no way of knowing for sure. But her grandmother's oatcakes were gone, and she had just six avocadoes stockpiled in her shed, all of them unripe. She felt desperate for something to eat, and suffered in other ways — bad dreams, loneliness, jitters.

She checked her food stash again and, no, there was nothing to eat. She cast a longing glance toward Citrus. *Martrell's oranges are so close I can taste them.*

Lemon trees came first, many rows of them, then orange trees laden with fruit. She grabbed a ragged bag near Martrell's shed.

Martrell's shed? Surprised how far into Citrus she had come, Muzz raced to fill the bag with juicy oranges.

She had picked nearly a dozen before voices reached her. *What horrible timing! This fruit is contraband!* Muzz sped with the bag back to her own territory, and stopped to catch her breath.

"Hepu Muzz! Show yourself," a male voice called. Muzz peeked from between leaves, and saw half a dozen cave guards armed with sharp staves.

A man with his back to her wore the unmistakable headdress of a Beacon, and next to him stood Mrs. Whitford in all her miraculous, ancient strength.

Mrs. Whitford called, "Muzz, do show yourself, and don't be frightened. We're here to help." Muzz ducked down fast.

"Is that you, Muzz?" Mrs. Whitford was looking straight at her.

Muzz stood up an inch at a time, stopped short when one of the guards pointed at her and chuckled. The other guards laughed, too. *Do I look wild-eyed or something?*

Her eyes met the Second Beacon's, who said in his gravelly voice, "Come here, Muzz. We need to speak with you." He looked impatient and imposing.

Mrs. Whitford called, "We're here to help you, Muzz. It was my idea. Come on over."

Though Muzz could not read Mrs. Whitford very well from there, her voice felt like a caress. So she set the oranges down, and went.

Mrs. Whitford gave her a huge hug, drew back to look at her. "Tattered, but safe," she said, and glared at the Second Beacon.

A faint frown flickered across his face. "Every inch of our Cave is safe." He turned to Muzz.

"You have Mrs. Whitford to thank for this visit." He sniffed loudly. "We haven't dealt with your sort before. But Mrs. Whitford has informed us about certain human practices with prisoners."

Mrs. Whitford nodded. "You see, any incarcerated human — any prisoner — was entitled to decent food, clean water, a bed to—"

"No need to explain. Guards, set down the sleeping roll and urn."

Three guards from the rear stepped forward, placed a woven mat, a thin blanket, and a clay water urn on the ground.

The Second Beacon nodded. "We're done here."

"What about food," said Mrs. Whitford. She gave Muzz a secret nod that the rest of them missed.

"All right. Give her what you have."

Mrs. Whitford pulled a bundle from her silk cape. "This is from your mother. Enough yam and collard stew for two nights, a packet of walnuts, and a dozen oatcakes." She turned to the Beacon. "I'll put these items in her shed. Come along, Muzz. Show me where you want them."

When they were alone, Mrs. Whitford clutched her, whispered, "I have something to teach you that will help you survive — a technique I use called 'delving deep.' It isn't the only way to enliven the mind, of course. But it's a good one. Helps me stay calm and centered. Whitford taught it to me back on earth, a special word and a special way to use it that's *infinitely* helpful when the world you're used to falls apart."

The Second Beacon appeared at the door. "Come along. You're taking too long."

"Blast it!" Mrs. Whitford hissed. She left the shed with Muzz close behind.

The Beacon scowled and smoothed his robe. "One last thing, Muzz. In nine days you'll be banished forever." *Nine days?* It bothered Muzz to have missed another day in her calculations.

He continued, "I urge you to reconsider your decision. Drent is a fine, healthy young male destined for a meaningful Calling. He might even make it into the cave guards, for all you know. Think what an honorable life awaits you. The alternative is hardly a life at all."

"Yes, by all means, give it some careful thought, Muzz," said Mrs. Whitford. When their eyes met, Mrs. Whitford shrugged the tiniest bit, and said, "We'll be back soon."

The Beacon turned to leave, and so did everyone else.

"One last hug!" cried Muzz, rushing to Mrs. Whitford.

The Beacon shut his eyes and sighed while Muzz threw her arms around Mrs. Whitford's neck. As their cheeks touched, Muzz said softly, "Please send someone? Jerith or Tendra?" Mrs. Whitford stiffened, and Muzz knew she had heard.

They all left. At the last possible moment Mrs. Whitford turned and waved. Then Muzz was alone.

In the shed with her booty, she unrolled the mat and blanket, flopped onto her new sleeping nest, yanked the wrapping from the packet of food. Soon she had everything spread before her.

One oatcake had a note on it saying, "Eat this first." She bit and her teeth hit something hard — a shiny object. *Mother's precious silver pillbox! She must want to encourage me,* Muzz told herself.

Two tightly wadded clumps of parchment fell out of the pillbox and she undid one, a letter in Chell's handwriting:

Greetings, Outcast — I guess you know you've caused a huge stir. The whole Cave is talking about your 'insolent, traitorous' behavior, as the First Beacon likes to call it. At first, I was angry with you because of my Calling. I pictured a heavenly future with Tendra, and the son and daughter we imagine together. But now, as you may have heard, Tendra is betrothed to Jerith against all our wishes. Is it symbolic that it happened the day of the tremblor? I'm doomed to marry Fluelle, and talk caveball and Lab food forever!

Q: How much does a small thing like my Calling matter now?

A: Much less if Tendra and I are doomed.

Q: How much does my sister matter to me?

A: As much as ever — a whole lot.

Though on the surface Tendra, Jerith and I make the best of all this, we are seething inside. As I think you know, Jerith loves you. So all our hopes are dashed.

Father is sullen, Mother mute. Even Em's tail has lost its wag. What bright light the Beacons shed on all our lives! Tendra, who is helping me write this, promises to scribble a note of her own soon now that Mother can provide you with food.

I'll close by saying we miss you much.

Stay well, dear sister,

Chell

P.S. Plantains and avocados? Eat beyond your share.
(:

CHAPTER EIGHT

The second letter read:

Funny One — Chell saved some news for me — not good, but worth telling. We are all frozen solid that not even Chell and Tendra will have the satisfaction of sharing their lives. Since the Beacons betrothed Tendra to me, some of the students in Higher whisper how unfair Hepu Dorne's decisions are this year.

47

The rest are quiet, but with smoldering eyes. In past years Hepu Dorne and the Beacons tried to please us with their choices. Now they want to oppress us. H.D. acts twice as smug in class. I can hear you say "impossible," but believe me it is possible.

As if that's not enough, I've been shifted to my Calling early. I'm a Garden Scout collecting refuse from ten tunnels (all but Tropical and Forbidden) and grinding it for mulch. Though mulching matters, it was never considered a Calling before; it's so dull and repetitive. I'm sure Dorne had his hand in this. He knows I'm much disappointed in my betrothal and want to help you however I can. He devised this new "Calling" to thwart me.

To make matters worse he wants Chell, Drent and me to leave for our Walkabout before graduation with windy season in full force. No previous sixteenth yearling males have had to face that, as you know.

The Beacons dismiss our parents' objections by saying we'll be testing new, warmer walksuits invented by none other than Hepu Dorne. Drent thinks he plans to freeze us solid and be done with us. I think he wants to show the Tribe just how much the son of the First Beacon can push everyone around. We leave in less than two weeks, a month earlier than usual. Lessons and mulch leave me no time to line my boots with fake fur. My father, praise Whitford, is doing it for me.

Speaking of fur, Emily misses you much. I see her with her head on her paws whenever I pass your grottoette. Her poor doggy mind must be much bewildered! Last week she was asleep with her legs racing. Dreaming of adventures with you, no doubt, and who can blame her? Chell says at lightdown she lolls on the floor near your bed and crawls in when no one is looking.

Missing you,

Jerith

The letters left Muzz less lonely despite their bad news. But when more days passed without Mrs. Whitford or the friends Muzz had asked for showing up, her mood darkened. And after several days of seeing no one but pompous, spiteful Ninskor, she felt miserable.

On the twentieth day he showed up to ask one last time if Muzz had 'learned what from what' yet. When she shook her head no, he read her a decree from the Beacons saying she was out-and-out banished for good. He delivered another packet of oatcakes and fresh drinking water, hoisted the empty urn and marched off.

Muzz felt a surge of misgiving. She wanted to shout "wait!" at him, to run after him, to beg to be accepted back. But she dreaded facing the life Hepu Dorne and the Beacons required even more than the lonesome, steamy doldrums of Tropical. So she went to her shed, plunked herself on her mat, and checked each oatcake for messages. There were none.

Nothing, though one oatcake was broken in half. That had happened at least twice since the first time. *Does that miserable cave guard swipe my mail?* Muzz wondered, remembering Tendra's promise to write.

At odd moments when her chores were done and she was not sneaking to the orange grove for a change of diet, her shed was a nest where she roosted, hoping to hatch some plan that would crack the egg to a better future. There she reread her letters, and counted notches. She calculated that within just a few days the sixteenth yearling males would be leaving.

Walkabout!

It was the time each year when the three newly betrothed males left the warmth and safety of the Cave as they arrived at the threshold of adulthood to spend a solid week in the frigid, wild terrain of The Planet. They would grapple with the forces of cold and wind on The Planet's dark, barren surface. For the trek they received scant supplies: a tiny burner for warmth, some freeze-dried food, a single three-Hepu tent, a rudimentary map to guide them to infamous Lookout Rock, and a miraculous Lamp to light the way that no one but the adult males was allowed to see.

Only adult males could see, touch, or use the Lamp. Only they set foot outside the Cave, made the arduous trek to Lookout Rock. To prove they had made it, each year the three carried a pickaxe and returned with a chip of the deep red rock that lay beneath the icy crust up there. Muzz knew the winds would make the whole trek more difficult. *Treacherous,* she thought, picturing Chell, Jerith and Drent huddled in a fierce storm.

Lately she had started doing something new to express herself, something she felt better about than talking to herself the way Witherers did when they started forgetting.

She had seen this in a film Hepu Dorne aired once to show how competitive, cruel, and corrupt humans could be, a film called *West Side Story*. When the humans in it felt strong emotions, they broke into song and dance, and that was what Muzz had started doing in Tropical.

Sometimes she used tunes from the film; sometimes she made up her own. This time she tripped among the avocado trees singing a made-up tune: "I need helllp, I'm alooone, and I'm baaanished, got no hooome." She swung a half circle around an avocado trunk, let go, used a series of leaps to return to her shed.

"Can't reach Tennndra, can't reach Chelll. Want to exxx-plain this is helll." She twirled dizzily and landed on one foot.

Muzz froze for a moment, gripped by a feeling of being watched though she had neither heard nor seen anything unusual. As her gaze darted around, she spotted two tiny red beads of light beaming from the rafters of Tropical.

She blinked, rubbed her eyes, stared.

The bright red dots slid along the ceiling and halted directly overhead. Horrified, she ran to the plantains and dove in.

The lights crisscrossed the ceiling.

Ever so slowly they zigged one way and zagged the other, gliding closer to her hiding place. Just as they were about to slip by overhead, she lost her balance and shook a frond. The dots hesitated, began moving again a little to the left, a little to the right, and stopped right over her.

"Frosted froth," she hissed under her breath. She ran for her shed, dove, pulled up the covers. She waited a long time before sticking her head back out. When she peeked, she saw the red lights on the lintel of the shed door!

Muzz stifled a yelp that surfaced as a high-pitched "meeerf!" and the beads of light vanished. She lay there trembling.

It took a long time for her breath and heart rate to normalize. When they did, she crawled out from under the covers, her eyes riveted to the spot where she had last seen the luminous dots.

"What *was* that?"

Sticking her head out her shed door, she examined every inch of the Tropical ceiling as far as she could see. Nothing. Then a terrifying question came to mind: *What if I imagined them?*

"Something's wrong with me," she half groaned, half sobbed. *Life in exile with nothing but whirring fans, damp air and incessant grow lights might drive a banished Hepu crazy.*

She was lost in this labyrinth of worry when she recalled what she had been thinking right before her hallucination (*if that was what it was*) began. Her eyes lit up. In an instant she was back in her shed digging through the jumpsuits and pulling out her Gronthor disguise. A new plan was forming in her mind.

She donned the Gronthor suit, hardly caring if it looked convincing, and set out boldly for the Great Hall. She reached the tunnel after lightdown, and pressed on. It felt good to be walking, so good that she forgot to limp until she was well into Tribal territory. Luckily there was no one to notice. At the Great Hall entrance, she passed a slumbering guard who sighed deeply as she tiptoed past, but predictably did not wake up.

She slipped into a dark nook to plan her next move, tucked some stray scalp hair into the hat. From her vantage point near the edge of the underground stream, the Great Hall looked and sounded wonderful to her. Warm water spilled from one pool to the next with the gurgling ripples she had come to love. Her eyes teared up over all she had been missing — the delicious chats with Tendra, the reassuring hubbub of Lessons, Em's joyous bark when they played fetch, the laughter of Chell and Jerith somewhere close. A draft made the lantern light on the rocky walls quiver spookily, and she loved that too. She bent to dip her hand in a warm pool, and watched it bend and glisten where she touched. She crossed the stream as stealthily as she could. *There's Jerith's tunnel.*

A guard with auburn face hair who played caveball on her father's team snoozed, arms folded over his broad chest and stave propped against the wall. He let out an explosive snore that sent her scurrying. Then she was passing darkened doorways.

Jerith's was the fifth on the left. His pup, Samuel Johnson, was outside and jumped her, tail wagging so furiously that it hit the grottoette door. Muzz heard sounds inside and ducked into shadow.

The door opened. "Quiet, boy," a voice whispered.

"Jerith!" Muzz breathed. The door opened wider, Jerith's head popped out. He eyed her and the dog through the darkness, then checked behind him, came out, grabbed his dog's collar and lowered him resolutely to the floor. Then after hugging Muzz, he guided her away from his door.

"Whitford's wisdom, what are you doing here? Your disguise looks pathetic. What if they catch you?"

Muzz shrugged. "Listen, Jerith. I need a new disguise. I want to look like a *young* male."

"Oh, no! What for?"

She would have to say it. "To come on the Walkabout."

Jerith's mouth dropped open. "No way! It's only for the three of us. There are public ceremonies. You know that. Besides, it'd be dangerous." He shook his head. "What were you thinking?"

"I can't stand being cooped up in Tropical anymore. I think I'm going crazy, and besides, I want to see what's out there."

Jerith's whispered "no" seemed to explode in the quiet tunnel.

"Jerith?" his mother called from within.

He motioned Muzz toward deeper shadows, whispered, "I'll come back if I can."

"Lie down, fellow," he said more loudly, and then, "Samuel was whining."

He went inside. Muzz heard more talk and a loud shushing sound before everything went quiet in the grottoette. She waited a long time in the shadows, careful not to make eye contact with Sammy for fear he would cause another commotion. After a while she started to worry. *What if lightrise comes and I have no place to hide?* She was almost ready to give up and leave when Jerith reappeared.

"You're mentally disturbed, Muzz. But I've thought this over. Tell me more about what you have in mind."

"Hmmm... I don't have all the details worked out yet, but I think Mrs. Whitford will help. When I went to visit her, she supported me about betrothal. She doesn't like all the restrictions. Also, if anyone can get hold of one of the old style walksuits, she can."

"Then what? Drent and Chell would never go for this. How could she sneak you out?"

Muzz shrugged, her eyes big with excitement. "As I said, I don't have all the details worked out yet, but I'm certain it can work. Please, Jerith, please give me a chance."

Jerith studied her face and then shook his head. "Okay, sure, I'll try to help you even though — Who knows? Maybe we'll *both* be banished."

"So you'll give me some clothes?"

"Not now. My mother sleeps lightly. Besides, we need a decent plan to make this work. First off, *no* one, not even Chell, can know what you have in mind."

Muzz grinned. "Well *I* won't be telling anyone."

"You might if you were captured and interrogated."

Muzz shook her head hard.

Jerith searched the shadows. "It's only an hour until lightrise. I'll come to Tropical very late tonight. Don't wait up; I'll wake you. Meanwhile you'd better devise a foolproof plan."

He hugged her, and tiptoed to his grottoette door.

"Thanks, Jerith. This makes a hard day exciting."

"You think this is hard! Just wait until you're climbing Lookout Rock."

Muzz nodded excitedly. *My first real adventure.*

At a bend in the tunnel to Tropical, she heard voices. Two guards loaded with armor rattled into view, and she ducked into a hollow.

"... mustn't let Dorne know we couldn't find her," one was saying in a gruff voice that sounded like Framp or his brother Ninskor. The other guard grunted.

"What with all the unrest in Higher, he wants to know where she is day and night," the gruff voice continued.

"I hear the Beacons plan to come down hard on all of 'em."

Someone snickered. "Yep, no more coddling anyone."

"Culling's what I heard. You too?"

"Right, ha ha ha, her, and anyone else that gets in the way."

Footsteps. "That's why we can't just *hear* her rustling around in the brush anymore. We need to *see* her. Day and night. Day and night."

More footsteps. "That female's way more trouble than she's worth. If the Highers know what from what, they'll forget this nonsense and be done with her."

His partner whistled softly. "If..."

Muzz strained to hear more, but as they rounded a bend, their clacks and words tapered off.

She had heard Tribe members bickering over what was safe to tell authorities, or listing penalties for misconduct before. But this had a more sobering ring, and having it about *her* made her petrified.

CHAPTER NINE

All that day Muzz waited for Jerith in a state of suspense and watchfulness, partly from what she had overheard, partly from trying to concoct a 'foolproof' plan. He had said not to wait up and she wanted to comply. So as lightdown approached she settled into her 'nest.' But she was still awake when he arrived, and sat bolt upright, spoke his name out loud.

Jerith poked his head in and silenced her with big eyes and a finger on his lips. "We need to talk."

Muzz saw he was empty-handed. "Where's my disguise?"

"Relax, if you can. In fact, relax even if you can't."

"Be serious if *you* can."

"I am serious." Jerith sat cross-legged on the ground facing Muzz, folded his hands, leaned closer.

"I didn't bring anything for you because it's either you or me, and 'me' makes so much more sense. A walksuit is the only disguise that will work, and I refuse to give you mine because *I* want to go on the Walkabout."

"But there must be a—"

"There isn't. Only one of us can go, and I've been waiting for this since I can remember. Not going would be devastating for me — disappointment and disgrace."

Muzz stared into space, slumped, sighed loudly at this sickening development.

"Also," Jerith said, in a slightly louder whisper, "even if I gave you my walksuit, someone would surely see that you were you during the Sendoff."

The Sendoff was the annual ceremony that took place right before the three sixteenth yearling males left on their expedition. Muzz pictured what happened at the Sendoff and had to admit Jerith was right. The three stood on the stage in their walksuits, each holding a giant fake fur-lined helmet. Everyone in the Tribe came to see them off. A few older males told stories — some funny, some scary, all cautionary — and offered advice. The mothers wept and hugged their sons, and the fathers shook their hands and thumped their backs.

"Besides," Jerith went on, "This whole scheme is way too perilous."

"I'm not afraid of a little ice and wind, Jerith."

"Well, maybe you should be. We've had survival training. There's ice, wind, and also major climbing. It's steep out there and rocky."

Muzz closed her eyes. "It's rocky in here."

"Don't get huffy, Funny One. The weather and terrain matter, our training matters, but these dangers may be small compared to how seriously angry with you Dorne and the Beacons are."

"If you were to go, as soon as they found out — and there's no doubt that they *would* find out — they'd declare out-and-out war against you and anyone in league with you."

Muzz stared at a scramble of plantain stalks. "There *must* be a way."

Jerith pursed his lips, shook his head. In the silence that followed, she could hear the noisome whir of the overhead fans.

Muzz pointed upwards. "Do you hear that?"

"What?"

"That incessant whirring?"

"Of course. And the reason you're mentioning that is...?

Muzz looked directly in his eyes. "Because it's driving me crazy. I can't stand it anymore."

"Sorry, Muzz, but if we want food, there's no way to fix that."

"Mmmmm," said Muzz. A smile of pure joy transformed her. "I have it!"

Jerith folded his arms and cast her a suspicious look. "Yeah?"

"After the ceremony, what happens?"

Jerith shrugged. "We leave."

"And *how* do you leave?"

"We go out through the exit chamber."

"Right. And how do you get out?"

"Through the hatch, of course."

"You're being difficult." Muzz sighed.

"Well, what are you driving at?"

Muzz jumped to her feet, her hands in the air. "The key. Where do you get the key?"

"From Mrs. Whitford, of course. The Key Bearer gets the key, we use it to exit, and he carries it in a banana leaf pouch tied to his ankle, inside his boot, the entire time we're gone."

"And who watches you do this?"

Jerith flipped his hands palm up. "Only Mrs. Whitford, but—"

"Right," said Muzz. "The tunnel narrows so much by the time you get to Mrs. Whitford's that you're walking single file. No one can see you. Then there's a bend in the tunnel just before her grottoette. She leaves the Sendoff early to go back and get the key, right? So she's waiting for you at her door. *Alone.*"

Jerith frowned. "What are you thinking of doing to that poor—"

"Not anything *to* her. Mrs. Whitford thinks the Beacons are too hard on us, especially on the young females. She told me so herself." Muzz paused to let that sink in. "She'll help me. I know she will."

"OK, say that's true. How will she help?"

"Here it is. She lets me wait in her grottoette. Then you volunteer as Key Bearer and when you knock, she invites you in. Chell and Drent wait outside. I jump into your walksuit and go in your place!" Before Jerith could object, she added, "She has another walksuit waiting for you, one of the old reliable ones. So pretty soon, you follow us out."

"Assuming Mrs. Whitford agrees to all this, what am I supposed to do when I get out there? Chell and Drent can count, you know."

Muzz shrugged. "You lag behind with a much dim light for a few hours."

"What about the light on my visor?"

"You dial it down. You follow close enough to see our light, but with such a small light of your own that we can't see you. Even five minutes behind ought to do it."

"I don't know." Jerith grimaced and held his forehead. "Let's say I lag behind the entire day without Drent or Chell noticing. Now it's time to camp and they discover I'm you. They're angry as twisters. Meanwhile it's so cold outside that I have to come into the tent. What's stopping them from insisting we all go back?"

"We'll have to sleep there no matter what. By the time they wake up, after they've dreamt on it, their feelings will settle. Trust me."

Jerith sat quiet, arms folded, staring through rather than seeing Muzz. Finally he looked directly at her and shook his head. "Funny One, I'm sorry. I care much for you and want to help. But this is big trouble."

Muzz saw that Jerith would not change his mind. Before he left she remembered to ask about Tendra's note, learned that she *had* sent one that someone intercepted. Mrs. Whitford had sent one too. Knowing her mail was being intercepted made everything worse. Long before the Tribe began stirring for the day, Jerith went home.

"Withered wasp wings!" Muzz muttered when he was out of range.

She pondered, but could not think of another plan. Then, after Lessons the next day, she ran into Martrell heading for Citrus. To her surprise, Martrell stopped to talk.

"Muzz, I am much glad to see you."

"You are?"

"Much." Martrell stood in front of Muzz with arms limp, eyes wide open and soft.

"I have wanted to speak with you ever since the time I gave you the snub. A guard was watching me. I knew if we spoke I'd be reported."

Muzz glanced around. "Is it safe to talk now?"

Martrell nodded. "The cave guards are meeting with the Beacons."

"What about?"

"You, me, all of us. It's about what you started, the conflict over Hepu Dorne. Nearly all of us are with you now. There is much unrest in Higher and the Beacons know it."

"There is?"

"Yes. They want us watched from lightdown to lightrise and the cave guards are stirred up about it."

Martrell tensed her shoulders. "What they don't know is that we're having a meeting ourselves to plan an insurrection." Martrell made it sound like a small miracle.

"That sounds much dangerous."

Martrell shrugged. "We're meeting at midnight to get organized."

"Where?"

"I promised not to tell."

Muzz looked crestfallen. Then her eyes lit up. "Will you take a note to Mrs. Whitford for me? Right away? Not about this, of course."

Martrell agreed to do it.

"Fine, I'll go and write it. When it's finished, I'll leave it right here." Muzz lifted a mossy clump of soil with the toe of her shoe.

Martrell nodded, "I'll get it on my way out." They hugged, went their separate ways, and by suppertime the note was on the move.

Muzz did not know which fact upset her more — Jerith's refusal to help or the Highers' plan. A little before midnight, she threw on her Gronthor disguise and, by the time midnight rolled around, had sneaked past snoring guards at two checkpoints. She followed the underground stream to where she guessed the Highers would meet. And she was right; she found about a dozen of them sprawled together in the shadows outside the drying room.

Tendra saw her first, and pointed. Loud whispers broke out at the sight of her. Tendra stood, threw her arms wide open, started bouncing excitedly. But Chell stood too and raised a hand to quell Tendra's excitement.

He said, "Muzz! What are you doing here?"

"I have something important to say."

Chell glowered at everyone. "Who told you we were here?"

Before Martrell could confess, Tendra said, "I may have hinted at something in my letter."

Chell slumped, shook his head. "Be my guest," he told Muzz with an exaggerated sweep of his hand.

"You are much brave to join us," said Tendra. Even Drent's cousin Jeeklo nodded at that.

Muzz knelt before them, looked around. "I want to discourage you from this plan."

Chell folded his arms and frowned, but she kept talking.

"I overheard two guards talking recently. The Beacons are ready to come down hard on all of us. Hepu Dorne's father is the most cutthroat of all. He's talking about culling rebels. I'm first on the list, but everyone's in danger."

Jerith spoke up. "I don't know how you heard about this, but you shouldn't have risked coming here. And you won't discourage us."

"We're determined to fight," said Tendra. Everyone nodded.

Muzz felt frightened for them. "I'm ready for whatever they want to throw at me. But why should anybody else get hurt?"

Tendra looked sullen. "Too late, Muzz. Our minds are made up."

"This is only a strategy meeting," said Chell. "Nothing's going to happen until after the Walkabout."

They all nodded. Tendra stood and held out her hand. "Get up, Muzz. You should go. We won't change and you're risking too much by being here."

Jerith cast her a cross look. "Muzz loves taking risks."

Reluctantly Muzz let Tendra pull her to her feet. She faced them. "Okay, I'll go. But I know how unbending the Beacons can be. I wish you'd find other ways to express your anger."

Chell scoffed. "Poetry, maybe? Melodies?"

Jerith and Tendra walked a few steps with Muzz.

When Tendra hugged her, she whispered in her ear, "I said it all in my letter. I get it now, Muzz. I see what you were trying to do."

Muzz closed her eyes and held her friend tight. "Be careful" was all she said.

Jerith took his turn, holding Muzz at arms length, a range of emotion crossing his face. "Don't fret, Funny One. We'll plan carefully and wait until after the Walkabout to act. We won't strike until the right moment. If we can garner support, we will. And keep in mind this is for you as much as for the rest of us. So take good care of yourself, promise? I'll contact you when we get back." With eyes closed, he gave her a warm hug.

CHAPTER TEN

Less than thirty hours later, again as Gronthor, Muzz sat facing the lovely painting in Mrs. Whitford's grottoette. She was not thinking about the human with the white face hair or the charming sailboats in the picture. Instead, she was attuned to the mix of sounds — some loud, some muffled — pulsing round the bend in the tunnel to Mrs. Whitford's door.

A roar of laughter welled from the crowd in the Great Hall.

When will Mrs. Whitford arrive, she wondered, *and will she be alone?*

The Sendoff had been underway for nearly an hour with the band playing "The Walkabout Bounce" and other favorites. The milling crowd on its way to the ceremony provided excellent cover for Muzz's Gronthor move.

But one thing bothered her: since Mrs. Whitford was already in the Great Hall, there had been no chance to talk. Faithful to Muzz's wish, however, the door to the dear old woman's grottoette was unlocked.

But is *it faithful?* Muzz shifted uneasily in her seat. She did not know whether Mrs. Whitford ever locked her door. *Maybe she didn't receive the note. Maybe she received it, but doesn't want to help. And even if she does, what if some guard comes back here with her?* Deep doubts tugged at Muzz as she imagined the range of reactions Mrs. Whitford might have had to her note, plus all the other problems that could arise.

She heard footsteps and jumped to her feet, ducking behind Mrs. Whitford's table. The door opened and there she was. *Alone!* Muzz held her breath.

Mrs. Whitford shut the door and wheeled around. "Muzz? Are you here?"

A wave of relief washed over her. "Yes," she cried, showing herself. Mrs. Whitford came up and clasped her in a hug.

"Chilblains! I hardly recognize you in that get-up. You're a perfect Witherer. But we haven't much time."

She moved to the screen in the corner, and motioned Muzz to follow. "The Sendoff's nearly over. Come see what's in store for poor Jerith."

Mrs. Whitford snatched a long, uneven rope from a hook on the wall. It was made of her crocheted wool stockings knotted together. Muzz uncoiled it, yanked to gauge its strength.

"I used square knots." Mrs. Whitford looked pleased with herself.

Next she pulled something bulky from a basket and held it up. "See this? It's the insulation for under your walksuit. Get into it."

Muzz grabbed the bulky thing, stepped in, pushed her arms through the sleeves, fastened it.

There was a knock on the door. "I'll bring him in and sit him down," Mrs. Whitford whispered. "It's up to you to do the rest."

Muzz crouched behind the bench as Mrs. Whitford opened the door. "Chell! What are *you* doing here?"

Muzz covered her mouth. *Chell will ruin everything.* She kept her head low.

"I'm here for the key, Mrs. Whitford." Muzz could hear Chell shift from foot to foot.

"Forgive me, Chell. I was expecting Jerith. I distinctly recall that Jerith is to carry the key."

There was a silence in which Muzz pictured Chell biting his lip as he did at such times.

"Jerith!" he called. There was a pause, and then he and Jerith talked.

It ended with Chell saying, "To avoid delay, *you* take the pouch and get the key. I'll wait outside."

Mrs. Whitford said, "Welcome, Jerith." The door closed.

"Sit right down. And please close your eyes. The key is in a secret spot."

"Certainly, Mrs. Whitford." The bench creaked as Jerith sat on it.

Mrs. Whitford crossed the room and mouthed "Go, go!" silently at Muzz while whooshing her hands.

Muzz sprang forward, quickly looped the rope to catch Jerith's arms at the elbows, tied it to the bench back, tightened and knotted it.

"Wha—" he yelped. "What's—?" Mrs. Whitford stuffed a sock in his mouth. "Really sorry to do this to you, Jerith. But it's for a higher cause. So keep quiet, and you won't get hurt."

Muzz looped the rope again so that the second loop caught him at the shoulders. She had trapped all but his flailing hands. She yanked the rope tight and wound the rest of it around his ankles fast, drew that tight, too.

"Hold completely still," she commanded. "I need your walksuit." She felt a lot of glee at two females subduing a strapping sixteenth yearling male.

And one of us over ninety at that!

"Mourf," Jerith gasped, struggling to get free. Mrs. Whitford lifted her brass lamp. "Calm down, or I'll have to bop you one."

Neither Hepu knew the word 'bop', but her meaning was clear.

"Please don't hurt him."

"Leave him to me and get that suit on."

The walksuit, slippery and lightweight, was challenging — but not impossible — to slide in and out of the ropes. Muzz peeled Jerith to his insulation. He gave up the struggle, clasped his hands, slumped. *I might feel sorry if he hadn't refused to help.*

"There's another walksuit for you," Muzz said as she pulled his on. Jerith shrugged and stared at the floor in silence.

"Don't forget the pouch," said Mrs. Whitford, still towering over Jerith, lamp in hand.

In the ruckus, Jerith had flung the pouch away. Muzz spied it on the floor at the far end of the table.

"And the helmet."

Muzz hardly noticed how heavy the helmet felt or how unwieldy Jerith's fur-lined boots were for her.

Mrs. Whitford set the lamp down, went to the door. "Helmets on, chaps, it's time to go." She watched Chell and Drent fasten their helmets, opened the door just wide enough to let Muzz out, squeezed her hand, and shoved the key into it. "Success!" she cried with a bright smile.

Muzz spotted Jerith's pack on the tunnel floor, swung it on her back, motioned toward the exit chamber and led the way without a word, unlocking the inner door. *It's a good thing I'm not short. They haven't noticed anything.* The three of them stepped into a small booth.

She closed the inner door behind them. "Ready?" she asked in a voice as deep as she could make it. She was glad for the helmets, which muffled everything. She was glad for the suit's bulk, too, for it seemed to conceal even her smaller size. When Chell and Drent said they were ready, she felt safe, at least temporarily.

She unlocked the hatch and held it open, followed them onto the icy surface of The Planet. Ice crunched beneath her boots. There was neither wind nor snowfall, just stillness, ice, darkness. She could only guess how cold it was. Locking the door, she slipped the key in its pouch, and reached into her boot to secure the pouch to her ankle.

Chell and Drent switched on their helmet lights, pulled something from their pockets.

"Check your maps," said Chell.

Muzz fumbled, managed to switch on her helmet light, tugged a folded paper from her pocket. "D'you have your bearings?" Chell's tone roused an old annoyance at his way of lording it over her. *Think like Jerith,* Muzz told herself, and that idea kept her calm.

"Ready?" Drent grunted and so did she. "Then switch on your tanks. Breathe *naturally*. And above all, stick together. Let's trek!"

Muzz had never been more excited. *I am walking on crunchy ice!* As far as she knew, she was the first female ever to leave the Cave.

The map was hardly necessary since there was only one way they could go. Her helmet light was too dim to reveal much, but Muzz could tell they were entering some sort of canyon. Soon its frosty walls rose up sharply on one side of the path. A light snowfall chased silken currents of air up toward the invisible clouds.

Muzz wanted to take her helmet off, inhale the crisp air that haloed The Planet. But once a sixteenth yearling male had done that and collapsed from lack of oxygen. The moral of the story: The atmosphere out there contained oxygen, but not enough, and too much volcanic dust.

To Muzz, each step crunched like a mouthful of walnuts, and she welcomed the change from the hard floors inside the Cave. Still, a layer of ice beneath the crunch lent a sneaky slipperiness to every step. Jerith's boots had sharp cleats that kept her from slipping as long as she imitated Chell by lifting her knees, then slamming her boots down to cut footholds. Leg high—slam—cut—step—repeat. It was a tiring way to walk, but it kept her vertical.

Once she was used to stomping along behind the others, she noticed how different from the ring and echo inside the Cave this trek sounded from inside her helmet. Every footstep and every puff of wind seemed to sweep up and away.

When a gust of wind whipped through the canyon, they had to lean into it to avoid falling. Muzz knew she should detest it, but she loved the feel of this true air. *Maybe it's too thin to keep me level headed, but it's helping me somehow!*

From sheer joy she flapped her arms like the birds she had seen in films.

"Something wrong, Jerith?" Chell's amplified voice ringing in her helmet startled Muzz.

She realized they all had microphones, touched her glove to her mouthpiece, and — afraid to use her voice — shook her head in reply.

"Don't shake your head. You might loosen the seal. If your phone's not working, move your right hand up and down for yes, side to side for no, remember? And make a fist with your left to signal that you agree."

Muzz made a fist.

"So your phone's not working?"

How could she have prepared for this? Hidden in the helmets, their faces were not distinguishable, and she had counted on that. But Chell was her own brother! *If I use a microphone, even with a fake voice, he's sure to recognize me.*

She soundlessly mouthed, "Something's wrong with my speaker."

"What?" Chell moved closer, much to her dismay. "Is it your speaker?" Muzz made her right hand nod. She pointed at her mouthpiece and added some shrugs for good measure.

Chell eyeballed something on her belt. "Strange," he said. "The switch is on." By then Muzz had a lump in her throat that would have stopped her from speaking even if she wanted to.

He switched her speaker off and on. "Try now." Muzz silently mouthed, "Can you hear me?"

Chell folded his arms. "Maybe we should go back and get this taken care of."

Muzz shook her right hand forcefully. *No way should go we back!*

"No?" said Chell. He turned to Drent. "What do you think, Drent?" *No! No! Please say no!*

"After that huge Sendoff, going back sounds much bad. Besides, we have the repair kit."

"True," said Chell. "We'll fix it tonight in the tent."

Muzz made her hand nod, breathed more easily.

"But stay in sight, Jerith. You'd better walk between us."

They set out again with Drent in last place. It bothered Muzz to lose the comfort of that last spot. But, for the time being at least, her secret was safe. *No one knows it's me and that's the main thing.* She vowed to be extra careful not to draw more attention to herself.

They continued along the canyon wall, and started climbing, still on something like a trail that stayed wide, rose gradually. Once they crossed something with a drop of five or six feet on either side; Muzz wanted to aim her helmet light over the edge for a better look. But Chell kept a fast pace and there was nothing to do but follow.

She felt her breath coming faster, like hunger in her lungs, and wondered if she was getting enough oxygen. Chell stopped suddenly, turned back toward the Cave.

"Did you see that?... In the canyon? I... thought I saw... a flicker of light." He was breathing hard himself.

Muzz spotted a faint shaft of light, quickly there and just as quickly gone. *Jerith!* Her breath caught in her throat. *If Chell figures this out now, he'll make us go back.*

"I don't see anything," said Drent. "You sound out of breath."

"Did you see it?" Chell asked Muzz, ignoring him.

She studied the dark terrain, remembering a curve in the path. It was probably blocking the light for the moment. She made the 'no' gesture with her right hand.

Chell kept looking back.

Drent said, "Maybe you're... seeing things from tiredness. Want me... to take the lead?"

"You seem a little out of breath yourself, caveball champ." Chell was probably smiling. He scanned the darkness once more and finally set out, slowing the pace.

Muzz wondered if Jerith could see them. Would he slow down if they did? Would he stay in range, but not too close, as Mrs. Whitford must have cautioned? *I hope he's planning to wait till we stop tonight to unmask me.*

She forced herself not to look for him.

A rumble began behind them, low at first, then gathering force. It reached a crescendo, echoing until it stopped. Muzz could feel it through her feet — in fact, right through her body like a huge drum roll.

"Tremblor or avalanche?" asked Drent.

"Avalanche, I think," said Chell.

Muzz strained to recall what an avalanche was.

"Rocks falling, or only snow?" Drent asked.

"Probably both." Chell said, "There's no one out here but us, no help, no way to tell without going back."

No! Muzz thought inside.

"Remember what we were told to do if there's any kind of slide nearby. Get low and stay low. Shield yourself behind the biggest rock or snowdrift you can find. When the stuff stops falling, move out fast."

Muzz made a fist.

As they trekked on, she tried not to think about what might be looming above them, ready to break loose, or of Jerith back there, and what might have happened to him. The trail they were following — for it seemed like a trail even though Muzz knew it had been used only a few dozen times over the years — kept curving and rising until it had grown quite steep.

She had watched a film of humans climbing the highest mountain on Earth. There was snow and ice there, too, and heavy wind. She felt an awful pang of fear and regret that the three of them could not see their whereabouts well, and she hated not knowing where Jerith was.

They pressed on and time passed. The wind picked up and the trail flattened, but only briefly. Muzz could see in the light of Chell's helmet that they were coming to a steep downward slope. He stopped and said, "The perch!"

Muzz noticed that, from the vantage of this so-called 'perch', the path sloped in both directions. *The trail ahead looks much steep.* She was glad when Chell found a seat-sized rock nearby and sat down. "Time to eat."

For once Muzz was glad her big brother was in charge. They switched their helmet lights to low, solving her problem of sitting face to face. Each of the males took out a small packet that contained frozen oatcakes, unappealingly hard and frosty, and so did Muzz.

Next they unsnapped the wrist guard on the inside of their left glove, and stuck an oatcake in. She did the same. Chell took his free hand and pressed the oatcake into his palm through the glove. "Whitford, that's cold," he said.

Yikes! Everything inside my food pack must be cold. Warming the oatcake in her palm made her nearly lose her appetite. But she followed her brother's lead, pulling a switch to slow her oxygen, opening a small slider near her mouth and feeding herself, then closing it, pressing a straw inside her helmet to her lips to drink a warm, sweet beverage.

"Mmmm! That tastes much good!" Drent licked his lips.

"Yeah, but let's not get distracted. It's been five minutes. Amp up your air."

"You don't have to tell us every single thing, Chell. We took the training, too."

"In case you haven't noticed, Drent, Jerith seems a little out of it. I think it's the problem with his speaker. Am I right, Jerith?"

Muzz made her right hand nod. She tried to picture Jerith back there by himself. Had the avalanche scared him? Was he safe? She realized now that Walkabout meant companions, safety in numbers. *But I forced him to go it alone.*

She sipped again, and was so soon engrossed in the delicious hot drink that she did not notice a light approaching until Chell jumped up. She turned and saw Jerith climbing the last few yards to the perch.

"Thank Whitford I made it in time!"

Drent was also on his feet. Almost in unison, they looked from the real Jerith to the phony one. Then they jumped Muzz, and threw her to the ground, pinning her shoulders down.

"Let her go," said Jerith, his tone so firm that they did.

"*Her?* Who *is* this?" boomed Chell, poking her with his foot.

"Come on, Funny One, get up." Jerith held out his hand and pulled Muzz to a sitting position. He brushed off some snow. "Are you okay?"

Chell stiffened. "Funny One!" He peered into her visor. "Muzz! You've sabotaged our Walkabout." He began to pace. "You put Jerith up to this, didn't you?" Drent moaned and clenched his fists, while Chell folded his arms and stared fiercely at his best friend.

"No! He wouldn't help me. But I found someone who would."

Jerith raised a hand. "That 'someone' wants to be left out of this," he warned her. "And I promised she would be."

"*She*?" Drent began waving his arms. "It's a female conspiracy!"

"It's not a conspiracy," Muzz scolded as Jerith switched her speaker on. "It was almost entirely my plan."

"It was one hundred percent her plan. There is really no other Hepu to blame for this."

Mrs. Whitford was not a Hepu. Muzz noted that he spoke the truth. "He's right."

Drent stiffened, turned to Chell. "Your dumb sister has ruined our Walkabout. I'd like to toss her off a cliff."

"Of course we won't do that," said Chell.

"Well, what are we going to do with her?" demanded Drent.

After a long pause, Chell sighed deeply. "We'll go back. We have to take her back."

Jerith blocked that idea with his hand. "I've had quite a while to think this over, and I don't think we have to do that."

"We can't just leave her here, can we." Chell stared so fiercely at Muzz that she had to fight not to hang her head. "You don't belong here. No female does. Which is why we have to take you back."

"You know perfectly well I am smart enough and strong enough to be here."

Jerith said, "It's not as if she'll go back and tell everyone our secrets. She's banished." He paused. "And don't you see, Chell? Once they learn she's out here, taking her back will seal her fate."

"Will I be culled?"

Drent muttered something Muzz could barely hear about how that might be a good thing. Chell scowled at him, then turned to her. "Did our mother help you do this? Because if she—"

"No, no, not Mother. She's too—"

"Then who in Whitford— "

Jerith shook his head. "Trust me on this. Don't pressure her. She, and no one else, is responsible ."

Drent glowered at Muzz, shot both hands skyward. "Freeze me!"

"Whitford knows this is less than ideal," said Jerith, "but let's just take her with us. We have a long way to go. We can figure the rest out later."

Chell considered that. "Do we have enough supplies?"

"Plenty," said Jerith. "What freezes me is that there's no hot chocolate in my thermos."

Muzz pointed at her straw. "Hot chocolate? Is *that* what this is?"

She had heard of it, read about humans drinking it on cold winter nights, but had no clue there was any on The Planet. "Where did it come from?"

Drent snorted. "It's a special Walkabout treat."

"Completely hidden from the females?"

"Until now..." Chell sounded both annoyed and somewhat sheepish.

CHAPTER ELEVEN

Muzz could tell that everything about her irked Drent. *He is still much angry with me.*

"Come on," he said, opening his pack. "Let's get on with this. It's way past time to light the Lamp."

"The *special* lamp?" Muzz asked.

Drent sighed and Chell eyed her sternly. "No time for questions. Just watch and follow our lead."

Jerith patted her arm. "You'll know soon enough, Funny One, and then you'll see why I had to catch up."

Drent took a large cylindrical object wound in blanket-thick silk from his pack. Chell helped him set it down. It looked quite heavy.

Chell said, "We leave our packs here, carry only this and the timer." The others obeyed at once. It took willpower for Muzz not to ask about the timer.

Drent said, "Only one of us carries the Lamp from here. Since I'm used to the weight, let me do it this time."

Chell picked up the timer and moved in behind Drent. "Do everything I do," he told Muzz. "Light Station Number One is a precarious ledge. There's a steep drop and of course the path is icy, so stay far to the right. Dig in hard with your boots. Got it?"

From habit, Muzz made the fist.

"I'll be right behind you," Jerith told her.

"And don't forget, any of you," Chell went on, "no matter how appealing the view, we get five minutes of light, no more. There are three Light Stations, Muzz, and each of us" — he pointed to Drent and Jerith — "will time one and steady the lamp for one."

He pointed at Muzz. "Your job is to keep out of trouble, if that's possible, and watch."

No one laughed. Muzz was impressed by their seriousness of purpose, even Drent's. *But does Chell have to act so bossy?*

When they reached the ledge, Drent eased out. The ledge was about five feet wide, encrusted with layers of snow-covered ice. Where it widened, Muzz could see what a good platform it made. Running a free hand along the wall, Chell followed Drent. Muzz calmly copied him.

In dim helmet light, Drent and Chell smoothed and leveled the crusty snow about three feet from the edge.

Chell said, "Okay, we're good. But don't set the Lamp down till I have a solid grip on the safety chain." Drent unwound a length of chain connected to the Lamp and passed it to Chell, who secured it around his wrist. *What if it's so heavy that it drags Chell over the ledge?*

Drent uncovered the lamp and put it down. Muzz had never seen a cylinder that shiny and smooth, let alone one with such a huge, peculiar bulb. *It looks wooly inside.*

He unfolded four short legs, one for each quadrant. Next he took out a level, adjusted the legs until the thing sat perfectly upright, and said, "Okay! Ready for the first switch."

As he flipped it on, Chell started the timer, which made a ticking sound. From where he stood by Muzz, Jerith told her softly, "Humans invented this weird contraption during the Last War for fighting at night. There's only one on The Planet, and in three hundred hours it'll burn out. We need to use less than thirty minutes each year to make it last. Do the math. It'll last a long time."

Later for the math, thought Muzz.

Chell said, "When Drent switches that thing on, the bulb is going to lift up from the base and float. Don't ask how it works, Muzz, it's too hard to explain. But after it starts floating, it'll flash on. You need to have your eyes shut then because it's blinding at first. And when you open them, squint, and keep your visor between you and the bulb. Never look directly at it."

"Never?"

"There's nothing in the Cave anywhere near this bright. Trust me, look around, but *never* directly at the bulb."

Drent was shifting from one foot to the other. "Okay, let's do it."

"Spread out so everyone can see," said Chell. "Brace yourselves, and, remember. No matter what, stay put. Okay... go!"

Muzz heard a click and saw the bulb rise like some miniature mutant airship. It hummed and hovered and then, just as she closed her eyes, flashed on with a ferocious whir. The light on her closed lids went from green to orange to gold.

After a while she gradually opened her eyes and saw far below, bathed in pale light, a vast sweeping valley floor.

They all gasped. Jerith staggered backward and leaned against the rocky wall.

A long silence followed as they tried to grasp what they were seeing. *This Lamp is its own small sun*, Muzz shouted inside as she made sense of the wide sweep of land below, *and this valley a huge world.* She let her eyes soar across the open space. They came to rest on far off, dimly lit mountains with grayish snow on the peaks. She had seen similar — albeit much whiter — winter landscapes in Book Storage, but with no real sense of the immensity.

Chell broke the silence. "Hoar ice!"

Jerith shook his head and groaned. "The hoariest."

Muzz had nothing to add. Barely able to breathe, she noticed Drent was trembling. "Drent, are you all right?"

"Fine," he croaked, his voice giving him away. Then, "Look, Chell," he said. He pointed weakly in the direction that their path would take them.

The ledge they were standing on curved by degrees so that the next part was visible for the first time. Below was an astonishing drop.

"Whitford's wishes!" hissed Chell.

Muzz felt light in her tummy, as if she might fly or fall. She backed up and clutched Jerith's arm. Chell and Drent inched back, too, until they all stood glued to the rocky wall with their hands flat against it.

Then they simply gaped until a bell dinged that their time was up.

"Make mental notes," Chell instructed. "For the report."

Jerith said, "That plain down there? It's broad and scooped like a..."

"*What* did we learn?" Drent asked.

"Like a basin," said Chell, pointing. "With a long rim of mountains on the far side. See?"

"Much long," said Muzz.

"Right," said Chell. In the wild beauty and gleaming light, he sounded less older-brother annoying to her. He sank to his knees, edged toward the lamp.

"*Everybody* stay put," he ordered, flipping the switch. The bulb gently whirred into its base.

In the sudden darkness, Muzz teetered and exclaimed, "I can't see!" Jerith grabbed her and they wobbled precariously, managed to steady themselves against the wall.

"Great Whitford! Everyone hold still. Let your eyes adjust." Chell stayed kneeling by the Lamp. Out loud he counted to one hundred, then flicked the other switch. The whirring stopped.

"*Crawl* out here, Drent. Bring the bag, but leave your pack. And go easy." Slowly, carefully, the two of them covered the lamp, dragged it back, stowed it in Drent's pack.

Drent insisted on carrying it as they returned the way they had come. They all sat on rocks looking dazed and then, without conviction, Chell announced, "We'd better push on."

Nobody moved. Jerith sighed audibly. "The ledge is wide enough," he said. "All we have to do is strap on our packs, walk carefully and keep our minds off the drop."

"True," said Chell. "But how?" There was a pause.

"Maybe we could sing," said Muzz. She remembered a song the Lowers had learned in a film Hepu Dorne disapproved of because it didn't demonstrate 'the destructive nature of the humans.' Their teacher in Lower liked it anyway — enough to show it every year — and he had taught them all the song.

"Remember that song about snow. The one with the four-part harmony?" she asked.

Drent scoffed loudly, but Chell rose to his feet saying, "Fine, let's all sing. Maybe it'll help. C'mon, we need to make this happen." He hoisted his pack, helped the others do the same. They stood single file at the verge of the ledge, and he placed his hand on the wall to the right, had the others do the same. "As long as you're touching this, you're a safe distance from the edge," he told them. Muzz thought, *Please let that be true.*

Chell took a deep breath and came in on a low note. "Snooooooow!" They all followed, with Muzz taking the highest "Snoooooow!" And even though *their* snow had a grayish tint instead of holiday white, they sang the song as they had heard Bing Crosby sing it in that favorite film in Lower. Even Drent sang, and in about five minutes they had conquered the ledge that introduced them to The Planet.

To Muzz it felt infinitely scarier to walk in the semi-darkness after seeing that drop firsthand. The predictable web of tunnels trod by Hepus every day could not possibly prepare her for the vast expanses outside. *I'm cowering with puniness,* she told herself.

70

After they crossed the ledge, dips in the trail sometimes forced them to crawl and claw their way forward. At one point, an enormous boulder blocked their path. The only way past was over the top, so they boosted and tugged each other. A few hours later, they made camp, and in their bulky walksuits pitched the tent awkwardly, ate huddled together inside. After figuring out how to fit four in a three-Hepu tent, they set Muzz's sleeping bag perpendicular to their own by their feet. She climbed in, closed her eyes, worried that slumber inside a helmet would elude her, and promptly fell asleep. When Chell's alarm went off, they all emerged complaining about their aches. It had snowed during the night, a thin layer of whitish gray that fluffed around their feet.

Drent rubbed his calves. "Even caveball didn't train me for this."

For Drent that's admitting a lot, thought Muzz.

To stay on schedule, they had to get moving. Lookout Rock, their final destination, was still far off. But partway through that second day they fired up the Lamp for a distant glimpse of the Rock. It dominated the far end of the long valley strewn with boulders and shards of ice that they were skirting. Ahead they could see traces of their path threading two or three hundred feet above the valley floor. Luckily the aches Muzz felt early in the morning softened to twinges after an hour at their brisk foot-slamming pace, and everyone seemed less awed by the occasional drops and the hefty boulders that sometimes blocked the way. They were making good time.

After the second firing of the Lamp, a brief snowfall swirled around as they stopped for lunch, which consisted of oatcake with avocado, and five squeezes of some flavorless paste from a 'nutrition tube.'

"The First Settlers ate this stuff on the way here," Chell told her.

She made a face when she tasted it. "Sixty-year-old leftovers. Yuck!"

Jerith nearly choked with laughter.

"It isn't funny, Jerith. I mean it! Yuck!"

"That's what the hot chocolate's for, you thief," he told her, shaking a fist in mock resentment.

Seeing Jerith smile at her, Muzz felt a nameless pang of something in her chest, but before she could name it, it was gone. She took a swig of the tasty, sweet, and still warm chocolate, a perfect antidote to the bland nutrients in the tube.

Chell signaled that it was time to go.

When they started walking again, she made a game of stomping her boots into the prints his made in the fluff of fresh snow.

That was what she was doing when Chell stopped with a cry. They all stared where he was pointing.

"Footprints!"

"Huh?" Jerith leaned down for a closer look.

"Impossible!" said Drent.

"And yet, seeing is believing." Chell knelt, touched the closest print.

In the newly fallen snow, a line of prints crossed the path. They came from below, and vanished from sight up beyond some boulders.

"Human boots," said Muzz. "Look at the tread marks!"

It was Chell's turn to say "impossible" in his most exasperating older brother voice.

Muzz made wavy motions with her hands. "I saw rippled soles like that in a catalog in Book Storage!"

Chell ignored her. "This must be a trick," he said, shaking his head. "A test for us."

"Yeah!" the other two males replied in unison. Muzz chafed at their unwillingness to listen. *I spend more time in Book Storage than all three of them combined, and they* still *won't listen!*

Chell set his pack down. "Everyone wait here." He lowered himself over the side of the path, slid down, disappeared behind a mound.

Muzz waited breathless until he came back into view. He kept glancing around, tensing and releasing his fingers inside his gloves.

"Well?" called Jerith.

"It's *definitely* a trick. They come from somewhere down there, cross our path, and keep going." Chell pointed up. "Two sets of prints — made by Hepu feet of course — even though they're wearing some odd sort of boot." He gave Muzz an in-your-face stare intended, she knew, to discourage further comments about humans. She grit her teeth. *I said 'human boots', not humans.*

"So what next?" Jerith asked. "It's a test we need to pass." As the three males talked, Muzz simply listened, confused by the whole puzzle.

Chell thought to take Jerith and follow the footprints uphill to see where they led while Drent stayed with her and guarded the lamp. But Jerith pulled Chell aside and, after a muted, but heated talk, Drent went with Chell and he stayed. As they left it started snowing again harder than before.

"Chell's so stubborn. What did you say to him?" Muzz asked.

"That I didn't trust Drent alone with you. He's still too mad at you in my opinion."

Even though she thought she could fend for herself, Muzz thanked him for wanting to protect her. Then they just sat watching the snow.

After a while, they heard voices. Jerith said, "With all this snow, they may have trouble finding us. I'll go meet them. Wait here." Not long after that Muzz heard him shout, "No! Stop!"

"Shut up," a gruff male voice ordered — not Chell's or Drent's — and Muzz hit the ground, dove behind a snowdrift, crouched as low as she could.

Jerith bellowed, "Humans! These are *humans*!"

"Ha! No one can hear ya. Your mates walked right past our hiding place. They won't be back for hours." Muzz heard scuffling sounds.

"Hey! I bet you'll taste pretty good." There was a loud thud, and a groan. "You're coming with us."

Muzz peeked over the drift, and saw in the pale light of Jerith's helmet two dark figures dragging him by his arms. He was slumped over, clutching his gut. They passed close enough for her to see blood on his forehead and their hardened, frooseless faces.

Hideous *humans,* she thought. *But how can that be?*

Their voices died away, and all Muzz heard for the longest time was her own smothered sobs.

Then Chell broke the silence. "What's happening? Where's Jerith?" He and Drent towered over her where she crouched.

"Thank Whitford you're back! Humans came. *Humans!* They attacked Jerith and dragged him away." She pointed where they had gone.

"You know that's impossible," said Chell, bending to brush some snow off her walksuit.

"Hoar ice!" said Drent. "If Muzz hadn't crashed our party, this never would've happened."

"That doesn't even make sense," said Muzz.

"I have to agree, Drent," Chell told him. "Use your logic. If we'd left Jerith alone, we wouldn't even know what happened to him."

"So you *believe* her?"

"Not the human part, of course, but I believe he was kidnapped. By Hepus, of course."

Though she told them everything she had witnessed, they refused to believe the human part.

Even the last small signs of Jerith's skirmish did not convince them. Chell called the kidnapping 'some kind of test.'

"We need to report this at once," he said, and Drent agreed.

Muzz had no choice but to rush back to the Cave with them, even if that meant not chasing the kidnappers, and even if they would all be punished for allowing a stowaway — a banished female at that — to join the Walkabout.

She worried all the way back, especially about Jerith. *Were they serious about wanting to* eat *him?* she asked herself, judging it a fate much worse than being culled.

As they approached the Cave, the snowfall intensified, lopping down huge gray flakes that appeared almost silver in their helmet light. Muzz had the key that allowed them to enter, and they went at once to Mrs. Whitford's grottoette where she let them in with a startled, but kind expression, and listened intently to their story.

CHAPTER TWELVE

"They *were* humans, Mrs. Whitford. Jerith said so, and I saw them with my own eyes."

"Impossible, Muzz." Chell gave an exasperated stare. "Would you please stop saying that?"

Mrs. Whitford sat firm and tall on her grottoette bench looking down at them with wide perplexed eyes where they sat cross-legged on the floor. She tapped her fingertips together and gazed at each of them in turn through her red-rimmed spectacles, finally settling on Muzz. "Surely your brother and Drent know what from what. Their conclusion that it's impossible must be respected."

Muzz wriggled with frustration and dropped her eyes to her hands, while Mrs. Whitford tapped hers some more, apparently lost in thought.

"We need to go to the Beacons. Now," said Chell.

Muzz put up her hand to fend him off. "Think what they'll do to me, to all of us!"

"It can't be helped," said Drent with a hard scowl.

"Oh, but it can," responded Mrs. Whitford. "No one knows Muzz went with you and no one needs to know."

Drent stiffened and narrowed his eyes. "The kidnappers know by now. Besides, Muzz deserves whatever they do to her."

Mrs. Whitford shook her head. "Leave Muzz to me. You two can deal with the Beacons without her. Meanwhile, sooner or later the kidnappers, or testers — if that's what they were — will have to bring Jerith back. They can't stay out there forever."

"So we'll say we don't know what happened to him because we left him to guard the lamp?" asked Chell.

"Exactly."

"Withered Whitford! We'll catch trouble for that," said Drent. "If Muzz had followed the rules, this never would've—"

"Muzz had nothing to do with the kidnappers. Now, you two need to get your story completely straight. You saw tracks, decided to follow them, left Jerith with the lamp, returned and found signs of a scuffle. That's all."

Though Drent seemed reluctant, he and Chell looked at each other and nodded.

"Was it still snowing when you arrived?" All three nodded. "Then your tracks are buried. If they want you to lead them back there, the tracks will have disappeared."

Moments later the two young males stood at the door.

"Avoid adding details to your story." Mrs. Whitford hugged each of them, and Muzz came to the door and hugged Chell, but not Drent, who backed away to make his opinion of her crystal clear.

As soon as they were gone, Mrs. Whitford said to Muzz, "I need to tell you something important."

When they we sitting face to face on the bench, she said, "It's time for you to know that you are right. You *did* see humans."

"I did?" Muzz scrambled to comprehend.

"Yes," said Mrs. Whitford. "Chell and Drent can't know what you're about to learn, at least not for now."

Muzz tried to grasp what Mrs. Whitford was saying. "So, are you saying some humans live on the Planet, too?"

"I'm saying that this place where we are *is* the human place. You see, Muzz, The Planet is Planet *Earth* —" she shrugged sadly — "what's left of her."

"You mean we—"

"I mean we never left the earth. There was nowhere else to go. Oh, we did fly up in a spaceship." She waved her hands skyward. "We circled the globe for almost a year. And there were some humans with us. Mr. Whitford and some others."

"You mean Whitford, right? *Doctor* Whitford?"

Mrs. Whitford smiled. "Yes and no. Mr. Whitford was my husband, but I have to admit to you that I am the doctor."

"*You're* Dr. Whitford?"

"Stranger things have happened in this world."

"Oh, Mrs. Whitford — I mean, *Doctor* Whitford — I am much confused." Muzz covered her face with her hands and shook her head.

"As anyone would be, my dear Muzz. But please don't call me 'doctor.' I'm used to 'Mrs. Whitford' after all these years."

There was a loud knock on the door and they both jumped to their feet.

Muzz darted behind the dressing screen.

"Open up, Mrs. Whitford. We need to talk to you."

"I'm not dressed yet." Mrs. Whitford threw her bathrobe over her clothes, and opened the door a notch. Muzz cowered behind the screen.

"Why, Framp! Tronkold! To what do I owe such an early visit from you?"

"It's almost noon, Mrs. Whitford."

Mrs. Whitford yawned and stretched. "Hmmm! I guess I overslept!"

"We're here to take you to the Beacons. They suspect Jerith was kidnapped by Muzz."

"Kidnapped? Muzz?"

"No one has spotted her for days and one of the old walksuits was stolen."

"Stolen! How could Muzz have stolen anything from that secure locker?"

The guards shuffled some and shrugged.

Mrs. Whitford has a real knack for pretend surprise, thought Muzz.

"I'll need a quarter of an hour to dress. Please come back then." The guards said they would wait outside, and Mrs. Whitford shut the door.

"I knew something like this might happen," she whispered.

Muzz clutched her throat. "Will they arrest me?"

Mrs. Whitford shook her head. "They'll never even see you. Listen carefully."

She put her hands on Muzz's shoulders. "I'm going to do something that won't make much sense to you. I'm going to make a call with my cell phone."

Muzz had heard of them. "You have a cell phone?"

"Yes. Remember this *is* Planet Earth and, believe it or not, cell phone service between the various outposts is still pretty decent."

"Outposts?"

Mrs. Whitford sighed deeply. "Oh, Muzz, there is so much more I'd like to explain to you. But you'll learn soon enough for yourself. There are around three thousand outposts on earth now — small communities that survived the Warming, some quite successful, some just hanging on. Many are friendly, a few are not."

She pulled a small silver-gray object from under her Lab hair mattress, opened it like a tiny book, pressed some buttons. "This one's friendly."

Muzz heard bleeping sounds. Then Mrs. Whitford spoke into the thing. "Thea? The time has come. (Pause) Just Muzz. (Pause) How fast can they get here? (Pause) I'll have her out there. (Pause) Yes, yes, she'll be there."

She closed the phone and stuck it back under her mattress.

"We have to rush, so listen up." She pulled something from a chink in the wall and held it out to Muzz.

"This is an extra key to the exit hatch." Muzz took it from her.

"See my clock?" Mrs. Whitford pointed at it as she flung her robe to the floor.

"Wait here and don't make a sound for thirty minutes. Not one sound. Then put on your helmet and get out of here. A copterjet — you know what a copterjet is?" She pointed upward and whipped her finger around. "Part plane, part helicopter?"

Muzz remembered seeing a film with some president of the Ewesay flying in a helicopter. Wide-eyed, she nodded.

"Good. And can you picture that space outside the Cave where it's open and flat?"

"Yes."

"As soon as thirty minutes have passed, get out there. Be sure to secure both the inner and outer doors as you go. Wait way over to the side by the biggest boulder."

"When you hear the copterjet, don't move. Its propeller —the part that spins around — is lethal! You need to stay put until the craft lands. Wait for someone to get out and help you board. It will be a human, but don't be afraid. A crew of friendly humans will take you to a safe place."

Muzz must have looked frightened because Mrs. Whitford pulled her close, gave her an energetic hug. She held her at arms' length and said, "Believe me, there are plenty of good humans left in the world. And the place you're going, a settlement called the Bubble, is home to quite a few."

"But, Mrs. Whitford? There's something I don't get. Knowing all you do, why don't you come with me? Why stay here when you could be with other humans?"

Mrs. Whitford swept her arms around, a wry smile on her lips. "I mustn't, I can't. I masterminded this cave-world, strange as it is, and I care too much about what happens to the Hepus ever to abandon it."

Mrs. Whitford's eyes went sad. "I'll miss you, Muzz. But keep dreaming and dream big." She laughed softly. "You're strong, intelligent, and mature now. I know you'll do well out there."

"I'll miss you, too, Mrs. Whitford. If I didn't know you to be an amazing human, I wouldn't dare do as you say." Mrs. Whitford gave her a gentle kiss on the cheek and one last squeeze before she stepped out to join the waiting guards.

Muzz saw them move in on either side of her as the door closed.

Using her helmet light Muzz found the open space, stood waiting by the big boulder. The snow had stopped and the air was still. It felt colder than ever out there, but before she left she had grabbed her shawl and stuffed it inside the walksuit, and she fancied it was helping her keep warm.

All she could hear was her own breath. Then a drone in the distance slowly turned into a roar. Overhead a copterjet burst through the thick layer of cloud. It had bright white lights. She detected small green and blue lights, too, and then a searchlight swept and fixed on her.

Light, noise, wind! The helicopter flooded her senses. It was so loud and huge that she wanted to dart away. But the door slammed open, and a human came down, pressed toward her through the flurry of air.

A gloved hand grasped her shoulder and nudged her forward. As the whirring blade churned nearby, another gloved hand reached through the door and pulled her in. There were at least two dozen empty seats in rows. The two humans guided her to a seat near the front, strapped a belt across her lap. The copterjet rose in a torrent of wind and slipped into darkness.

The human who had pulled her onboard, smaller than the first one, piloted the craft, turning knobs, pressing buttons on an array of peculiar instruments. There were lighted dials in hues she had never seen — vibrant greens and pinks, luminescent violets and blues.

Muzz could tell that the larger human had the squared-off features and light brown mustache of a 'man.' He swiveled his chair and faced her while the aircraft rumbled higher. In light from the dials she could make out a broad smile on his face.

He seemed intent on being noticed, waving and nodding at her, pointing at the sides of the craft. Then came a sudden roar followed by thuds. Wings slid forward, locked into place.

The man nodded, smiled again, pointed upward. After several small thonks up above, the propeller folded and the newly streamlined craft sped through the darkness.

While he watched her, he said something to the pilot. She could not hear his comment, but sensed that it was about her. Then the craft broke through the thick cloud layer, and Muzz experienced daylight for the first time ever. Plump gray clouds below and a bowl of pale blue overhead. She studied the view for many minutes. It made her heartsick to know that down below, terrain that must have been home to so many kinds of life B.W. languished in chill darkness.

After a long while, during which Muzz dozed and awoke to the same scene many times, she opened her eyes to something remarkable. The cloud layer below them had thinned, and through it she saw something rippling and reflecting down below. *Water. I must be looking at a huge body of water.* Her eyes widened and she could not help looking directly at the man.

She found him watching her and, when their eyes met, he broke into another of his unnerving smiles. He undid his seatbelt, crossed the aisle, took the empty seat beside her and motioned for her to take off her helmet. "Beautiful, isn't it."

Muzz nodded in spite of herself and took the helmet off. "Is that an ocean?"

"That's the Arafura Sea down there. Have you heard of it?"

"Maybe once in a book."

"My name's Tom, by the way. I know you're Muzz." He paused. "So the Cave has books?"

"In a room called Book Storage. Hardly anyone goes there though."

"But you went there sometimes?"

"I went there much."

Tom thought that over, nodded, and then pointed. "Look! There's land."

Muzz's mouth dropped at the sight of a gray-green prominence up ahead. "Where are we?"

Tom shook his head. "That's called New Guinea. We'll fly right over it."

It was not long before Muzz could see where the sea met the shore. She spotted a line of white that seemed to be trembling along the edge of faintly green terrain.

"What's that white stuff?" she asked.

Tom grinned and his eyes sparkled.

"Those are ocean waves coming ashore. They're white with bubbles — foam — as they splash in."

Muzz recalled the occasional bubbles that splashing in the underground stream made. "That foam must be made of millions of bubbles."

"Zillions," said Tom, widening his eyes.

Muzz had never heard that word before. *Hmmm... I wonder if there's a zillion of anything in the Cave?* That thought pulled her mind right back to the Cave and, to her surprise, she felt a wave of compassion for almost everyone there. *Mrs. Whitford is keeping so much hidden from the poor Hepus. She's kind and she means well, but is she right? How many Hepus besides the Highers feel trapped and oppressed? How many feel hopeless when they think of the harshness of The Planet? And what if the Highers follow through with their dangerous plan? That could get all of them culled, and their families crushed by the Beacons' fury. Everyone would suffer, not just one recusant who refused her betrothal. Whatever else I do out here, I mustn't forget the Cave. I need to think of ways to help.*

She was distracted from those thoughts by more green — deeper green that looked like hills, and then a thick line of pure white. "Is that snow?" she asked.

"Yes, a mountain ridge dusted with snow. And, see? Lots of trees down there, and other wildlife."

"You mean animals?"

He nodded. "Mostly scrub brush, that sort of thing... but small animals too."

Before he could say more another craft zoomed in along their side and seemed to bump it. There was a jolt, a whir. Tom jumped up, pulled something metallic from his jacket, ran to the door.

"Don't shoot!" called the pilot. "They've locked in. They're coming aboard."

So that's a gun, Muzz told herself. *What in Whitford is happening?* The door opened, and she could see a narrow passage connecting the two crafts. Three armed humans in tan uniforms thundered aboard.

"Drop that," one shouted, pointing at Tom, who let his gun clatter to the floor. The man seized him and, dragging him further back, forced him into a seat and handcuffed him there.

Another rushed to the front of the plane, shoved the pilot aside, while the shouter ran forward, dragged the pilot back, handcuffed him the same way.

The third took the seat next to Muzz. In no time she, too, was in handcuffs.

"We're taking you down."

Muzz caught a glimpse of one of the captors blindfolding Tom before the same thing happened to her.

CHAPTER THIRTEEN

A pang in the pit of her stomach told Muzz the craft was making a spiral descent. Then came dizzying turns in mid air. Her ears clogged — a shock for a novice flier, and popped clear one at a time. She heard Tom say something to the pilot. He was promptly told to "shut it" by their guard. The craft touched down on a rough landing strip, pitched and rolled to a stop.

Someone unclasped Muzz's seatbelt, yanked her to her feet. "Make any trouble and I'll slug you hard." He pulled her blindfolded toward the door.

"Your abductors won't get to keep you long," Tom called as she stumbled away. She heard a thwack and a grunt, knew he had been slugged.

There was a loud click. One of the captors barked, "Don't waste the ammo. We have their fuel cell and supplies, and their radio's in smithereens. Let 'em starve to death. Just uncouple and get us the hell outta here. Now!"

Doors opened, slammed behind her. As they bumped back into the air, someone secured her wrists again. Sometime later they removed her blindfold. The craft sped over water for a few more hours, then some land, before another sharp descent.

Once down two of them disembarked, and the third kept watch on Muzz. She saw snow-clad hills dotted with pointy, frost-laden trees, and eyed them in wonder — her first woods. The two returned with another prisoner in tow who was wearing a dark green uniform, limping, fighting every step of the way.

"You think you'll get away with this? Because I don't," the captive said. Muzz was surprised to hear a gruff, angry, but clearly female voice.

When they sat her next to Muzz, she moaned, "Not a furball. Spare me. Spare my nose!"

All three captors exploded in mean laughter, ignored her plea.

Muzz's cheeks burned beneath her froose. *Do I really smell, and if so how bad?* She shrank from the outspoken woman, and did not so much as glance at her again.

They flew a long way. She dozed and woke several times, and nibbled at a meal she was served of completely odd, unrecognizable food. Later they were crossing pale green hills. She spotted two large structures and then a dirt landing strip appeared.

"Get in, or we'll drag you in," a guard told the woman, who resisted mightily, claiming she could not stand sharing a cell with "a stinkin' furball." After a tussle, she was inside. Muzz sat on a dilapidated cot glumly watching the struggle.

After the guard locked up and left, the woman removed her hat. She had messy, dull blond hair, a tan, weathered face, and piercing brown eyes. She shoved her hat under the other cot, shushed Muzz with a conspiratorial finger to her lips, and tiptoed to the cell door.

She was still limping, and one of her legs seemed shorter than the other. She had a stumpy body too, like a dwarf's, only larger. She stuck her nose through the bars, looked both ways. Next she examined the cell walls and low ceiling, running her hands across rough patches and cracks, tapping here and there. Then she crossed to the empty cot and sat facing Muzz.

She grinned and in a low voice said, "Sorry about the 'furball' talk. I was doing some paradoxical work." She chuckled softly. "I figured we'd have a better chance of ending up together if they thought I detested you. I guess I was right."

Muzz brightened. "Then I don't really smell?"

The woman mock frowned. "Ha! *I* probably smell. In fact, I'm *sure* I do. Some of our captors' pals nabbed me two days ago before my shower and left me tied in a leaky lean-to. I thought I'd be eaten alive. At least these guys got to me before the bears did."

"Bears? What bears?"

"The bears formerly known as polar."

"Is *that* where we picked you up? Don't they live in a place called the Arctic?"

"Guess again. I'm one of the rangers assigned to reintroduce polar bears." The woman shook her head and laughed. "Actually they're hybrids — part polar bear and part grizzly. 'Polzzies' is the name coined for them — big, white beauties. Anyway, we're introducing them to our newly established Glacial Wilderness near the Sea of Japan. Right where South Korea used to be." Muzz squinted, she was that confused.

The woman jumped to her feet. "You need a geography lesson, don't you. I'm going to sketch an invisible map on the wall with my hand. See if you can picture this. Here's where you started."

She sketched in a shape on the lower right. "Now, look. Here's Eurasia." Higher up she enclosed a big oval the length of the wall for Eurasia, then added a smaller oval on the left end of it.

"And that sea *there*"— she pointed at the smaller oval — "is the Mediterranean Sea. That's where you were headed. To the Bubble. It's located on the northeastern edge of what used to be Spain. A city call Barcelona was near there."

The woman swept her hand across the top. "That's the Arctic. It's under ice so thick polar bears can't live there anymore." She walked back to the upper right side of Eurasia and pointed. "Right here is where you picked me up — the Korean Peninsula."

"Are we still there?"

"No, no. I *think* we've flown way down here to a place that used to be called Cambodia. It used to be warm, moist, tropical back in the day. The climate was a lot warmer everywhere, for that matter.

"I see." Muzz bit her lip. "At least I think I do... Things cooled down?"

The woman slumped to her cot, facing Muzz. "That's a major understatement."

She leaned forward with her elbows on her knees, shook her head. "The earth had huge shifts in every climate indicator imaginable. Heat waves, floods, droughts, tornadoes, and a little over forty years ago a major worldwide cold snap."

Muzz sighed and shook her head. "Wow!"

"'Wow' is right. Cambodia's more like Pennsylvania used to be minus most of the foliage. D'you ever hear of it?"

"I think so. In the Ewesay?"

The woman nodded.

Muzz asked, "What's *that* like now?"

"The USA? I don't even want to talk about it. Too depressing."

Muzz thought some more. "But there's actual wilderness out here, right? With wild living things?"

The woman pursed her lips, slowly shook her head. "Mostly bedraggled scrub brush with a few hardy trees, some insects and prairie dogs. Frogs, garter snakes, other snakes you *never* want to meet, stuff like that. But they're working on it just the way my crew's working on Korea. Did you see a pine forest as we left my post?"

Muzz nodded.

"That was planted a little over thirty years ago. Not quite what used to be called 'wilderness.'"

"Do the Polzzies live there?"

"Close. Sometimes they wander up to the pines. But they prefer ocean. Ice. The Sea of Japan's frozen and still under cloud a good part of the year. It supports kelp beds, krill, and other sea life — fish, some seals. And now the bears."

She closed her eyes, moved her head slowly from side to side.

"Building an ecosystem involves a lot of trial and error, even for Mother Nature. Ours looks as if it's going to take hold with her help. We have to nurture it every step of the way. That takes lots of work, of course, and time. Lots and lots of time." She rubbed her eyes and stretched her arms. "But enough of this! Right now we need to strategize."

The woman reached out her hand. "I'm Deborah. Call me Deb."

Muzz found it strange to offer her froosey hand, and let the woman flop it up and down. She had read about handshakes in Book Storage. "I'm Muzz."

"I know," said Deb. "An alert about you came in, so when I saw a Hepu onboard, I knew they'd nabbed you."

"*You* know about us too?"

"Hepus? Oh, yeah. We all do. Or, I should say, we *think* we do. The Cave is common knowledge, but there are rumors about what goes on in there that I personally don't believe. Human sacrifices, cannibalism, that kind of thing."

Muzz gasped. "*Human* sacrifices? There's only one human in there and she's—"

"Only one? That's a matter of debate, of course."

"What do you mean?"

Deb shrugged. "I've heard Hepus are human."

Muzz stiffened and held her head high. "Then you heard wrong! Hepus hate humans much. Humans wrecked everything. And as for Hepus being cannibals, that's just—"

"Hogwash, I know." There was a silence.

"How did that alert come in, anyway?" asked Muzz.

"On my iGadget. It's so small that when I was captured I had it hidden in my mouth." She took a thing the size of half a walnut from inside her cheek and held it up. "Too bad it's out of power. We could really use it about now."

Deb got up, looked through the bars, came back.

"But listen. Any minute now they're going to come for one of us, so you need to know what's going on. Not far from the Cave there's another outpost — Tumbarumba — founded by prisoners and a few guards and locals who banded together during the Warming. They captured a canning factory with a giant warehouse, lay in supplies, and survived for decades on dried and canned food. In fact, they multiplied. But unlike most settlements, they'll be helpless soon. Their food supply is almost gone."

"I heard there are three thousand settlements. Is that right?"

"Close to three thousand worldwide. Not all of them that successful." Deb gestured around their cell. "And, obviously, not all of them that friendly."

Muzz frowned. "In Lessons we learned about the Warming, but not about ice or darkness. What made the earth this way?"

Deb's lips formed a grim line. "It's hard to grasp, kiddo, even for the experts. The atmosphere got hotter and hotter, and there were storms, big ones — tornadoes, floods, droughts. And, sure, the sea level was rising. But beneath the surface the planet transmogrified — changed bizarrely."

Sitting on her cot, staring at the floor, Deb scowled deeply. "Earthquakes and volcanic eruptions."

She cast Muzz a sidelong glance and flopped to a lying position. "I think of Mother Earth now as having an illness. You know how bad fevers cause chills, then hot spells and more chills — maybe even boils — as the body tries to regain its balance? Well, that's what many including me think has been happening to Mother. We infected her atmosphere, which made the weather more and more extreme. And without realizing it, by giving her a fever, we wound back to a time when tectonic plates moved more freely. D'you know what they are?"

"No."

"The crust of the earth is made up of big plates of rock that slowly shift around. Eons ago, when the earth was warmer and the crust thinner, everything shifted faster. So by reheating the planet we've caused Mother's skin to start erupting again the way it did in prehistoric times. At least that's my way of describing what many scientists say has been happening. And whether that's entirely right or not, volcanoes are much more active now, pumping black ash into the atmosphere. And oddly, that's probably what triggered the sudden cool-down."

Deb faced Muzz, elbow braced on her cot to prop her head up.

"In less than two decades, we had massive upheavals. A new land mass forming off Australia at an alarming rate, the sky down there darkening with smoke and ash, the darkness spreading. Even the prevailing winds changed direction. The final straw came when a little thing called the Ocean Conveyor — think of that as Mother's heart — started pumping the seas in new patterns. An ice age swept Eurasia, Canada, and much of the northern USA. New Zealand and most of Australia too. With that and the darkened sky, nearly every life form on the planet took a serious hit." She made circles with her hands. "And bada-bing! This is what's left."

She took a deep breath, sat up and faced Muzz again, clutched her forehead and looked down. "Look, Muzz. The Tumbarumbans are starving. They want to invade the Cave. They want it all to themselves."

Muzz gasped. "Could they do that?"

Deb raised just her eyes gravely. "They're desperate, they're scrappers, and they'd have the element of surprise."

Muzz gulped. "Because no one in the Cave even knows we're on earth except for Mrs. Whitford."

"Sad, but true. And now it's becoming *our* problem. Yours and mine. You see, our captors are their pals. The fact that they captured you means they intercepted key messages that were circling the globe."

"About *me*?"

"Not just you, but sure. Didn't you think it was weird that they only kidnapped you? That's because they want information about the Cave to make it even more vulnerable. They want to get that information from *you*."

They heard footsteps, and Deb jumped up. Whispered words fairly shot from her mouth. "Someone's coming. If they take you for questioning, don't tell them anything true. They're thieves. Liars. That's how their kind survives. They'll try to trick you, confuse you into revealing facts about the Cave. Lie to them, but keep whatever you tell them simple. You need to be able to repeat it over and over, understand?"

Muzz bit her lip, nodded, willed herself to keep calm.

"Now tussle with me," Deb grabbed Muzz by the arm and jeered "you miserable, stinkin' ball of fur" just as a guard arrived.

The windowless, stale-aired room they took Muzz to had a rickety table, a few dilapidated chairs, and nothing else.

The guard who brought her told her to sit. He opened the table's only drawer, a squeaky one, pulled out a pad of paper and a pencil, and slapped them down in front of her.

"See this? Your first assignment is to draw a detailed map of the Cave. Take your time, and make it as close to perfect as you can." He scoffed. "You might as well. You have nothing else to do." He left and locked her in alone.

Muzz wanted to pace and ponder, but a slit in the door kept her seated for fear of being watched. *If any of them has been there, they know where the Cave's mouth is, maybe saw where the underground stream comes out.* With that in mind, she started with the mouth and stream, then drew a large square room with some living quarters and gardening plots as different from the Cave as she could reasonably make them.

After that she waited a long time, considering what Deb had told her. *What will they want to know?* she asked herself. She kept rehearsing what to tell them.

Then the door rattled open. Two strangers entered, a tall, bald man and a plump one with a round nose and short, black hair. The bald one had a gray mustache, which he rubbed while he eyed her. The plump one grabbed a chair, sat right beside her at the table, leaned in close. Muzz clenched her teeth.

"So!" said the plump one, pushing his bulbous nose into her face. "I'm Bill and this is my partner, Larry. Let's have that map." He ripped the map from the pad and handed it to the one called Larry, who studied it in silence, and ripped it in two, then four. Muzz felt her stomach twist as he tossed the torn map down in front of her.

The plump man swept the pieces to the floor, as if to undo what Larry had done. "We have a couple questions for you, Muzz, and if you answer them honestly you'll be treated well."

Muzz disliked the oily sound of his voice, resented that he knew her name. *Deb must be right! They've captured me to pump me for information,* she thought. She forced a breezy reply. "Ask away."

He asked her a series of personal questions about her age and family, her school, and even her Lab. She was surprised how much he seemed to know about the Cave, and even her, already.

Larry had been pacing around, arms folded, a frown on his face. He moved in closer and asked, "How many Hepus live in the Cave anyway?"

"I'm not sure."

"Come on, you must have some idea — at least a good guess."

"I'd guess about four thousand," she lied.

"Really! We heard something very different from your friend."

"My friend?"

"Bill, what's his name again? Beriff? Territt?"

Bill pondered the question with an oddly jocular smile and little shakes of his head. He snapped his fingers. "Jerith!"

Muzz felt a wave of shock. "Jerith? Here?"

"Just answer the questions." Larry resumed pacing.

"At least three thousand," she lied.

Larry wheeled around, shot her a hard stare. "How many are your age?"

"Thirty," Muzz shot back.

She hoped her overblown numbers sounded plausible.

"Hmmm." Larry pulled a piece of paper from his pocket, unfolded it, and set it down in front of Muzz. "*This* is the map Jerith drew."

Muzz was shocked at the accuracy of some parts of the map. The Great Hall was there with the underground stream flowing right along one side, and there were some tunnels and smaller rooms drawn in, along with a couple of the cultivation enclosures.

Her mouth went dry and she had to fight the urge to gulp. She laughed, she hoped derisively. "That's completely wrong. He must have been trying to trick you."

Bill, still beside her and watching her closely, said, "Draw your map again."

Thank goodness Deb warned me to keep things simple, Muzz thought as she redrew the map. *This is good. Drawing it twice will help me memorize it.*

They kept her in there so long recycling the same questions and throwing in an occasional new one that, when they finally delivered her back to the cell, it was dark and Deb was snoring. Muzz felt hungry, numb, scared. Jerith's map worried her most. As Deb had cautioned, she kept everything simple and incorrect, but from their comments she thought Jerith might not only have drawn the real map, but might have told them way too much.

As soon as the guard's footsteps faded, Deb's snoring stopped.

"How'd it go, kiddo?" she whispered.

"Oh! You're awake... Not great."

Deb had saved her a bowl of porridge, which she ate while they talked.

"So you stuck to your story. Good! Because whatever they know, I doubt Jerith told them."

"But they said— "

"Lies. He was kidnapped by the Tumbarumbans, true."

"Really!"

Deb nodded. "But I heard the Bubblians snagged him before they'd taken him ten kilometers, and delivered him to the Bubble. I doubt those rogues got much out of him, if anything at all."

"Then where did they get such an accurate map?"

"How accurate was it?"

Muzz shook her head, closed her eyes, "I don't know. It was far from perfect, but not far enough. If Jerith didn't make it, where did it come from?"

Looking gnomish and lopsided, Deb jumped up, walked to the bars, and held them with both hands. *She's strong*, Muzz thought, *determined*. Deb began limping around the cell, thinking aloud.

"You can't worry about that map. Forget about Jerith and what they claim he said. All you need to do is keep your version of the story the same, time and time again. We need to keep going over what you told them so it stays fresh in your mind. And," here her eyes darted around the dark cell, "we've got to get out of this place. Fast."

CHAPTER FOURTEEN

Weeks later little had changed. Bill and Larry kept pulling Muzz out for questioning; she stuck to her story. They kept telling her stuff they said Jerith had told them, and some of it sounded plausible. She and Deb ate porridge three times a day, and exercised in a cramped, sunless yard. There wasn't much else.

On their daily airings, it amazed Muzz to have breathable air. Deb told her, "Everyone north of the equator wore oxygen masks outdoors till about thirty years ago. By then kelp beds and patches of forest had made a comeback, photosynthesis picked up, and the amount of oxygen in the atmosphere more than doubled. I've lived mask-free for years."

Muzz said, "In the Cave, we know *some* oxygen is out there, but no one thinks it's enough."

"Down Under it probably isn't. You felt sporadic rumbling in the Cave, right?"

"Much rumbling."

"Remember that huge new land mass I told you about — the one forming in Oceana? It triggers earthquakes galore and volcanic eruptions that spew tons of ash into the atmosphere. The air near the Cave's not just cloudy, it's pretty thin on oxygen."

Deb pushed her hands down. "Lucky for the rest of us, prevailing winds keep most of that stuff below the equator."

"So the Cave is near Oceana?"

Deb looked hard at Muzz. "You don't know where you come from, do you."

Muzz felt herself blush, and was glad her froose covered it. "Not exactly."

"Australia. The Cave is in the mountains of southeastern Australia. Tumbarumba's about a hundred kilometers north of the Cave. The Tumbarumbans survive because they're marauders par excellence — human locusts devouring everything they can. They've overrun three other outposts down there. The Cave's the only one left, which is why without it they're sunk."

After their talk, Deb sat cross-legged on her cot, leaned against the wall, eyes closed. This was not the first time, and Muzz felt curious to know why. But Deb's pose said she wanted separate quiet time, so Muzz shut her own eyes, soon dozed off.

She dreamt a lively mixture of Tendra, butterflies, and Labs.

After a while Deb rustled around and woke Muzz, who did not like having her dream interrupted. She yawned and asked, "Why did you sit with your eyes closed that way?" trying not to sound grumpy.

Deb gave a funny laugh. "I was practicing something called 'delving deep' — 'delving' or 'diving' for short. It's an enlivening, restful mental technique."

"*You* were delving deep? Mrs. Whitford wanted to teach me that. She told me so when I was banished, on the only day they let her visit me. But there wasn't time to teach me. The Second Beacon made her leave."

"D'you want to learn it now? I know how to teach it."

Muzz shook her head. "Not really. It looks kind of dull, to be honest, like everything in this prison that isn't downright miserable."

"Delving is about *you*, Muzz. You dive into *yourself*. It would be dull if *you* were dull inside, but you're not. You're lively. Get what I mean?"

"Sort of."

Deb tilted her head at Muzz. "Tell me. What do you do to help yourself when you feel cross or bored or worse?"

"Fall asleep, I guess. At least that's what I did in the Cave." She yawned. "Maybe I need another nap right now."

Deb shrugged. "Maybe. But delving gives you deeper rest, which makes you livelier. It may even make time move more quickly here in prison. It can do wonders for people."

"I don't see how."

"Of course you don't. How could you?"

Muzz looked at Deb long and hard. *Her eyes look clear and bright,* she thought, *and I feel wiggly and flustered.* She pursed her lips. "Okay, maybe I'll give it a try."

Deb nodded. She had Muzz throw on her shawl, which the guards had not taken from her, and sit not quite facing her. It felt a little strange, but pleasant to hear the instructions. Delving involved a sound word chosen for *her,* and a special way to use it. She tried it.

Afterward she opened her eyes, blinked, and gazed around the cell. She felt calmer, lighter. *As if I've been wading in the underground stream, or playing fetch with Em and my friends.*

She said, "I like it." Deb nodded.

"But I have a question."

"What?"

"I think Mrs. Whitford said something about other ways to feel lively. Do you know what she meant?"

"I know someone who has a long list of ways," said Deb, smoothing a lump out of the blanket on her bed. "Basically it includes anything creative, expressive, and restful — even, say, painting a picture or walking in the woods. Most of the activities on the list can't happen very well here, LOL."

"Elloell?"

Deb smiled. "That's an acronym. The letters LOL stand for 'laugh out loud.' Sometimes I forget what you know and don't know. Sorry."

Muzz thought that over. She shrugged. "Anyway, I like diving."

"Good. Keep doing it."

That night Muzz told Deb stories about life in the Cave and Deb told her about her 'boyfriend', as she called him (even though he was a man). He was a ranger like her, an expert in a field called bioengineering. After the stories Muzz dozed deliciously until she dreamt about greedy Tumbarumbans plotting their raid on the Cave.

When she awoke she could not help pitying everyone — her family, Em, the Highers and Lowers, the babies in buntings, adults going about their tasks without a hint of what was in store for them, her grandparents and the other Witherers. *The Highers' revolt looks tame compared to an invasion. Everything might be lost.* She remembered how Hepu Dorne craved the banana ices served at celebrations, and knew that if an invasion wreaked havoc on the Cave, she might even pity him. *No! He never pitied us,* she thought to talk herself out of it, but there it was.

Time passed, and then more time. One day several weeks later, she and Deb were lolling on their cots after a dismal lunch, daydreaming about tasty foods, when two red dots like the ones she had seen in Tropical sprang onto the ceiling.

Muzz gasped and pointed.

Deb looked where she was pointing, said, "Oh, wow! An Infrareader!"

"A what?"

"You know what that means, don't you?"

"Those little red lights?" Muzz sat up and squinted at them. "What did you call 'em? "

"Not 'em.' 'It.' An Infrareader. You must still be wired."

"Wired?" Muzz looked down at herself with big eyes.

"No, no, not actual *wires*. 'Wired' means you have a tiny doodad in you somewhere and those red dots mean she's found it."

"Who has found what?"

Deb sat up and grimaced at Muzz. "What else don't you know about the Cave? It's so big and dark that Dr. Whitford has a chip installed in every newborn Hepu in case one gets lost. She uses an instrument called an Infrareader to track toddlers. Infrareaders are used in lots of situations by lots of people. They track pets, children — things like that. I've used them in the wild to follow Polzzies around." Deb's eyes shot around the cell. "There's probably a satellite involved."

"In here?"

"No, a satellite. You know, out in space. That's the only way the Cave's Infrareader would work at such a distance."

The red dots slid directly over Muzz.

"That has to be Dr. Whitford," Deb insisted. "Go ahead, kiddo. Wave. Say something to her."

Muzz stood and waved frantically. "Doctor, uh, Mrs. Whitford?"

The dots moved up and down — a nod. "So you know where I am?" Another nod.

Deb came and stood beside Muzz. She saluted the red dots.

"Enviro-Ranger Deborah Norton at your service, Dr. Whitford." The dots reacted to that with lots of fast nodding.

"We're prisoners, maybe at Bayon Holding. S'that right?"

The dots nodded again.

"Do you know how to get us out of here?" The dots moved first from side to side, then up and down, then side to side again.

Deb furrowed her brow. "Hmmm. That's how *I* feel about it. I have a plan that might work with your help, but it's not ready."

She raised both hands. "You see, warmer weather's on the way soon and, when that comes, we may be able to get out during an electric storm. I'm working on it. Can you contact us again in a couple of weeks?"

The up-and-down motion that followed warmed Muzz to the core.

"Better go. Someone coming." The lights vanished. Both of them pounced on their cots. It was exercise time. A guard arrived to usher them to the dingy courtyard they circled each day.

There were three other prisoners in the yard by then, a stocky man with reddish scalp hair and disheveled face hair, who always looked miserable and said nothing, and twin boys in their teens — both tall and skinny, with sallow cheeks and big, dark, empty eyes. None of the three ever spoke to or looked at Muzz and Deb, but the twins traded looks that seemed like talking. Muzz thought they might be eye-talking about Hepus and her in particular, though of course she could not be sure.

On a regular basis — rain, sleet, or shine — all five of them trod first one way for fifteen minutes and then the other way for fifteen. A tall, sullen guard with a bushy brown mustache that wiggled when he chewed oversaw their routine. He habitually had his radio tuned to monotonous chatter punctuated by whistles and beeps.

That day in the courtyard dark clouds wafted by and, when a shard of lightning flashed, Muzz shot a look at Deb. Deb nodded ever so slightly at a distant rumble that followed. For once the twins' big eyes expressed something, and they ran and clutched each other, then reluctantly returned to their assigned places, all under the guard's heavy scowl.

Right then the only electric light, a drab little sconce on the courtyard wall, flickered and went out. So apparently did the guard's radio. He began moving dials, cursing, and jabbering into it. Meanwhile Deb stopped to fuss with her shoelaces and, when Muzz caught up, kept her hands on her shoe, but pointed with a baby finger.

"Don't look now, but see that fence?" she whispered.

Muzz gave an infinitesimal nod.

"It may be climbable. Notice the barbed wire on top? Take a good look."

"Hey, you two! Get moving," called the guard, "now!"

Deb planted a fake punch on Muzz's shoulder, snarled, "You mangy pelt! Get away from me."

They quickly resumed their tedious routine. He eyed them with a cagey expression and fiddled some more with his radio.

When Muzz was sure his mind was elsewhere, she examined the fence. It was made of steel mesh with barbed wire looped along the top. It looked impenetrable, but the crisscrossed mesh had finger and toeholds, and she spied a small gap where the barbed wire met the wall.

Back in their cell, Deb said, "That storm came pretty close. You saw how it knocked out the lights and the guard's radio? Power outages are chronic here every spring. I've been waiting to see how a storm would play out for our dear, sweet-tempered guard."

She sat on the edge of her cot and rubbed her hands, narrowed her eyes. "He sure was preoccupied with that radio of his. And did you see that gap right by the wall? If the electricity dies again, we may be able to scale the fence, run like hell, and make it up to that brush at the top of the hill before our doltish guard even notices."

"But—" said Muzz.

"No buts about it. It's our only hope. And since we know you're being tracked, we can count on—"

The door to their cell rattled; two guards stood outside. "You! Stand up!" said one, pointing at Deb. He ordered her to gather her things. She said, "Thanks for getting me out of this rotten fur shop," and did not glance at Muzz, though she slipped a hand behind her back and waved a finger. Then she was gone.

From that point on, Muzz saw Deb only during exercise. She started to worry that the Infrareader might be hooked up somewhere in the prison. *What if Larry and Bill are using it to get inside my head?* Then a plan emerged: She would test the Infrareader with questions no one in the prison could answer.

One day the red dots appeared again on her ceiling. "Mrs. Whitford, is that really you?" she said in a hoarse whisper. The dots nodded.

"I need to make sure. I want to test you with questions no one here could possibly answer, okay?"

The dots nodded.

Muzz stood right under the dots. "Okay, ready?" There was a nod.

"First, is my Lab named after a famous human poet called Elizabeth Barrett Browning?"

The dots answered "no."

"Right. And second, did I bring you a big bunch of plantains last year?"

"No," said the dots.

"Right, I brought two, didn't I."

"No," came the reply.

"Excellent. Now third. Is my best friend Tendra betrothed to someone who's not in the Cave?"

"Yes."

"Right again since Jerith's been kidnapped. Fourth, is your comforter covered with purple taffeta?"

Yet another "no."

"Red taffeta?" "No." "Green?" "No."

"Fine."

"And last, is Gronthor my brother?"

A final "no."

Muzz grinned. "You passed my test with flying colors."

The dots bounced around.

Muzz flung out her arms. "Oh, Mrs. Whitford! I don't know what to do. They took Deb — the Ranger — away."

The dots started bouncing up and down furiously. Muzz asked, "Are you saying escape is hopeless? Because it seems that way to—"

The dots moved from side to side.

Muzz sighed, flopped on her cot, and stared at the dots. They resumed their frantic bouncing.

"So what should I do?" More bouncing from the dots. "I can tell you the part of the plan I know." Big nods from the dots.

Muzz told all she knew. "Hmmm! So if the power fails again, I guess we could go ahead. But if we make it, will you be able to locate me?"

She pictured them hightailing it to the brush at the top of the hill. "I mean both of us?" The dots gave a huge nod that made her warm and hopeful.

For days, distant thunder made the lights flicker sporadically. Then late one night lightening knocked the power out and the prison went pitch black. But the timing was all wrong. Another time the skies rumbled while they were exercising, and she and Deb exchanged a look. But no break in the power. Muzz felt half-crazed with eagerness.

Then one afternoon, when the guard turned his back to sniff a bowl of soup he was using to torment them, Deb darted over, handed Muzz a slip of paper, and darted away. Muzz crumpled it and kept walking, stone-faced. She tucked it under her arm.

Later, alone in her cell, she read: *If Dr. W knows our plan, we need to make a run for it ASAP. Things are getting dicey. The next time we exercise, cough twice if she's ready.*

Muzz thought, *ASAP must be another acronym, but what does it mean? After saying please? Acting swiftly against prison?* Still, she got the gist of Deb's message. The next day, her throat all warmed up, she gave a loud double cough that made Deb's eyes sparkle. Muzz could feel her own eyes brighten, and her gait quicken. In fact, she walked so fast that she gained on the twin in front of her. His dreary scowl sobered her right up.

Then came more waiting, and something worse: During a session with her, Bill and Larry started in about truth serum. Bill held up a tube with a long, shiny needle at the end. "Hmmm! Where should I stab her with it?"

Larry said, "Scared, are ya? Then why don't you draw us the real map instead of this stupid doodle?" He waved in her face the counterfeit map.

"That map is *correct.*"

He shoved his face so close to hers that she flinched. "The Tumbarumbans don't think so. They've surveyed the outside of the Cave — every foot of it. They claim your map doesn't jibe with what they found."

Picturing the horrid Tumbarumbans sneaking around outside the Cave made Muzz almost nauseous.

Bill approached her with the needle poised to jab into her arm and rasped, "Roll up your sleeve."

But Larry said, "Hold on. That stuff'll cause permanent brain damage. Before we shoot her up, let's give her one more chance."

He turned to Muzz with an odious smile. "I'm sending you back to your cell. Sit there and think this over. Next time we get you, you either draw an accurate map and tell us all you know, or we give you *this.*"

Bill let his breath out fast, scowled deeply. But Larry had overruled him. Alone later, flat on her back, eyes shut tight, fists clenched at her sides, she whispered, "We need to get out of here. *Please* let's get out of here!"

She heard distant thunder, and her eyelids flashed open. She held her breath, listening. She was pretty sure it was almost exercise time.

There was another rumble. She sprang to her feet and paced her cell, wondering what to take with her just in case. She had left her breeding beads and her mother's silver pillbox on the first copterjet. All she had was her shawl and, tucked in its hem, the card with the small bird with bright-red plumage.

She grabbed the shawl, slipped it inside her uniform, and secured it around her waist so it would not slip.

As she and the guard entered the yard, a close clap of thunder made her tingle all over. Deb came into the yard too.

She gave a miniscule nod, raised her brow, glanced at the vulnerable gap in the fence. If the bulb in the sconce went out, Muzz knew it would be time to act.

They circled as usual. Muzz saw the twin ahead of her stick out his tongue to catch a few drops. Pretty soon the rain picked up and, true to form, the guard ducked under an overhang, grinning as his charges trudged through the sloppy downpour. Getting drenched had never been so appealing to Muzz, she was that hopeful.

Soon the storm became an out and out deluge — all water and no thunder — until a big flash of lightening triggered the loudest clap of thunder Muzz could imagine. The light in the sconce went dead.

The guard let out a grunt of annoyance and started fiddling with his radio. Muzz looked at Deb, and they darted in unison to the weak spot in the fence.

"You first," Deb more mouthed than whispered. She cupped her hands at knee level to help Muzz scoot to the gap. When Muzz looked back, Deb pointed decisively over the top, mouthed, "Go!"

Deb started climbing and, from halfway down the other side, Muzz saw her swing her leg over the top. Muzz hit ground just as the guard glanced up.

"Hey!" he shouted. "Halt or I'll shoot!"

But Deb had made it to the ground and run out ahead. The two of them raced for the ridge. The downpour was a curtain of wet and noise. They heard a few shots, but by then they were near the brush, and the next thing Muzz knew they had made it; they were flat on their bellies in dense, wet grass peering back over the crest of the hill.

Still on her belly, Deb slid around. A few yards from them a runoff churned down a ravine. Deb signaled Muzz and made her way to it on all fours with Muzz crawling after. They scrambled into the ravine, and clung to some brush.

But the runoff had become a torrent that Muzz saw could sweep them away. Sure enough, a clump of earth under Deb gave way and she tumbled halfway down the eight-foot cliff.

Muzz shot out her hand, but Deb ignored it, grabbed some wet roots with all her might. Then the two of them, holding onto roots and grasses, stumbled and crawled down the side of the ravine as it curved first one way and then the other in a huge muddy S that eventually brought them to a creek.

"Good. I spotted this on the way in," Deb said in a choked up voice. "We'll follow it."

The thunder and lightening had abated, but the rain was still falling in sheets. They took refuge further down the creek under a little tree with wide, flat leaves. Crouched there Muzz hugged herself, tried to stop shivering and keep her teeth from chattering.

Deb said, "A lot of good your froose does in this stuff." She grinned, pulled up her muddy cuff, and gingerly touched a gash on her ankle that was oozing blood.

"You're hurt," Muzz cried. Deb held up a hand to silence her. She ripped a strip off her cuff, handed it to Muzz.

"Wrap that tight." Muzz wound the strip around Deb's injury and pulled. "More. Tighter," Deb told her. As Muzz complied, the bleeding slowed.

Deb turned her attention to their soggy surroundings. "Weather's too bad for them to track us by air, and the dogs won't catch our scent now. That works for us and against us. No one can get in to save us either."

CHAPTER FIFTEEN

Deb ignored the injury. Muzz followed her down the creek, which led to open meadow just as the rain tapered off.

Deb squinted, reconnoitered. "They'll use this break in the weather to unleash their dogs." She pointed to the far side of the meadow where the creek met a larger one. "If we cross that stream before they catch us, we have a real chance. Can you sprint?"

Muzz nodded and off they sped through tall, wet grass, Deb rocking wildly as she ran. They had a lot of ground to cover, and Muzz — who had never moved that fast or far — started gulping air. Her legs felt like noodles, and the gap between her and Deb kept widening. Finally she croaked, "Wait!"

Deb let her catch up. "We can't afford to rest, but *you* can lead. Watch out for stones and snakes."

The thought of snarling dogs with sharp teeth kept Muzz moving. Once a yellow slithery thing made her falter, but she recovered fast. She found an almost magical, steady pace.

They could hear faint barking. They reached the bank of the stream, too deep to cross, and huddled by a bush long enough to see a posse with a pack of dogs burst from the ravine.

"Let's go!" Deb slid down the bank and waded downstream in sandy, shallow water, her footprints vanishing behind her.

They reached a high, narrow falls with a drop pool. A board bridged it. "After you," said Deb.

Muzz looked in horror at the skinny board. She knew she had to just walk it. She teetered, scooted across.

Deb followed, ditched the board in the drop pool, and they sprinted to a stony road nearby — really just two ruts through tall grass.

"There's a ranger station to the right, and a ruin to the left. The ruin's better for us. It's much closer. There's a moat we have to cross, but coming from the east will make us difficult to spot. Lots of trees on the crossway."

"Okay, step only where I step, on rounded rocks, and even this light rain may cover our trail." Deb started limp-hopping from rock to rock. Soon an edifice loomed above squat, leafy trees. Muzz saw three towers glistening in the rain, and rings of water where occasional drops were landing in the moat.

"Is that a castle?"

Deb stopped to catch her breath. "Good guess. But it's a Wat, a kind of temple."

"This one's called Angkor. It was a ruin centuries before the Warming, a place for tourists, not worshipers."

"Frozen forebears!" Muzz cried as she spied a wide stone walkway shooting toward the tallest tower.

Deb burst out laughing. "You sure have a way with words." She pointed at the tallest tower. "We need to get there fast."

They came to an archway through a long inner wall on which Muzz could see a story carved, frame by frame. *I much want to stop and look.* In a frame nearby, Muzz saw soldiers marching one way with staves while a startled bird with a crested head burst from a tree and flew in the other direction. *Like the bird on my card! I wonder if this one was red.* Leading the march was a man on a powerful animal with a long, dangling nose and huge ears.

"Keep up your pace," Deb urged, and they pressed on past statues of graceful dancing women. "Those were called Apsarasas," Deb told her. "But you have to keep moving!"

They climbed worn steps to the tower, scanned the expanse beyond the treetops. "I see them," Deb said softly.

The posse with its dogs had reached the rutted road. "If they turn our way, we're finished." They both held perfectly still.

Muzz could see the dogs circling and sniffing, the posse conferring and facing first one way, then the other. Finally they set off toward the ranger station. Deb breathed a sigh of relief. That was when Muzz saw little red lights on the tower ceiling, and pointed at them. "Look!"

They moved under the dots. "Are you coming for us?" Deb's voice had a catch in it. *Is she scared,* Muzz wondered. *Exhausted? Or just out of breath?*

The red lights gave a nod.

"Are you close?"

The lights moved back and forth.

"More than an hour away?"

Another back and forth.

"Okay, less than an hour." Deb's eyes darted around. "The flattest place is Angkor's promenade, uh, walkway. Smooth, wide, solid rock. Inside the moat, but outside the inner wall. They're after us. But when we hear you, we'll be there. Agreed?"

The lights nodded, went out. "Did you get that, Muzz? When it's time to go, stay close."

"Okay."

"For now keep eyes and ears out for the copterjet. You may see it before we hear it. I'll watch the road."

The sun came out, weakly but surely, and Muzz felt it drying her froose. Looking down, she could make out massive steps with toothy guardian beasts on both sides. She moved into the sunlight where she could see steam rising from the ancient ruin.

"You sure you want to do that?"

"It's warming me up."

"Okay, whatever you want. But watch and listen."

It was a nerve-wracking forty-minute wait before they heard dogs barking and men's voices again. From her perch Deb said, "They're almost at the far side of the moat."

Muzz saw a silver glint in the sky. "I think I see it!" She pointed. They started to hear a faint putt-putt. Muzz's legs ached with wanting to run.

The posse must have heard too. There was shouting, barking. "They're running," Deb told her. "But don't move yet. Take my cue."

Muzz could hardly breathe she was so nerved up.

"The dogs are getting close." Deb jumped down, eyeing the copterjet, which was also getting close. "Okay, now!" she cried, and took off with the fastest hobble imaginable.

They were down the steps and racing toward the promenade when some dogs burst through the main gate, tearing toward them. The copterjet arrived with such a flurry of wind that most of the dogs cowered and retreated, but one kept coming.

The aircraft's door swung open just as Deb and Muzz got there. A hand shot out. Deb signaled Muzz to grab it and she was fairly yanked onboard by the same man the hijackers had left for dead in the snow.

Tom! I never thought I'd see him again. As he reached for Deb, the dog locked jaws on her injured leg, and they lifted her up with it clamped on. A hard kick from Tom sent it howling to the ground. The posse raged up, kicking dogs out of the way, shooting at the rising craft. While another of their rescuers began first aid on Deb's mauled leg, the craft zoomed high over the exercise yard and away.

The pilot — the redhead who Muzz also knew from her previous flight — turned the craft into a jet. They flew in and out of clouds for a while, broke through that layer, and Muzz got to watch her first sunset.

Tom, sitting nearby, leaned over and said, "Glorious, isn't it?"

He seemed to take Muzz's enthusiastic nod as an invitation to move next to her, where he sat watching in silence as the orange orb dipped below the horizon. It was the most impressive show of color and light ever for Muzz.

When the last orange glow had nearly vanished, Tom turned to her. "I understand that your captives interrogated you often. What was that like?"

"Threatening," Muzz told him. "But Deb explained what to do. I made up a good story about the Cave and stuck with it."

"Beachy!"

Muzz gave a puzzled frown. "Beachy?"

Tom laughed. "That's just a way to show enthusiasm that's used a lot in the Bubble. All I meant was that you did a good job. In fact, I'd like to hear more about it once we reach the Bubble and you've had a chance to rest. Is that okay?"

For the first time in weeks, Muzz thought of all the problems facing the Cave — the Tumbarumbans' invasion and the Highers' revolt, and said, "It is." Tom returned to his usual seat. As darkness engulfed the craft, the other rescuer helped Deb, wearing a clean white bandage on her ankle, to the empty seat beside Muzz.

Deb squeezed her arm, but said very little — just that she felt "pretty good."

Muzz noticed some froose missing from her hands and wrists.

"Snowballs!" she told Deb, "I must've torn my froose on those briars."

Deb grabbed a hand and had a look. "The froose is gone, all right," she said and then added, quizzically, "How long were you out in the sun?"

"I don't know. Why?"

Deb shrugged. "It should grow back in no time."

Muzz nodded sleepily.

Deb yawned and promptly fell asleep. Muzz slipped in and out of consciousness, with images of the lush foliage and crested bird from the stone carving at Angkor drifting through her head and then, finally, she fell asleep too. When she awoke the craft was leaning; bursts of red and blue lit up its wings. It whined and swooped till she could see through the haze, which had grown thicker again, a huge half sphere nestled in some whitish snowy hills. She knew right away it must be the Bubble. They turned into a copter again, Deb woke up, grinned, and clasped her hands in a gesture of triumph.

As they flanked the glowing Bubble, Muzz saw how vast it was. Then they sank and entered through a trap door that shut behind them. Inside she found rolling hills — green this time, and big shade trees, spires, a tiny bluish lake with boats, a whole small city protected from the cold, snowy world outside. They landed on a slate blue rooftop and two new humans helped her jump to the roof.

The humans hooked their arms in hers and led her down a ramp, through a windowless hall to a sign that read 'Decontamination.' The rescuers carried Deb on a stretcher straight through a door marked 'Bubblians.' They parked Muzz outside one marked 'Others,' and the door slipped open.

Dr. Deet, as her nametag read, met Muzz inside with a stethoscope, a clipboard, and too many questions. Did she have a cough, stomach ache, or pain anywhere? Did she feel dizzy, feverish, confused?

"I'm worn out and hungry," Muzz said more than once.

"Have you been in the sun?"

"Some," said Muzz. "Why?"

"It's just that your froose—"

"What?"

"Looks patchy."

"I must've caught my hands on briars."

"Okay, we'll keep an eye on that."

Muzz could not understand what all the fuss was over her froose.

"It'll grow back," she said, annoyed when the doctor did not answer.

After the examination, Doctor Deet's pen point vanished with an intriguing click. "You'll be out of here in about a week."

When Muzz stifled a gasp, she added, "Don't worry. Your room is comfortable. You'll have delicious meals and a chance to adjust."

She looked Muzz up and down. "Were you in the sun long?"

"I don't think so. It's still hazy at Angkor, though not as much as here."

The doctor nodded, turned, opened an inner door and motioned Muzz through. "Go ahead. Shower and get some clean clothes on. The tops are called 'tunics' and the pants 'leggings.' They won't be what you're used to, but they'll fit."

"May I have my shawl back?"

"It'll need washing."

"But washing will ruin it."

"Okay, I'll order the light treatment to get rid of any microbes you might have picked up in that horrid prison. And I'll send you your breeding beads tomorrow. Did you know you left them on the copterjet when you were captured?"

"I thought I lost them."

"Well, they're back, along with that pretty silver box you had with you."

Dr. Deet slipped out, shut the door, locked it.

Locked in again! Muzz paced, wondered if she would ever feel at home in this place. The walls and doors of the isolation chamber struck her as way too smooth for her liking. *Just like the humans with their bold, bare faces.*

Still, the warm water pouring from the wall felt good — good, that is, until...

"Wha—? Wailing Whitford! I'm molting!" Sure enough, her froose was falling off in clumps so thick that they were clogging the shower drain.

Muzz felt like shrieking; she bit her hand and jumped from the shower, dried off, only to see more froose rub off on her towel. By the time she was dry, just a few tufts remained on her shoulders, and she was trembling like a sapling in a windstorm.

She flopped across the bed and wept. When dinner came, she did not eat, and when the lights dimmed automatically, she lay staring at the ceiling with tears rolling down the sides of her face. By morning even the tufts were gone.

A little after lunch, someone knocked on her door and unlocked it. It was Dr. Deet. "Oh!" she cried. "What are you doing down there?"

Muzz was huddled in a corner on the floor, so appalled at her lack of froose that she wanted to fade into the woodwork. "Please! Don't look at me."

Dr. Deet moved closer. "Oh-ho-ho, it happened! Your froose fell off. You're gorgeous! Come and see." She held out a hand for Muzz, who let herself be led to the bathroom mirror.

A complete stranger stared back at her, a green-eyed stranger that touched its scalp hair when she did, and ran a finger over its bare cheek when she did, too. There was no denying who it was. And even though, as Dr. Deet had said, the face looking back at her looked nice, she scrunched it up and started sobbing loudly.

"This is a tragedy. I look human," she gasped through her tears.

"You're going to have to face it. You *are* human."

Muzz wailed harder.

"That's not necessarily a tragedy. It could have a happy ending. It all depends on whose play this is. If it were mine, I'd say this change is serendipitous."

Muzz sniffed and wiped her tears. "What does *that* mean?"

"Unexpected, but fortunate — like in a comedy. You're darling."

"But I'm *not* a human. I'm a Hepu. Hepus hate humans. We lived deep in the Amazon. Humans smoked us out. We—"

"That was a myth, Muzz, a very handy myth to help explain your predicament in the Cave, especially your froose. But the fact is that HEPUS stands for "Humans Engineered for Planet Under Siege. "

Muzz made her eyes large and wild, and she gripped the sides of her face. *Is the whole idea of what I am based on an acronym?* "You're making that up."

"Why would I do that, Muzz?"

Muzz threw her arms out. "So Hepus don't even know what HEPUS means?"

"That's correct, but that fact doesn't change anything. Face it! You're human. One look at you makes that obvious. And why would your froose fall off after less than an hour of actual sunlight? Because that's how you were engineered. You don't need the froose out here. You needed it for the dark, dank Cave. Out here, it's programmed to fall off. Handy genetics, if you ask me."

"Please don't call the Cave dark and dank."

"I didn't mean to offend you. I'm just saying what is."

Muzz scowled and shook her head.

"You're human, Muzz, and like every Hepu who leaves the Cave, you have to face that fact. Not all at once, however. Take your time. Think it over. I just need to finish your physical today, okay?"

Muzz turned her back on the mirror.

CHAPTER SIXTEEN

Each day the doctor took Muzz's pulse, checked her ears and eyes, tapped her knees, prodded her tummy.

"Your heart rate is up today. Are you okay?" she asked one day, and "You're not eating well," she announced another. She jotted something Muzz could not see on a clipboard after each of these comments.

Meanwhile, every time the doctor arrived, Muzz hoped it would be Tom. *I need to tell him the Cave is in danger.*

She asked Dr. Deet, "When will that man Tom who brought us here be coming to speak with me?"

Her only reply was, "I don't know anything about that."

"Well, could you please find out?" Muzz asked.

Dr. Deet stopped what she was doing and looked hard at Muzz. "If he needs to talk with you, I'm sure he'll find a way. That's all I can tell you."

So frustrating! Muzz often paced and imagined conversations with him. She asked for him more than once, and refused to give up.

After a few days Dr. Deet said, "You're not used to spices or variety, are you. We grow so many more foods here, and import some, too. Those green hills you saw on the way in feed over a thousand people and many animals. Cows, sheep, horses. Even birds."

"Some we eat, like chickens. Some just sing and fly around. You can learn more about the Bubble on the Internet. I'll show you how to use it today."

Muzz suppressed a groan. *The Highers may be risking their lives, an army of Tumbarumbans wants to invade the Cave, and she's talking about birds?*

Muzz mastered the Internet fairly quickly, launched a search for facts about the Cave. Many settlements and outposts were listed — some above ground, some below, some with special purposes like species engineering, medical technology, and grow-light production. A handful sold items such as sun lamps, synthetic fur, and that delicious substance 'chocolate' that Muzz enjoyed on the Walkabout.

She found Tumbarumba and Bayon Holding listed on a site about "rogue" outposts, learned they were part of a worldwide network of ruffians and thieves. By chance, she even learned what ASAP meant. But on the Internet, she could not learn anything about the Cave. It turned out to be as invisible from outside as the human world had been from inside the Cave.

Meanwhile, her feelings about the Cave kept undergoing changes. Worlds away and frooseless, she felt more and more allegiance to her roots. *I miss my family and friends much, and fear for their lives. I'm still more Hepu than human,* she told herself, *and I always will be. I don't just want to help Hepus, I need to.*

She found a site about the Bubble that showed its location near the northeast tip of Spain. One article said that, while almost everyplace north of the fortieth parallel languished under snow nearly all year, the Bubble's more temperate Mediterranean climate protected it from that fate. In fact, since the cloud layer above the Bubble had thinned over the past twenty years, enough filtered sunlight seeped through the clouds so that certain enterprising Bubblians had begun cultivating crops in an area outside the Bubble's shell during a four month growing season. Not only that, but the growing season seemed to be expanding a day or two each year. It was expected to start in about a month.

Made of a substance called "Sun-Plast" that was able to turn every trace of incoming solar energy into usable power, the Bubble's shell cost over a trillion Euros to build, the article said. Muzz guessed from the word 'cost' that 'Euros' had been some sort of money. She had a vague notion of what money was, and knew 'a trillion' was a huge number. *Is it more than a zillion?* According to the article the cost was worth it because, outfitted for the sudden cold that swept the globe, the Bubble had escaped the doom settlements faced that had only planned for increasing heat and drought. Humans in those places either migrated or perished.

One day mid-week, after Dr. Deet left, Muzz flopped across her bed in disgust, frowning, sighing, wiggling. She felt bored with the Internet, worried when she thought about threats to the Cave, betrayed each time she noticed how well her skin was adapting to frooselessness.

Then she remembered delving. *I stopped after we escaped from Bayon Holding,* she realized, and promptly propped her pillow against her headboard and shut her eyes. Afterward, gazing at the ceiling, she detected a faint source of light seeping from somewhere high in the bathroom.

She jumped straight up, dragged her desk chair in, climbed it, discovered a small window above the shower. She had thought the isolation chamber had zero connection with the outside world. *What an odd window — pale light through milky glass! But it looks as if it might open.*

She piled her pillows on the chair, stood on top, strained to move the window. It slid open and a shaft of light burst through. On tiptoe she could see a green lawn, humans walking on pathways, relaxing on benches, or eating and talking at picnic tables. *A town square!* It had a charming clock tower, a fountain in the center, a rack for bicycles, two big play structures loaded with noisy children, and flowers in neat, symmetrical beds. The women and girls wore leggings and tunics like the ones she had been given in a variety of colors, while the men and boys had leggings too, but long shirts instead of tunics. Everyone wore boots, and she had the impression that it was cool out there. Trees with silver-green leaves fluttered in a faint breeze. Children were swinging and sliding, or throwing lightweight disks. A squat black dog with pointy ears and lots of fluff barked at a man with a bouquet of floating colored spheres on strings. *What are those?*

For the rest of the week, when not pacing around worrying about Tom and the Cave, Muzz secretly studied the square to learn all she could about the Bubble. On the Internet, she learned the word 'balloon.'

When the week was almost over, a young man with dark hair emerged from behind the clock tower pushing someone in a wheelchair wearing a jumpsuit and, on closer inspection, breeding beads. There was a bandage wrapped around his head. *Is it Jerith?* As they neared the fountain Muzz could make out his handsome, angular face. She nearly fell off her perch. *It is!* She squinted for a better look. *His head's leaning to one side and his eyes are closed. He must be in terrible shape.* The young man guided the wheelchair directly to her building.

After that she spent an almost sleepless night. In the morning, Dr. Deet arrived with Muzz's beads and shawl, and the silver box her mother had given her. She set them on the bed and gave Muzz a worried once-over. "What's the matter, Muzz? You look so tired."

"I saw my friend Jerith in a wheelchair last night, and I'm worried much."

"How did you do that?"

Muzz had to admit she had been spying and explain how.

"It's a pity you saw him because it's your release day, and now you're upset."

"I'm fine. Really."

"You don't look fine."

"I just need to see Jerith... and also Tom."

The doctor jotted a note on her clipboard. "You're moving to a place where you'll learn more about our fair Bubble."

She shook her head. "But nothing has changed concerning Tom, and I can't let you visit Jerith. Not just yet. He isn't well enough for visitors. Those Tumbarumbans gave his head an awful smack."

"I know. I saw how he looked. Poor Jerith! Can I visit him soon?"

Dr. Deet looked doubtful. "As soon as he's well enough, I'll make sure that you do. But for now, I'm moving you someplace new — the Halfway House, it's called. I'm going to introduce you to a guide who'll take you there. He's waiting downstairs. His name is Alok. Come and meet him."

Muzz would have liked several rides in the elevator that lowered them to the ground floor. But Alok stood waiting and within minutes was carrying a satchel of her things across the square. He was the same dark-haired human she had seen with Jerith, which bothered her though she did not know why. Still, the light, air, and space out in the unique artificial world of the Bubble improved her mood. The light from the Sun-Plast dome felt surprisingly warm on her skin. *Like the real sunlight at Angkor.* At the center of the square, she stopped to take it all in. A soft breeze with a sweet scent brushed her face, made her sneeze.

"What's that smell?" she asked.

"Roses," said Alok. He stopped and breathed in deeply. "I like this most of all."

"What?"

He swept his hand around. "Showing people around like this." He studied her face. "You don't think of yourself as 'people' yet, do you."

Muzz shrugged and blushed. She felt awkward around Alok. *I can't seem to forget he's human. Is it my early training, the mistreatment at Bayon, or suspicion about this picture perfect artificial place? Or is it all three?*

As they walked on, Alok explained that she would eat and sleep in the Halfway House, and have a few weeks to explore. "Then what?" asked Muzz.

Alok said he was not sure. *Does he know things he isn't telling me?*

"Do you know the man named Tom from the copterjet, the one who brought me here?" she asked.

Alok nodded.

"Well, he said he wanted to talk with me when I was ready, and I am ready. How do I let him know?"

"You don't, I'm sorry to say. He's out on another mission."

"Will he be back soon?"

"I can't say. But—" Alok raised his pointer finger, cast smiling eyes on her. "I'll try to get a message to him. I can't promise anything, but I'll ask him to contact you as soon as he returns, and I'll tell him where you are."

Muzz wished she felt relieved, but she felt exasperated, annoyed that no one seemed willing to help her reach Tom. *Besides, Alok's smile makes me uneasy. It's too friendly, I think, as if he feels close to me. How could he when he doesn't even know me? That smile is just plain phony, and I need help — someone who can be trusted, not a hypocrite.*

"What happened to my cell mate Deb? How is she?" Muzz asked.

"I don't actually know. She's a Bubblian and I work with visitors — teenagers, mostly, and an occasional child. But I'll ask around and let you know."

"Thanks." Muzz felt somewhat better after that, enough to turn her attention to the various sights and sounds along their route — families on porches, bicycles whirring past, snippets of music here and there — but hardly enough to trust her guide.

The Halfway House stood on a corner a few blocks from the square. Two stories tall with dark green shutters, it had peach colored roses clinging to trellises around a generous porch. Like other buildings on their route, it sported a garden full of vegetables and flowers, as well as shade trees here and there. As they climbed the front steps, something shook a windowpane upstairs, and startled Muzz.

"What was *that*, a tremblor?"

Alok smiled, shook his head. "No, don't worry. The Bubble's artificial wind does that sometimes; it copies nature that well. It's always spring-like here to help things grow. The wind changes with the time of day almost the way it used to B.W."

He cocked he head at her. "You'll probably need a scarf at night. It's cooler then."

"I'll wear my shawl," she said, pointing at her satchel.

There's that smile of his again, she thought as they entered the Halfway House. Alok showed her to a corner room on the second floor with buttery walls and beige lace curtains. Her windows let her see down both streets — a new perch from which to study Bubble life, keep an eye out for Jerith, and plot ways to reach Tom or at least Deb.

After stowing her things, Alok said, "It's lunchtime."

Downstairs the cook served them bread with a delicious spread, and a bowl of tasty greens. Though Muzz enjoyed it, she did not let her guard down with Alok. "Who else is staying here?" she asked as they ate.

"No one now. Guests come and go."

"Are there ever other Hepu guests?"

Alok raised his brows and shrugged. "Not many," was all he said.

I'm not about to pressure him for news about Jerith. All I'll get is another mixed message served up with that smarmy smile. I need to figure things out for myself.

After lunch they took another walk. Little battery-powered pastel cars had begun moving with a slight hum on the Bubble's narrow streets. Each driver rang a bell to alert pedestrians. Muzz came out of her shell long enough to say she wanted to learn to drive one, but when Alok told her she was not old enough to drive yet, she slipped back inside, more suspicious of him than ever.

They strolled through neighborhoods, passed a schoolhouse with chatter bursting from the door, saw some shops and a few eateries including one with outdoor tables. One shop sold, among its many boots, a pair Muzz wished she could have, offered in a rainbow of hues. She liked the ones labeled 'russet' best that were a few shades lighter than her hair. Next door Alok bought something delicious called 'peanut butter cookies' at a fragrant place called a bakery, and they nibbled cookies in front of a store window where a woman stood motionless in a fancy purple gown.

In spite of herself, Muzz asked, "How does that lady hold so still so long?"

Alok grinned at her. "That 'lady' is a mannequin, an artificial statue of a human." When Muzz blushed at her mistake, he told her, "I thought the same thing when I first saw one."

"So you're not a Bubblian by birth?" Alok solemnly shook his head, which piqued Muzz's curiosity. But his expression stopped her from asking more. *There's that tricky little smile again.*

Back at the Halfway House he said, "I have to leave now. I hope you'll like it here. If you need anything, I have a cell phone. Be sure to contact me. Your housekeeper knows my number. But whether you call or not, I'll come to see how you're doing in a couple of days."

"And you'll remember to contact Tom?"

"I'll remember to try. Oh, and one more thing. You asked about Hepus? Actually, there's one living here I'll be taking you to meet soon."

Still suspicious, Muzz quelled the excitement that news made her feel.

CHAPTER SEVENTEEN

Weeks with seven days instead of ten and days with their own names were new to Muzz, but she learned she had arrived at the Halfway House on a Friday, and Alok was due back on Sunday. *So long to wait to see Jerith!*

On Saturday morning she studied Bubble life from her windows. She thought Bubblians spent a disturbingly large chunk of time laughing and talking. *Are they for real?* After lunch she took a book and went to the square for a closer look. She sat on a bench pretending to read. When children came up, their parents called them. *Maybe they know I'm a Hepu.* But many adults smiled at her. *Maybe they* like *Hepus.*

Late in the day as the artificial light faded to twilight, a bandaged head appeared at a third floor hospital window — *Jerith!* Muzz bristled with excitement as if she still had froose, her bare arms dotted with odd little bumps that eventually disappeared. *What were* those *about?*

As she watched, Jerith stood rubbing his forehead and eyes. Soon human hands gripped his shoulders and pulled him away. A slender woman in white with scalp hair lighter than a Lab's pulled down the blinds. Soon after that the crowd in the park thinned. Muzz closed her book, crossed to the hospital. *I have to chance it.*

She pushed her way in, found the greeting desk empty. She heard voices nearby, saw scads of confusing doors and one promising one — almost surely the elevator she had taken with Alok. *But riding it will make too much noise.* She spotted stairs, climbed to the third floor, snuck down the hall.

She stopped, hand poised above a doorknob, at the door most likely to be Jerith's. While she was debating whether to turn it or not — *knocking would be too loud* — the door opened. She and Jerith stood speechless until he dragged her in.

"Who are you, and why were you lurking out there?"

"It's me, Jerith. Muzz."

Jerith pulled her to where his lamp shone directly in her face.

"Who?"

"Muzz."

Jerith scowled and examined her closely. "You're not my nurse. The reason I'm supposed to know you is—?"

"It's me, Muzz from the Cave." Muzz had a sinking feeling.

Jerith scoffed, looked her up and down. "You're not even a Hepu, for Whitford's sake. Get out, get out!" He pushed her to the door and forced her out, but she wedged her foot in the gap.

"Shhhhh! I'm Muzz, a Hepu, your friend. Really."

Jerith scowled at her from beneath his bandage. "Liar!"

"No, no, I can prove it. You have a special name for me... remember?"

Jerith managed to push her foot out and slam the door. Through it his muffled voice replied, "I don't remember anything. Go away."

Muzz heard a key turn in the lock. She tapped the door softly and tried to twist the knob. "Please open up. I need to talk with you."

There was silence.

"I *am* a Hepu. I have my breeding beads to prove it."

After a long pause, the door opened a crack.

A single eye shown through, and Muzz took her beads from her pocket, held them up. "I was exposed to too much sun, and my froose fell off."

Jerith eyed the beads, then her, and shook his head. He turned, letting the door swing open, and staggered back into the room. "I've heard that can happen."

He held his head and crumpled on the edge of his bed. Then he pointed at his bandage. "I have amnesia."

Muzz knew about amnesia from Book Storage. "What happened?"

"If I knew that, I wouldn't have amnesia, would I!"

Muzz considered how unlike the old Jerith this cranky Hepu was.

She clenched her fists. "You'd better lie down." She was surprised when he did. She pulled a chair to his bedside.

"Do you want to know about your life in the Cave?" He groaned softly and nodded, so she started describing the Cave, his family and pup, then Chell. But she could see him looking more and more lost and unhappy. "This isn't helping, is it?"

Jerith stared at the ceiling and sighed slowly through his nose. "Nothing helps."

Muzz crossed to the window and looked at the darkening square.

"It's late. I'd better go."

When she glanced back at Jerith, he was pointing at the ceiling. "Look! See those little lights?" They were the red, beady-eyed lights of an Infrareader.

Jerith seemed ready to burst. "I see them much. Always at night on my ceiling."

"So you remember that."

"It happens *here*. I remember here."

Muzz felt skittish, wondered who was watching. *Mrs. Whitford or someone else?* "I'd really better go," she said.

Jerith got up slowly and followed her out. He closed the door, clutched her arm, whispered, "Creepy little lights? Imprisoned in my room? I think the Bubblians are the ones who kidnapped me and knocked me unconscious."

"I came to in a helicopter with someone bandaging my head. They brought me here. At first they were much kind. I lived freely in a nice place. But then they shut me in this room. I've been here... it feels like forever."

His eyes widened. "Do you know Alok?"

Muzz nodded.

"Alok comes to see me, but before they put me here, he used to take me for an airing almost every day. On one of those walks he showed me a building where a female Hepu lives who rarely shows her face."

"Maybe that was me."

"How long have you been here?"

"About a week."

"Isn't 'rarely' a long time sort of word?"

"I guess." Muzz felt relieved that his thinking seemed logical.

"She lives in a large wooden structure high in a forest."

"Really?"

"That's what Alok showed me."

Muzz said, "That is much strange."

"Strange, or worse! Who would stay hidden in a forest as a matter of choice? I think she's imprisoned like me. These humans pretend to be friendly, but I think they're fakes. Kidnappers and Hepu haters." Jerith emphasized his words by making a fist with one hand, and hitting the other.

Muzz thought of Alok's smile, closed her eyes and shook her head. "I hope not... Do you know where the forest is?"

"I know how to get there."

"Tell me."

"I'll have to show you."

"But how?"

Jerith scanned the room with unsteady eyes. "We can sneak there late tonight. But I've had a hard day. I need to rest up first. Besides, my nurse may come back."

"I saw her pull you away from the window earlier."

"She's nice, though, not a fake. She comes to see me often, and I'm really fond of her. She's the one human I like." Jerith's eyes brightened. "Maybe I can arrange to get too much sun like you. If I lose my froose, she may start to take me seriously."

"What do you mean?"

"She'll never marry someone with froose."

Muzz felt something twist in her chest. "You want to marry her?"

Jerith nodded.

"You used to want to marry me."

Jerith's mouth dropped open. "Are you sure?"

"Much sure."

"And did you want to marry me?"

"I didn't want to marry anyone, and it got me in a lot of trouble."

Jerith frowned deeply. "That cave place we're from sounds pretty weird, uh— What did you say your name is?"

"Muzz. I said it's Muzz." The twisted feeling deepened.

"Anyway, Muzz, if you come back tonight, I'll take you to that forest and we'll check things out. Meet me by the clock tower at midnight, okay?"

"I'll be there." Muzz started toward the stairs, turned back. "You'll remember this conversation, won't you?"

Jerith grimaced. "I told you, I remember *here* just fine."

Muzz felt strange. On her way back to the Halfway House, a host of questions surged through her mind: *Can the Bubblians be as bad as Jerith thinks? Are they holding him captive? What if they decide to lock me up? How could Jerith have become so devoted to a human? And did those Infrareader lights on his ceiling come from spies in the Bubble, trustworthy Mrs. Whitford, or someone else?*

As she walked Muzz thought over her discussion with Jerith about the Cave. Suddenly she wanted so much to see Tendra, Chell, her mother and grandparents, even her father in all his sternness. She did not like the way her past clung so dimly in the back of her mind. *Even Emily is going pale.* What's more, she wanted the old Jerith back. She could hardly tolerate this new one.

The time until they were to meet crept by. Muzz kept herself awake. About twenty minutes before their meeting time, she threw on her shawl, tiptoed out and slipped through shadows toward the clock tower. Jerith came toward her adjusting his bandage. "We need to hurry. They check on me at dawn."

Muzz asked, "Are you okay?"

He nodded. "It's great to be out of that dumb wheelchair. I've been exercising when no one's around. See how well I walk?" He took a few more steps, turned and eyed her inquisitively.

"You do seem to be walking pretty well."

Jerith put a finger to his lips, turned and led her past dozing shops and houses, each with its own small light. Artificial stars shimmered overhead. *How pretty this is*, Muzz wished they were on a midnight stroll instead of some secret mission. Soon they came to a path that led up the slope of Bubbletown's bowl.

The path wove through scrub brush and, after they climbed for a while, a gap in the bushes revealed the town twinkling below — trees, streets, houses, open spaces — tiny in the distance and gently lit. *So full of light, so different from the Cave.* But Jerith sounded out of breath, which worried her.

She was glad when he stopped and said in a coarse whisper, "There it is." He nodded at a grove of pointy trees, rustling in an artificial breeze.

Muzz peered around him, pulled her shawl close. Beyond the trees a large rustic wooden building sat in a clearing. *A log cabin! I've wanted to see one ever since I read about that nice human, Abraham Lincoln.*

"Follow me." Jerith clutched his head, crept forward.

Muzz took in details: the cabin's stone chimney, and multi-paned windows, the faint light that shone from within, and the warm, nutty fragrance of the trees. *Evergreens. But what kind?* she wondered. A gust of artificial wind set off a chime in the cabin's eaves that startled her.

"Relax." She noticed Jerith's breathing sounded ragged.

"*You* relax," she told him.

He ignored her, gliding from one dimly lit window to the next. Finally he stopped, stood up for a closer look. "There she is!"

They crouched, facing the window. Jerith scooted closer and Muzz followed, sliding noiselessly behind a bush. He angled himself so that he could see in. Then he turned, his eyes big with excitement. "She has on a creepy looking robe." He traded places so Muzz could look.

An older female Hepu lay sleeping on a low padded platform. Muzz could tell she had a froosey face even in the dimness, and saw her breeding beads. Sure enough she wore a pale green robe.

"Wow!" Muzz shook her head.

The female opened her eyes, sat up, gazed at the window. "Who's there?" she called. Seeing her features gave Muzz a strange, half-familiar feeling. *As if I've seen her before.*

Muzz ducked and stared at Jerith. They both cowered, and rushed back to the safety of the path.

"How in Whitford's winter did she hear me?" Muzz whispered.

Jerith tried without success to adjust his bandage. He shook his head. "I don't know, but she must be much desperate, trapped in there with nothing to do."

"She didn't seem trapped or desperate to me."

"No one to talk to, nothing outside her window? She's worse off than I am." He started down the hill.

Muzz hurried after, eying him closely. *I hardly know him now.* He was moving so fast that she had trouble keeping up. He rounded a turn in the path and went out of sight; she heard a loud thud. "Jerith?" she called, rushing to catch up and nearly tripping over him. He lay sprawled on the ground.

Muzz knelt, shook the sleeve of his jumpsuit. "Jerith? Jerith!" She eyed him closely. *He's breathing, but he's out cold!*

Unfortunately, as Muzz saw it, this was how her secret hike with Jerith came to light. She was forced to get help at the cabin — an emergency call to Alok by a woman who also wore a robe.

The rescuers brought Jerith to, and he rode the rest of the way down the hill on a stretcher. His nurse, with her copious golden curls and striking eyes, hurried alongside, her hand on his knee, and Muzz took up the rear.

At one point the nurse slowed to walk with Muzz. "Why were you out here with *him* in the middle of the night? I mean, with a Hepu?"

"*I'm* a Hepu, and Jerith's my friend."

"Oh... sorry. I didn't—"

"Simone!" one of the porters called, and she hurried back to her post. As soon as they stowed Jerith in the ambulance, Simone climbed in and they were whisked away leaving Muzz alone.

By late Sunday morning Jerith was back in his hospital room recovering, and Muzz was sitting by Alok on a bench in the square, debating what to tell him and what to hide.

She knew it all came down to whether Bubblians were friend or foe. *If only I could run this by Mrs. Whitford!*

Alok sat with his arms folded and eyes cast down, poking at a flagstone with his feet.

Finally he glanced over at her. "Muzz, I think you'd better tell me how you came to find Jerith and what you two were doing up there."

"I— I saw him at his hospital window," she said before her voice trailed off.

"And?"

"He didn't know me." She searched for what she could safely say. There was a pause.

"Look, Muzz. You're in some trouble, you and Jerith. So am I." Muzz lowered her eyes. "I'm sorry." She took a deep breath, and looked Alok in the eye. "Jerith doesn't remember anything until he woke up here."

"And he thinks we're the ones who injured him, doesn't he."

"Who did injure him?"

Alok shook his head. "I can't tell you yet."

Muzz thought he looked genuinely sorry. He bent and broke off a blade of grass, twisted it around his finger. "Jerith has grown tough to work with — way too easily agitated! And he keeps forgetting how weak he is. That's why he's where he is."

Alok shredded the grass and tossed it to the ground. "The last time I took him out, he acted so confused I had to rush him back to his room. Now he's not supposed to leave the hospital at all." A pause. "So, what were you two up to last night?"

"Exploring." Another pause.

"Not far from where he collapsed there's a place called The Retreat. Did you happen to see it?"

"Is it made of logs?"

"Yes."

"Then we saw it. That's where I went to call for help."

"A resident heard sounds outside her window. Was that you?"

Muzz shifted uneasily. "Jerith had something to show me."

"Do you know about the other—"

"Hepu? Yes, we saw her."

Alok thumped a hand on his knee. "This is my fault. I told Jerith about her once, but he seemed to forget. I was waiting for the right time to tell you."

"Who *is* she, Alok? Jerith thinks she's a prisoner, or something. What's she doing up there?"

"It's — as you say in the Hepunese dialect — 'much hard' to explain."

"Will I get to meet her soon?"

"Probably not soon."

"What about Jerith? When can I see him?"

"I don't know. Even I can't visit him now."

Muzz had felt more trusting of Alok during this talk, but when he smiled at her, she thought, *There it is again. Why does his smile do that to me? It feels exaggerated, or something. Like more than the situation calls for. I just don't trust it, and that makes me suspicious about everything he does and says.*

CHAPTER EIGHTEEN

For the next few weeks the female Hepu often appeared in Muzz's dreams, she had nightmares about Tom, more suspicions about Alok, all kinds of concerns about the Hepus, and gradually came to realize how immensely she missed the old Jerith from the Cave. With a growing mound of questions and problems no one seemed to care about the way she did, Muzz vowed to snoop more and try to do more on her own.

Her fourth Friday there marked the eve of the Bubble's Festival of Illumination, and everyone flocked to the town square including Muzz, whose snooping so far had been disappointing. Lights decorated the treetops and a band from a distant place —Vienna Woods — played tunes called 'waltzes.' Men in tailored jackets and striped pants twirled ladies with upswept hair and fluttery skirts, creating an odd, impressive sight. The audience cheered after every number and, if Muzz had not been so determined to continue snooping, she might have enjoyed the show. Instead she was scanning the crowd for clues. *Are there any Bubblians I can trust?*

She saw Alok up near the performers with a group of friends, and deliberately lingered toward the back where he would not see her. She saw Dr. Deet sitting on a park bench beside a man about her age. She was keeping an eye on a small child in a pink dress playing peek-a-boo from behind a nearby tree. Now and then the man would fetch the child and swing her until she giggled and shrieked. *Who can I trust?* Muzz searched for Deb, but could not find her.

Then some movement by the clock tower caught her attention. She saw a man's face appear from behind the brick façade, drop out of sight again.

A soldier with a uniform like Tom's. Just as a waltz ended with more cheers and applause, she edged to the back of the crowd, dodged a few grown-ups, made a beeline around the far side of the tower in time to spot the man walking down an adjoining street. In the dusk, no one noticed her follow him. He sped past homes with wide verandas and well-kept lawns, stopped at one, glanced around, climbed the porch steps.

She stood behind a hedge in dim light from the house's front porch and windows. From her vantage point she could see the man in a close circle with two other men and a carrot-headed woman, all in overstuffed chairs, and all wearing uniforms. Tom was not among them. *The redhead's my pilot, but who are the others?*

She could hear them talking. "A huge undertaking" was the first phrase she caught, and later "Tumbarumbans." *Ice chunks, does this mean they're in league with those rogues?*

A large map lay open between them, and a blond man with a trim beard was pointing at it. He had a thick neck and shoulders. "They're nearing the Cave as we speak. More than five hundred, well armed," he said. Another man — also stocky, but dark-haired— nodded. So did the one she had followed.

"Their weaponry alone will overpower the Hepus," said the pilot.

The pilot glanced outside. "Will somebody shut the window? This is top secret. We need to take every precaution." The dark-haired man came over, Muzz ducked, the window slammed shut. *Hoar ice and snowdrifts!* When she felt safe enough to look again, they were talking excitedly, even laughing. She saw the pilot hit the map with her pointer finger. To Muzz it almost felt as if the Hepus in the Cave were being struck.

Later, before they left, the humans paused to talk near the front door. Muzz scuttled to some bushes nearer the porch, listened, waited. The pilot and the dark-haired man stood facing the other two, all nodding and talking. When they came outside, one remarked, "So all our forces are ready for combat."

The pilot nodded. "Yes, Captain. If the weather holds two hundred soldiers will be airborne within the hour. We rendezvous with our allies outside the Cave tomorrow at fifteen hundred hours."

"Excellent," the stocky, blond man replied. The other three saluted him and left the porch, and he stood for a long moment twirling his mustache and gazing around.

Then Muzz watched him walk down the street until the darkness swallowed him.

Warring Whitford! It looks like they're helping the Tumbarumbans! Oh, you poor Hepus! If only I could warn you of the danger heading your way.

"Poor Mrs. Whitford has no clue what these humans have in store for the Cave." Muzz stood by Jerith's hospital bed early next morning recounting her adventure to him. "If only I could warn her."

Jerith eyed Muzz with a dazed frown. "I don't even remember who Mrs. Whitford is. But at least you finally get what I've been trying to tell you about these humans. They're liars! Villains! They want that cave you keep talking about for themselves." He pointed at his head. "This proves they'll do anything."

"How can we stop them? I mean, how can *I* since *you* need to stay put?" Muzz paced and paced, whirled around so fast that Jerith scrunched his eyes shut and clutched his covers. "I know!" she said. "Mrs. Whitford used an unusual name when she talked on that phone contraption. Meeya, Pleeya... something like that. If only I can find out who—"

Jerith stuck his hand out of the covers and waved it weakly. "Thea? Could it have been Thea?"

"You know someone named Thea?"

"Thea's the name of the older female."

Muzz tilted her head at him uncertainly.

"Thea," Jerith repeated. "That's what Alok called her."

"You remem— uh, I mean, I guess you're sure..."

Jerith groaned. "I already explained, Muzz, I remember *here*. It's *there* I have trouble with."

Muzz resumed pacing. "Stuck together ice cubes! How can I speak to her?"

Jerith sat straight up. "Please stop marching around. You're making me nauseous." He thought a moment. "Go back to The Retreat and demand to see her. Call her by name. Say 'I need to speak with Thea right now.'"

"Then what?"

"They've probably kept this from her. Once she hears what's going on, she can use the phone contraption to warn that Whitford person."

"Hmmm... Maybe you're on to something. It's worth a try."

From Jerith's room, Muzz climbed straight to The Retreat, pounded on the door, and asked the woman who answered to take her to Thea.

The woman made her sit in an antechamber and withdrew through an inner door.

Muzz waited a long time. Then she saw Alok scaling the porch steps. Noting his sneaky smile, she hissed 'Blighted berries' under her breath, went to meet him.

"Muzz! What's going on?"

"I need to talk to Thea."

"Thea? You know her name? You couldn't ask me to set something up?"

"This is urgent. I need to see her. Now."

Alok furrowed his brow. "I'm supposed to give you help, but you keep bypassing me."

Muzz wondered if this human facing her knew about the attack. She eyed him suspiciously. "I need to speak with Thea, that's all."

"It's that urgent?"

Muzz nodded.

Alok sighed, shook his head. "I'll see what I can do."

He knocked on the inner door and a face appeared, the same woman who answered it the first time.

"Oh, Alok. Thank goodness we reached you. Please come in." Muzz stood up. "Just Alok for now," said the woman.

Muzz sat again for a long time before Alok finally opened the door and motioned her in. They followed the woman down a long hall with gleaming wooden floors, their footsteps echoing in the quiet.

At the far end, the woman showed them where to leave their shoes and gave each of them a pastel colored robe. Alok slipped his over his clothes, helped Muzz on with hers.

"Why does everyone wear a robe around here?"

Alok beamed at her, shrugged, smiled faintly. "To save on heat. They keep the air so cool."

Muzz noticed it really *was* cool in there. Thea, seated, hardly seemed to have moved since Muzz last saw her. *And her eyes are closed.* Alok motioned Muzz to sit on one of the thick cushions. He sat on another and mouthed the word 'relax.'

Muzz felt like a pot of something bubbling on a stove. She studied the room, its pastel walls and drapes, its fluffy carpet. A graceful vase of roses and ferns made the room so unlike the prison Jerith had conjured that she shook her head in wonder.

After a few minutes Thea's eyelids fluttered and she opened them. *Her gaze reminds me of... something I half remember, but what?*

"Hello, Muzz, I'm much glad to see you. I hear you urgently need to speak with me?"

"Yes, I..."

Muzz glanced over at Alok, leaned forward, whispered, "It's about the humans, Thea. I'm afraid they're up to something."

Thea nodded and held Muzz firmly in her gaze. Her eyes looked so clear and deep that Muzz felt the funny bumps on her skin again.

Thea nodded toward the window. "This is about something that happened last night. You overheard something, didn't you."

How in Whitford does she know that? Muzz leaned toward Thea, pleading. "I eavesdropped on some humans. They're planning to attack the poor, defenseless Hepus. I'm sure you remember what life was like in the Cave. You *must* see that the Hepus need our help."

Thea broke into a smile and shook her head. "Oh, no, no, Muzz. The Bubblians are sending troops to Australia to *defend* the Hepus, not attack. A pack of outlaws is heading for the Cave, the same ones who kidnapped Jerith and injured him."

"He says the Bubblians injured him."

Thea looked Muzz squarely in the eye. "He's so confused. You mustn't listen to him. The outlaws are rogues from a settlement near the Cave."

"I know — the Tumbarumbans. My cellmate at Bayon Holding told me. But are you sure the Bubblians aren't their allies?"

Thea took a deep breath. "You need to understand, Muzz, that the Bubblians are heroes in this story, not villains."

"You mean they're not violent, greedy humans?" From the corner of her eye, Muzz gave Alok an apologetic look.

Alok lowered his head, closed his eyes, clasped and unclasped his hands, smiled the unnerving smile, let his eyes rise to Thea's. "Isn't it time she knew?"

"I guess so, Alok. Go ahead."

Alok turned to Muzz. He looked excited. "Muzz, you need to know that you and I have the same mother."

Muzz stared at him wide-eyed, clutched her face in both hands.

"You see, I was born in the Cave, but frooseless. The Beacons couldn't grasp how it had happened, and they didn't want to know. They wanted me culled."

There's that dreadful word again. "How were you saved?"

"The same way you were, I'm told — with Mrs. Whitford's help."

"I'll be it was intense."

Alok gave a big nod. "There were huge shenanigans, some sort of power struggle that ended with my father spiriting me out of the Cave and bringing me here. It all happened before you were born." He turned to Thea. "Am I telling this right?"

She nodded. "You are, Alok." She turned to Muzz excitedly. "Even the *Beacons* don't know what goes on in that puppy lab. Mr. Whitford was a geneticist. He figured out a way to use a gene from Labrador Retrievers to create froose. It's good for protecting Hepus from the Cave's dampness. But somehow the process didn't work for Alok and they thought he was some kind of mutant. How ironic considering that in actuality *they* — or I should say *we* — are the altered ones. A whole tribe of genetically modified humans hidden away in the Cave and protected from all kinds of knowing, including knowing what in reality we are."

"Frozen fraudulence!" Muzz exclaimed, and the other two laughed.

"Beachy ursp!" said Alok.

Muzz aimed for an empty cushion, keeled onto her back, covered her eyes. She lay there remembering the poor nameless puppy she had found in the Forbidden Tunnel. *Gene theft! So that's what was going on!* She felt sorry for the puppy until another thought gripped her mind. She turned excitedly to Thea. "Wait! Does what you two are saying mean that Chell had a *different* mother?"

Thea nodded. "You've got it."

Muzz thought of her father and the dark expression she always seemed to trigger in him. "What happened to Chell's mother?"

"She died from cave fever when Chell was just a yearling, and your father took losing her much hard. The Beacons wanted him to remarry right away, but he was so heartbroken that he stalled for over a year before marrying your 'widowed' mother."

"No one knew where my father and I had gone," said Alok. "They thought we were dead. It's been hard, not telling you.

So that's where the smile came from, thought Muzz.

Thea nodded. "It must have been, Alok. Thanks for waiting. The Tribe believes to this day that Alok died at birth and his father committed suicide."

"But no one ever speaks of it," said Muzz.

"It was forbidden." Thea paused. "We all remember it, of course."

"So you came here *after* Alok?"

"Yes, I had my own dispute with the Beacons. They thought I had too much power, especially among the females, who wanted to make me the first female Beacon."

"Wow!"

Thea nodded. "So just like you, they banished me and threatened to cull me, which was why my mother sent me here."

Muzz blinked and shook her head. "Your mother?"

"Mildred Whitford."

"Mrs. Whitford, your mother?" Muzz sat and, staring into space, slowly rocked back and forth. She moaned, "Oh, oh, I feel much mixed up inside... But I mustn't forget my other *serious* reason for coming."

"What's that?" asked Thea.

A clock somewhere chimed the hour and Thea checked her watch. "Forgive me, Muzz. Time to call the others in. Will you do it, Alok?"

As he left the room, Muzz rushed to explain. "The Highers are planning an insurrection."

"That does sound serious. But I'm afraid it'll have to wait. We don't have time to discuss it now. It's time to delve. I heard you've been diving for nearly half a year now, is that right?"

"Yes, but how did you—"

Thea pointed toward the door. "I heard from this amazing woman."

Muzz turned to see Deb coming in.

She took a seat on the cushion next to Muzz, threw an arm around her shoulder, squeezed. "Muzz, baby, it's been ages! How're you doing?"

"Deb!"

Deb framed her face with her hands. "Big as life," she said. Several others came in and sat in a circle on the cushions. "We'll have to catch up later, okay, kiddo?"

Thea leaned close to Muzz and whispered, "I know this isn't easy for you, but we need to face one crisis at a time, the Tumbarumbans first." She sat up straight and glanced around the group in a calm, deliberate way. "Let's close our eyes. The troops will be doing the same. It's less than an hour until touchdown for them, and they need all the support they can get."

She folded her hands, closed her eyes, and the others did the same. Muzz, her mind still churning with a hodge-podge of thoughts and feelings, reluctantly joined in. *How can 'support' from a bunch of divers thousands of miles away possibly help?*

She had never delved with a group before. At first waves of confusion and frustration overshadowed her mind, but soon the group's gentle power helped settle her. At some point she found herself floating in a pool of silence.

CHAPTER NINETEEN

Deb was still diving when Muzz finished, but Alok was watching her. He motioned toward the door and she followed him out. "They'll be a while. D'you want a tour of this place?" He smiled shyly, and this time Muzz welcomed it.

Alok showed her an art studio, a large, well-stocked library with computers and globe (showing where all the countries used to be), an exercise room and one for spinning, dyeing, and weaving various fibers, a large Retreat kitchen that also made great smelling bread to sell in Bubbletown, a tiny theater with fifty-odd seats, and further up the hill many small cabins nestled among trees. Near them stood a large music cabin with a piano and an array of other instruments, chairs and music stands.

The tour ended with a flower and vegetable garden in a spacious clearing nearby.

"I didn't know all this was here," said Muzz. "If I weren't so glued to what's happening at the Cave, I could really enjoy this place." She sniffed a daisy that made her sneeze, and when she recovered asked, "Who owns all this?"

"It belongs to everyone," Alok told her. "School children come here, grownups on leave from work, retired people... There's time set aside for just about every group in the Bubble. I came here twice a year all through school."

"And you stayed in a cabin?"

Alok nodded. Then he turned, arms folded, and looked at her hard. "You know, those troops Thea mentioned should be able to protect the Cave. When they defeat the Tumbarumbans, will you be able to relax and enjoy it here?"

Muzz tightened her hands into fists, dropped them to her sides. She bowed her head and grimaced. "But there's a problem *inside* the Cave too!"

"What's happening in there that has you so worried?"

Muzz knotted her brows. "Months ago, just before the last Walkabout, the Highers in the Cave — Do you know who the 'Highers' are?"

"Yes. What about them?"

"The Highers felt so angered by the unjust betrothal picks that they were planning a revolt."

Alok plunked cross-legged onto the garden grass, gestured for Muzz to do the same. He studied her intently. "Really!"

"Yes, and that isn't all. One day I heard a couple of cave guards talking. They already knew something about it. The Beacons ordered them to do anything and everything to stop it."

"Culling included?" He flinched pronouncing the word.

Muzz gave a large, serious nod. "'If necessary,' they said. And it sounded as if they could hardly wait." Muzz shook her head, a grim line to her lips. "During one of the Highers' early meetings I warned them to stop, but they wouldn't listen. My brother Chell's one of the ringleaders; Jerith *was* another. I'm sure Chell and the others haven't given up. The whole thing has me much perturbed."

"I see." The way Alok said that made it clear he did see. He stopped to think. "This hasn't surfaced yet. If it had, I'm sure Thea would know. She talks with Mrs. Whitford nearly every day. She would've said something. But now I see why you were so eager to speak to Tom and Thea."

"I told Thea about it before everyone dove, but she said it has to wait until the Tumbarumban crisis is resolved."

Alok furrowed his brow and sighed. "I guess she's right."

Both Muzz and Alok stayed for lunch served in the main dining room. The room had a fireplace and a view of the forest. Muzz sat with Deb trading stories at a circular wooden table. Deb had spent a few days in hospital recuperating from her injury, and several more with her family. "Yesterday I came here for a little rest and relaxation before returning to my post."

"Nice," said Muzz, sinking her teeth into a bite-sized bright red fruit. It was her first ever of whatever it was, and she had to stop and unravel the flavors.

"Strawberries." Deb held out the serving plate. "Good? Here, have some more."

Muzz took a large helping, and ate them with relish as she and Deb talked. She was thinking of asking if Deb knew anything about Jerith when Thea crossed the room.

"Our forces are about to land," she said with more than a trace of tension in her voice. "If you want to watch, Muzz, you'll have to hurry."

Muzz jumped to her feet, waved to Deb because her mouth was too full to speak, took a few more strawberries, and followed Thea to a nearby room. Alok came too.

The Retreat had its own Infrareader with impressive dials and tubes. Thea fiddled with the instrument panel for a while and said, "Here, Muzz, take a look."

Through an oblong viewing tube that encircled her eyes, Muzz saw the polished silver window of a copterjet. She could hear faint, rhythmic thumping — its engine.

Then the Infrareader zoomed in on several hundred humans below, all racing, parting, diving to hide behind boulders and mounds of snow from what must have been massive searchlights the copterjets were aiming at them. To Muzz these would-be invaders looked like frantic, itty-bitty insects, and she almost pitied them.

Muzz saw several copterjets land and hundreds of soldiers stream out to block the path of the scurrying invaders. Bubblian soldiers and their allies soon had them surrounded, and seized a few who looked like leaders. Muzz could not hear gunfire, but saw flashes of orange light. Scads of Tumbarumbans began throwing down their weapons, crawling from their hiding places with their hands up.

"We've got 'em," a woman's voice announced. But without warning, a band of them broke loose and burst over an embankment.

"This is Rooster Twelve. Unable to peck them," a male voice piped. "Repeat: Unable to peck."

On the Infrareader, Muzz saw a giant craft swerve in close to the breakaways, but they were on the run through a narrow, shadowy canyon too tight for the copterjet to maneuver.

"Pull up, Rooster Twelve, and block 'em at the other end," replied the woman. Muzz recognized her pilot's voice again and felt somehow proud this time.

Muzz's view through the silver frame shifted. Everything in it shrank in size as the craft apparently lifted. "Did you hear that, Alok? They're chasing runaways. Here, d'you want a look?"

Alok traded places with Muzz and peered into the oblong tube, making an occasional half-gasp or moan. Muzz could hardly stand the suspense. "What's happening?"

Alok held his hand up. "Just a minute. The copterjet has landed, our soldiers are disembarking, and... They're turning back and, yes, ... they've been ... the enemy's surrounded! The Cave is safe."

The three of them cheered and clapped until fear crept over Muzz and her hands froze in mid air. "How do we really know that? Maybe they've already invaded the Cave. Maybe they're—"

"No, Muzz. You mustn't worry. Here, we can show you."

Thea flipped a switch and pressed some buttons. Alok checked the view in the oblong tube. "Here, see for yourself."

Muzz could see inside the Cave's Great Hall from a vantage point somewhere on the ceiling. She could hear rhythmic thwarping and distant chanting voices. *Lessons!* Through the dim light she saw a cave guard lolling on his bench, and felt almost nostalgic.

"Oh! Can we look into the Lesson chamber at my brother? It's been so long."

"It *has* been long," said Thea. "Several months since your, uh, birthday dash."

I like that name for what I did.

"Chell and the other sixteenth yearlings were about to graduate when you left, remember? All the other Highers moved up, and they moved out. Now the three seventeenth yearling females who've been betrothed since they turned thirteen are preparing grottoettes for their marriages next year. Meanwhile the two remaining seventeenth yearling males — including Chell, of course — are employed elsewhere in the Cave. I don't have an easy way to find them. Instead, let's check back with the copterjets before we run out of power for the day."

Muzz quelled her disappointment. *So much has changed!* She gazed through the tube at Bubblian soldiers loading chained invaders onto copterjets.

Thea's eyes took on a resolute brightness. "The attack was thwarted."

"And no one in the Cave has a clue," said Alok, shaking his head.

"Doesn't *anyone* know?" asked Muzz.

"My mother knows," said Thea, "but she's still diving. We'll contact her tomorrow. After all, given what you told me, we must find out what Chell's doing."

Muzz had her own cabin for the night and, next morning, since it was still not quite time to contact Mrs. Whitford, Thea helped them "globetrot" via Infrareader, which meant dialing up the coordinates for whatever place they chose. "Nearly four million people here on earth and at least three thousand settlements keep our Infrareader busy. The rogues try to block us, of course, but hardly ever succeed," she told Muzz. After an hour or so of cataloging nondescript copterjet landings and 'dropping' into the schoolyards and offices of various peaceful settlements, Thea switched on a large screen that all three of them could watch at once and zeroed in on the exercise yard at Bayon Holding. The screen had a less clear picture than the viewing tube, but they could see the twins and the stocky prisoner circling.

Muzz's eyes enlarged as she turned to Thea. "Does this mean you were watching me and Deb exercise?"

Thea nodded. "That's our only reliable view of the prisoners —a blurry picture from a satellite. Of course, with your wire we could find you just about anywhere."

"Did you watch our escape?"

"Too stormy," said Thea.

Muzz broke into a wry grin, held hands to her temples. *Frooseballs, that prison was the absolute worst!* She pointed at the screen. "Now there's something I don't miss — weeks of circling with those three... But look! They have a different guard now."

"Yours was probably demoted for letting you two escape," Alok commented.

"Demoted or worse." Thea pursed her lips and shook her head.

Muzz did not have much time to dwell on that because Thea said, "My mother should be available now. Let's dial up the Cave."

She cast Muzz an impish smile. "If the Highers' revolt hasn't surfaced, it'll probably be pretty quiet around there. After all, the Tumbarumbans never did attack, and *you're* not there to stir things up."

Muzz grinned. She liked being teased by Thea. But as the Infrareader buzzed them into Mrs. Whitford's grottoette, she felt her insides flutter with worry.

Seated in her armchair, Mrs. Whitford was writing furiously in a notebook when a bell tinkled and startled her. She reached under her table and did something that made the ringing stop.

"Hello, Thea," she said, rubbing the back of her neck and blinking.

"Hi, Mother."

That sounded so odd to Muzz. *How can Mrs. Whitford be any Hepu's mother?*

Mrs. Whitford went to the back wall and removed her sailboat painting. Underneath it hung a lighted screen showing all three of their faces.

"Well! If it isn't Alok and... Is that *you*, Muzz? *Frooseless?*"

Muzz nodded. "So you recognize me, Mrs. Whitford?"

"I'd know my green-eyed Scottish princess anywhere! You look gorgeous."

"I was in the sun too long at Angkor. It's tough adjusting to my new self."

"I always wondered whether that sun reaction would work the way it's supposed to. It certainly worked for you."

She glanced from Muzz to Alok and back again. "Amazing how you and Alok are so—" There was a pause. "They know now, don't they?"

"That they're brother and sister? Yes, Mother," Thea interjected. "And while they're here at the Retreat, I hope they'll get more used to the idea."

Alok and Muzz exchanged a quizzical smile.

"Let's hope so. And I hear you learned to delve in prison, Muzz. Do you like it?"

Muzz said she did.

Mrs. Whitford nodded excitedly. "I taught Thea years ago. And I bet you can see now why it gets me through my day. Especially a day like today when there's so much trouble brewing."

More trouble?" Thea shot back. She cast Muzz a concerned glance.

"Much more. Yesterday we had the Tumbarumbans on the outside, and today insurgents on the inside — Tendra and Chell riling up the Highers, fomenting revolt."

So I was right! They didn't listen to me, thought Muzz. Aloud she said, "Ice storms and chilblains!"

Mrs. Whitford smiled faintly. "I had my Infrareader trained on them earlier, trying to figure out what they're up to so I can decide what to do about it."

"Muzz knows about it. They were already working up a plan before the Walkabout."

"I had no idea." Mrs. Whitford looked genuinely worried, and it relieved Muzz to see that she grasped the seriousness of the problem.

"Muzz says the Beacons suspect. Have you heard about that?" asked Thea.

"No, but it certainly makes matters worse. Shall we see what the Highers are up to now?" Mrs. Whitford flipped some Infrareader dials.

"Hmmm, it's nearly lightdown. Let me see if they're still where they were." When she punched the keyboard, her screen flashed criss-cross patterns, and then a snowy image of Tendra's face came on.

Seeing her adorable soft froose and crinkly eyes excited Muzz.

Mrs. Whitford hit another button, and the picture widened. Chell came into view. He was kneeling near a cultivation chamber wall facing Tendra. *My other big brother! Now I know why we're so different.*

"—no longer accept this," Chell was saying. "Every last Higher I know *wants* to fight. We outnumber the guards. Without them the Beacons will be powerless."

Tendra answered with quick, repeated shakes of her head.

"No, no, no. If we nab the Beacons *first*, tie and gag them and stash them somewhere, the rest will be easy."

"Nothing will be easy." Chell pursed his lips and lowered his brow. "But without the guards, what power do the Beacons have? We *must* go for the guards first."

Tendra shook her head fast many times. "But the Beacons have tradition on their side and the rules they've drilled into everyone. They have every Hepu over twenty-five, for sure. Don't trust *anyone* over twenty-five."

Mrs. Whitford clasped a hand to her mouth, her eyes momentarily mirthful for some reason Muzz could not guess.

"Check this out," Chell told Tendra, holding up a parchment scroll. "It's the plan Jeeklo drew up. It looks much feasible to me."

Tendra took the scroll from Chell, unrolled it. But before she started reading, she gazed into space and sighed. "If only Jerith and Muzz were here to help."

"Yeah." Chell cast his eyes down. "If only they were still alive."

"They'd have great ideas." Tendra seemed awfully sad.

Chell shook his head. "You know how much I miss them. But don't forget how down on all this Muzz was. And the way Jerith gave in to her during that Walkabout fiasco? I doubt he could've stood up to her."

Muzz felt Thea and Alok turn and gaze at her. She blushed, did not gaze back, and continued to listen, relieved when they focused their attention back on the screen.

Tendra read the scroll, dropped it to her lap. She glanced around and suddenly stiffened. "Ice me!" she cried, pointing directly at the Infrareader. "Look, those red dots again! What in Whitford *are* they?" She let the scroll snap shut.

Chell mumbled something Muzz could not make out.

"Okay, let's get out of here," said Tendra.

They crept along the wall of the cultivation chamber. Muzz wanted to shout, "Stop! Jerith and I are alive. You don't know how much I miss you, or what trouble you're going to cause."

Mrs. Whitford switched their three faces back to her screen. "That's it. They moved into a blocked zone. Thea, this is pure trouble, isn't it?"

"It will be if it surfaces." Thea paused, and Muzz could almost read her mind it was churning so hard. "Maybe it's time to start putting that idea we've been tossing around to the test. Where are you with your research, Mother?"

"I wanted more time," said Mrs. Whitford, shaking her head. "But perhaps you're right."

"For it to work, we'll need—" Thea turned toward Alok and Muzz.

"We'll need to tell them, I know," said Mrs. Whitford. "Everything." She paused. "I hope they're ready."

Alok and Muzz glanced at each other wide-eyed, and shrugged. Meanwhile Thea gave them both a long, slow once-over. "It's a risk, but I agree. Better sooner than later."

She drew herself up and took a deep breath. "Hold onto your seats, you two. My mother and I have more surprises for you.

"About who we are?" asked Alok.

"That, and why it matters," replied Mrs. Whitford.

Muzz slumped into a nearby chair and literally held onto her seat, while Alok, arms folded, leaned against the wall with studied nonchalance, and said, "I think we're ready."

Thea looked solemnly from one of them to the other. She pulled a strand of breeding beads from the pocket of her robe and held it up. "It has to do with the clear bead. You see, you have it, Alok, Muzz has it, and so do I. It's time to complete your family tree for you: the mother you share is my daughter."

Muzz's mind raced. "What? So mother is— You're our— And Mrs. Whitford is—" She whirled toward Alok. "Did you know all this?"

Alok closed his eyes and slowly shook his head. "This is a total surprise to me, Muzz. The short answer is 'no.'"

Thea said, "Alok's father has always thought that the less he knows about the Cave, the better he'll adjust to life in the Bubble, hasn't he, Alok."

"Yes. So now I have one *gigantic* adjustment to make?"

"Just like me," said Muzz. "Our mother told me the clear bead was only for *females.*"

Thea said gently, "None of this is easy. But you both need to know how you're connected because—" she paused, seeming to search for the right words.

"Because we need your help," breathed Mrs. Whitford. The Infrareader did not hide one iota of her excitement.

CHAPTER TWENTY

Thea turned to Muzz and her soft, glowy eyes made Muzz feel oddly excited again. "When we dove in the group this morning, you had a powerful experience, didn't you?"

Remembering, Muzz said, "I dove someplace... much difficult to describe."

"That's because it's so indescribable," said Thea. "Sages who've experienced it say it underlies all creation, and dipping into it calms and enlivens a person's mind."

Alok sat on a cushion and hugged his knees. Thea gazed at him intently and back at Muzz. "You've both experienced something inside when you dive — more calmness, more strength? Your thinking is clearer, yes? And you feel happier?" They nodded. "Well, you're becoming more conscious, more aware inside. You can say you're growing in consciousness. Think of consciousness as the bowl that holds your thoughts and feelings — your whole Self. Each time a person dives the bowl expands a little. Slowly but surely it comes to hold clearer, gentler, more lively thoughts."

Alok turned to Muzz. "I think I feel that happening sometimes, do you?"

Muzz nodded. *I'm almost sure I know what Thea means.*

Thea said, "So that's diving's inner strength. But it also has outer strength." She turned to the screen. "Am I heading where we need to go with this, Mother?"

Mrs. Whitford bit her lower lip, thinking, until a spark came to her eyes. "I'll tell them what I discovered in Book Storage."

Thea gave a brisk nod. "Go for it."

"Well, Muzz and Alok, not long ago I found a dusty folder there under a heap of encyclopedias. It was a scientific paper from way back around the year 2000 showing how delving affected large groups of people. It made even those who were not doing it more positive, happier, more peaceful."

Thea said, "She means they found that it even affected people who were not doing it themselves. Small groups, large groups, even entire cities, depending on the number of people among them diving."

"Whole cities?" asked Alok.

"That's right," said Mrs. Whitford. "Cities became safer, and the inhabitants a bit more calm and content."

"Yes," said Mrs. Whitford, "safer when just a very small percentage of the people dove. And the whole population a bit more calm and content. So you see what that means? Each time a single person's bowl of consciousness expands, *everyone's* bowl expands a little."

Muzz considered that. "But didn't you tell me once that diving is just *one* way to enliven people's minds?"

Mrs. Whitford flashed her a smile. "So you remember that conversation, Muzz, even though the cave guards rushed us so? Delving is one way. Thea has a whole list of ways to enliven minds. She adds new ones all the time, don't you Thea?"

Thea nodded. "Anything kind, funny, restful, fun, satisfying, creative *expands* the bowl of consciousness. It's just that delving is so effective and reliable."

Alok brought his hands to either side of his head. "I know, Thea! You and, uh, Great Grandma want us to sneak into the Cave to calm the Highers, right?"

Muzz pictured that. *If they spot us they'll think we're ghosts. That could be fun.*

Thea shook her head. "Good guess, Alok, but not this time."

"We need you to take a more unusual trip," said Thea.

Alok dropped his hands. "Where to?"

Thea took a deep breath. "To—"

"Before we get into that," said Mrs. Whitford, "I want to sketch our purpose more clearly for the kids. Muzz, Alok, I'm sure you know I'm among the oldest surviving humans. I recall the world we had and lost."

"During Warming humanity took its last crazy joy ride on a fast train heading for a cliff. The passengers on the train numbered nearly nine billion, with cars, trucks, roads, trains, tracks, airplanes, toys, games, books, jewels, clothes, equipment, tools, houses, furniture — *all the human riches* — as baggage."

"Meanwhile, a few people noticed that Mother Nature was in trouble due to the speed of the train and all the stuff onboard. But the people in charge made the train pick up speed just when it should have been slowing."

"Why couldn't they see what a dangerous ride they were on?" asked Alok.

Mrs. Whitford shook her head sadly. "They were either too caught up in the ride to see the danger, or powerless to do enough about it. Right up until we careened off the cliff, lots of people hardly knew there *was* a cliff."

Muzz closed her eyes. "How tragic!" She shook her head. "But what does that train crash have to do with us here now?"

"That's a key question. Back then scientists *warned* people, but they didn't really understand that research I mentioned on how to *change* people. So they couldn't build the political will needed to pull the safety brake and stop the train short of the cliff."

Hepu Muzz

"Wait! What's 'political will'?" Alok wanted to know.

"Hmmm!" Mrs. Whitford thought that over and replied, "A group of people's commitment to reaching their goals — their deep desire to bring about a change — is political will."

"And during that train ride the desire to put on the brakes just wasn't strong enough. That's where the need for expanding the bowl of consciousness comes in. There just weren't enough people enlivening their minds to expand the bowl enough. And that bigger bowl of gentler, livelier thoughts and feelings is what you can help create."

"Us?" Muzz gave Alok a confused frown that he mirrored back at her.

Alok dropped his head, closed his eyes, made his open hands a wall of protection. "Whoa! I need some time to think this over."

Thea nodded, smiled, sniffed the air. "Smell that delicious bread?"

Muzz had been too engrossed in the talk to notice. Sure enough the room had filled with the fragrance of baking bread.

"How would you two like some bread fresh from the oven, and some tea?"

"Mmmm." Alok jumped to his feet, stretched, smiled at Muzz. "C'mon, let's get some."

Soon they were heading for the porch, each with a giant chunk of freshly baked bread smothered in butter and a mug of piping hot cinnamon tea.

They sat together on a dark green bench, taking sips of spicy tea between bites of the delicious bread. There was a slight breeze rustling through the pines, and Muzz closed her eyes and took a couple of breaths of the cool, sweet air.

Then with bright, wide eyes she looked at Alok. "Wow, I'm seeing something."

"What is it?" Alok asked, glancing around.

"No, not out there. In here." She pointed at herself. "I'm thinking about all that's happened to me since I turned thirteen. Maybe all along it had a deeper purpose, and maybe this was it."

Alok tilted his head at her and smiled. "Maybe." He thought about it more and nodded. "I hope you're right."

A while later they were back inside with Thea, and Alok was asking, "So you're saying Muzz and I can help somehow?"

Thea nodded. "You see, the more people dive, the more they'll want to help the earth *and* each other."

She turned to Alok with a quizzical smile. "A while ago you asked where we wanted you to go. That's the easy part. The Klamath Mountains."

Muzz had not heard of them.

"But aren't those mountains under a hundred feet of ice?" asked Alok.

"They are."

"Then how can we—?"

"They didn't used to be. We need you to travel back in time."

There was a long silence. Muzz felt strange inside, a little dizzy, agitated. She saw that Alok was sitting with his mouth open staring at Thea.

He was about to speak when voices struck their ears from down the hall.

"What's that commotion?" asked Mrs. Whitford.

"Uh-oh, the high school band is here," said Thea. She stretched, took a deep breath. "They've come for their weekend retreat." She held her hands out to Alok and Muzz. "This is an odd time to take a break, but..."

Alok moaned. "And I'm supposed to greet them." He stood and walked in a small circle. That made Muzz loosen up and laugh, and Alok sort of smiled.

"Luckily we have over a week before travel day," said Mrs. Whitford.

"Travel day?" Muzz felt tension grab at her.

Thea closed her eyes, smiled, nodded. When she opened them again, she had clearly changed gears. "There's an optimum window of time for you to travel. It has to do with the seasons, the lengths of days and nights then and now, that sort of thing. But nothing's final about this. You need to ask all the questions you have, and you need to be honest with yourselves and us. This is huge. We can't force you to do it, and we don't want to. We'll talk more soon, all right?"

"And I need to talk more about the Highers," said Muzz.

"Of course. That's essential. We mustn't forget them," said Mrs. Whitford.

"Thanks," said Muzz. *I can tuck them further back in my mind, but only for a short while.*

Thea stood up. "How about the three of us greeting these high schoolers together?" She turned to the Infrareader. "Shall we contact you after the weekend, Mother?"

"Of course. I'll keep an eye on developments here. And Alok? Muzz? Thea's right to say that nothing's final. Mull this over. You'll have questions, comments, concerns. Keep track of them. We'll pick up with those after the weekend, okay?"

"Okay." Muzz stood up, yawned, blinked her eyes, shook some tension from her arms and shoulders, and followed the other two from the room.

The band of around twenty high schoolers brought luggage including lumpy instrument cases and fancy clothes on hangars. They stood chatting and milling around the front hall of The Retreat.

Muzz liked how good-humored they seemed. After greetings and introductions, they stowed their stuff in their cabins and began trickling into the big music cabin a few at a time.

Their instructor, Mister Oakfield, was a jubilant fellow whose face stretched long under rust-colored curls, horn rimmed glasses, alert brown eyes. She and Alok helped him pass out sheet music. Meanwhile the high schoolers squeaked, hummed, and tapped their instruments into tune. When Mr. Oakfield rapped his stand with a thin white stick, the cacophony ceased and everyone eyed him eagerly.

"Let's give Muzz and Alok a preview of our concert." They beamed at him, raised their instruments, broke into a medley of spirited tunes.

"You like this stuff, don't you," whispered Alok. "Have you heard it before?"

Muzz shook her head.

"It was popular during Warming." Alok and Muzz were sitting together on a bench from which they could hear and see everything. It made her smile the way the band members swayed and bounced through the songs as if they could scarcely keep their seats. *So many instruments and so much fun!*

She felt a small twist in the pit of her stomach. "I wish Jerith could be here," she told Alok. "Did you know he plays flute and keyboards? He wanted 'musician' as his Calling back in the Cave. He would love this."

Alok folded his arms, nodded, tapped a foot to the beat. Muzz began listening again. At the end of the medley, she and Alok clapped and cheered, and the horn soloist gave a gigantic mock bow that produced a cascade of laughter from the band.

Muzz had only seen friskiness like that on films back in Lessons, when Hepu Dorne would scoff, "Wasteful, foolish humans!" She felt angry with him all over again, but not for long.

More tunes lifted her mood, and afterward everyone walked in the garden, laughing and talking until nearly suppertime. She more observed than joined in, but she liked it. Then they all went back to their cabins to get ready.

For Muzz, part of getting ready meant diving; this time she ran into that twist in her stomach she had felt earlier, which turned out to be twistier than she had thought. From deep inside an image of Jerith floated up that would not drift away. His long ago words, "I know you don't want to be betrothed. Not even to me," echoed through her mind.

Jerith had looked so sad that seeing him in her mind's eye made her sad. *Diving is supposed to be peaceful,* she thought. But there the sadness was. *He loved me, and I ignored him. What was I thinking? What if he never recovers? Or what if Alok and I never come back from that weird time trip?*

Afterward, Muzz doused her face with cool water at her sink. She stared into the mirror and whispered, "Jerith." There was something she was learning about herself, but what?

At dinner she sat next to Deb again. "Say, Muzz, you don't look so great. Anything the matter?" Deb asked.

"Something bothered me right in the middle of diving. Has that ever happened to you?"

"Sure." Deb leaned closer to speak softly. "It's a funny thing about it. There's a lot of peace. But if something's bothering you, it can pop right to the center of your mind. That happens. It happened to me sometimes at Bayon Holding. But whatever comes up, it's always about *you*. It *is* you — whatever's *in* you. You can't dive and hide things from yourself, but the diving can transform those things. So, for instance, that's where I felt the most miserable about being a prisoner, but it's also where our escape plan came to me. It popped up and I sorted out the details later."

"Problems you wish would leave you alone and solutions when you least expect them?" Muzz asked.

Deb gave a giant nod. "Diving isn't something you can plan or control. But I always feel a shade or two brighter and lighter *afterward* than I did before I started."

While eating generous helpings of green, deep red, and purple salad leaves, bowls of savory chili, lemon cream pie, they turned their talk to Polzzie habitat and Deb's plans for the Glacial Wilderness. The food and conversation soothed Muzz, and afterward there was band music again for the rest of the evening.

Later, though Jerith and the Highers slipped into her dreams in half-forgotten snippets, she slept soundly most of the night.

CHAPTER TWENTY-ONE

"We want you to travel back to Klamath Falls in the year 2010," said Thea in a matter-of-fact tone. The weekend with its delicious concert was over, and they were back on the Infrareader with Mrs. Whitford. "I know that sounds impossible. And we don't even have a time machine. No one does."

Alok shifted uneasily. "What *do* you have?"

"Dreams," said Mrs. Whitford. "Dreams and that indescribable place we spoke about last time."

Thea nodded at her mother through the Infrareader. She looked from Alok to Muzz with deep intensity. "Minds — especially peaceful minds — can move in surprising ways, even through dreams. That's what the clear bead is about, the bead all four of us have."

Muzz said, "Wait! My... I mean *our* mother" — here she smiled at Alok — "told me only females have the clear bead."

Alok pursed his lips, raised his brow, pointed at her. "Chell didn't have it because you two are related through your father. And she couldn't tell you about me."

Thea pointed at him. "Right, Alok."

"Wait a minute!" cried Muzz. "Does this dream power explain how come I dreamt about the Beacons' wardrobe before I actually hid in there? A much scary dream that came true?"

Thea thought a moment. "That makes perfect sense. A premonition. Our family has had this dream power for generations. Here's another taste of it: A few months ago I visited one of your dreams, Muzz."

Muzz clutched her head, closed her eyes, snapped them open fast. "*That's* why I keep having a funny feeling around you. I half remem—"

Thea raised her hand. "Wait, Muzz. As a kind of proof for Alok, let *me* describe the dream. Let's see if I have it right."

"Okay, go for it," said Alok, and Muzz nodded.

"You dreamt about finding a tunnel, very low, with a secret cavern at the end. You found me in there, right?"

"I *knew* when I saw you through that window that it wasn't the first time!" Muzz frowned. "But you were *frooseless* in that dream!"

Thea grinned. "Sometimes in dreams I lose my froose."

Alok leaned toward Muzz as if to leap inside her head. "Come on, Muzz, are you sure it was Thea?"

Mrs. Whitford piped up, "Of course she's sure. And as I've told Muzz, she's a powerful dreamer. So are you. That's what the clear bead is about. Go on, please, Thea. I like where you're taking this."

Muzz and Alok glanced at each other and shrugged good-naturedly.

"Okay, so have you two heard the term 'clairvoyant'? People who perceive things that aren't visible to others?"

"I think so," said Muzz, and Alok nodded.

"Clairvoyants have some unusual power — not magic, but not for everyone. And, in the same way, all of us with the clear bead could be called 'clair*revant*,' to coin a term. 'Voyant' means 'seeing' in French, and 'revant' means 'dreaming.'"

"So are you saying we have *unusual* dream power?" asked Muzz.

"That's exactly what she's saying," cried Mrs. Whitford. "All of us. Now and then you've both been half aware of it — dreaming something before it happened, having a dream that seemed surprisingly real, *that* sort of thing."

Alok sighed softly, shook his head. "Okay, I kind of get what you're saying. But, Muzz, how can you be sure a frooseless Thea was in your dream before you ever set eyes on her?"

Muzz used her hands to frame an empty chunk of air.

"I'll bet I can prove it," she said. "Thea, there were two kinds of animals in my dream. What were they?"

Thea nodded, gazing hard at Alok.

When Muzz followed the gaze, she saw how confused and maybe even suspicious he looked. Thea said, "Listen, Muzz, take Alok out in the hall, and tell him in advance so he won't think we're making this up. And be sure to whisper." All of which Muzz did.

When she and Alok returned, he folded his arms. "So, two kinds of animals. What were they?"

"Lab puppies."

"Right. That's a pretty obvious one."

"And butterflies. Blue and green butterflies that sort of glowed."

"Yes!" exclaimed Muzz. "And, remember, Thea? I didn't know what butterflies were until you told me. Right there in the dream she named them for me, Alok."

Alok looked wide-eyed for a moment. "Pretty wild," was all he said.

Muzz turned to him. "Okay, Alok. Do you accept this dream thing? Because even if you don't, we should go with what they want us to do."

"I don't know…" Alok sounded pained by the question and shifted uneasily in his seat.

"Because, don't you see? Whatever they want us to do, it'll either work or it won't work. What happens *after* will be our proof of whether or not it works. We'll either be back here in this cold, miserable world or the world we return to will be better."

Mrs. Whitford said, "A word of caution: Even if it works, we may not be able to measure or observe the proof."

Alok frowned, shook his head. "Why not?"

Thea looked wistful, serious. She gave a slow, deliberate nod. "Because if we succeed, our "after" will be completely changed. Everything that happens in between then and now will have changed, too. Oh, you may still be brother and sister, still my grandchildren, you may even have some of the same friends. But if the dream travel works, in the world we help to save, the climate change train will have slowed — maybe even stopped — before the Warming becomes irreversible. No cliff, no train crash, no huge climate distortions. no desertification, no Ice Age, many, many more survivors, probably no need for settlements. And all this will seem like a nightmare that we've awakened from."

Alok flopped around on his cushion and closed his eyes. "Are you saying no Cave, no Hepus, no Bubble, no Bubblians?"

"Exactly." Mrs. Whitford's voice fluttered with excitement. "If our plan works, the world will have lived an entirely different future between 2010 and now."

"What year is this, anyway?" asked Muzz.

Alok lifted his head and gazed at Muzz, more or less shocked. "2103 just started. You didn't know?" he whispered.

Thea said, "A whole different future."

There was a long pause while Muzz and Alok considered that. Muzz was back in the Cave in her mind, recalling the tunnels, the grottoettes, the cultivation enclosures, and especially all the unhappy faces. *So dark and stifling!*

Finally she said, "I'm in, Alok, are you?"

Alok remained where he was with his eyes closed. He sighed. "Something else is bothering me. If the researchers back then already understood what delving could do, how come we're where we are now?"

Mrs. Whitford said, "To reach a tipping point for the entire planet, they needed more delvers — a small percentage, but more than there were — or something else equally enlivening. It didn't happen."

Alok thought that over a long time before he sat up and rubbed his eyes. "When do we start?"

He stood up, strolled to the window, called back over his shoulder. "I'm still listening."

"I thought we could count on you two." Mrs. Whitford started clapping.

"What a relief!" said Thea. She glanced at her clock. "But look how late it is. We need a good night's sleep. We have at least a day or two, don't we, Mother?"

Mrs. Whitford nodded. "And we mustn't bungle this by moving too fast. The perfect window of time is still a few days off. For now, sleep soundly, dream well!"

That night Muzz dreamt she was swimming through waves white with foam, alarmed one moment, thrilled the next, churning through the Great Hall, Bayon Holding, Lab runs and Tropical, the Forbidden Tunnel, the copterjet, the Walkabout, all awash in a deep, wild, splashing sea. The faces of Hepus from the Cave bobbed one after another through the roiling water. Some greeted her with a smile or nod, others called to her with outstretched arms. Even the Beacons and her father seemed friendly as they floated by. The last to show up was Jerith, asking for something. Seeing him gave her that strange, almost sweet feeling inside again, and she woke in darkness with him in her mind. After a while, she dozed off again, woke up completely calm. But the sweet sensation lingered. *Have my feelings for Jerith changed... Is this what love is?* she wondered. *Even if it is I may never see him again. And I'm so worried about him! He's such a mess right now.*

At breakfast Alok's cell phone rang. He took the call outside, afterward came directly to Muzz. "Hey, Sis." He grinned shyly. "Guess who's been asking for you."

"Who?"

"Jerith. And Dr. Deet okayed him for a visit. Do you want to see him before..." He glanced furtively at the others around their table, lowered his voice. "...before you-know-what?"

Her sweet feeling for Jerith increased. *Calm yourself.* To keep the feeling in check, and hidden, she nodded with studied nonchalance.

"Beachy!" said Alok. "You can visit Jerith this morning. I'll walk down with you." He leaned closer and whispered, "I want to contact my father in case this weird clairrevance scheme actually works. Because if it does, there's no telling where on earth we'll end up, if we end up anywhere at all."

Muzz closed her eyes, shook her head, opened them, sighed softly.

"I have to believe we'll end up *somewhere* just to have the courage to do it," she said. Alok gave a firm nod.

Later, as Muzz walked with him down to town, she hardly saw the yellow suncups crowding the path, the birds rustling and tweeting in the brush, or even Alok beside her, lost in his own thoughts.

Then Alok pointed... "Look! A red-winged blackbird, my father's favorite. I wish I could be with him before our mission — or whatever you want to call it."

Muzz studied him closely for the first time that day. "Are you as nerved up about dream travel as I am?"

Alok gave her a sidelong glance. "I guess... I mean, I'm hardly used to the idea that you and I are brother and sister, let alone that we're related to Thea and Mrs. Whitford. And now on top of that there's this plan to have us use special powers we didn't even know we had to dream ourselves into some major change on earth."

They walked in silence for a while before Muzz laughed tensely. "Which is tougher? All that, or the fact that our lives might be so different if we succeed that we won't remember any of this?"

"I don't know. If this plan works, it's pretty strange, and if it doesn't work we have a couple of pretty strange relatives."

Muzz smiled, rolled her eyes. "I hope they really know something. The worst part will be if there's *nothing* that can undo the train crash."

"Right. But I really won't be surprised, no matter *what* we dream, if we wake up right back where we've always been."

Not long after, Muzz stood outside Jerith's hospital room. The door swung open and his angular, froosey face appeared with no bandage on his head and his eyes clearer than she had seen them since he was kidnapped.

"Funny One! I've been waiting for you. I saw you and Alok in the square. I'm so impatient to tell you. My memory is back! That fall did it."

Exuberant, Jerith threw open his arms, Muzz jumped in, and they hugged. Then he held her at arms length, and looked her up and down. "You make a much pretty human."

"Thanks." Muzz shook off a blush, walked in, sat down. "Wow, Jerith, am I ever relieved you have your whole self back!"

"*You're* relieved. Think how *I* feel. I've been remembering all sorts of stuff about the Cave. It makes me miss everyone."

Surprise tears welled in Muzz's eyes. "Sometimes I miss them all, too, even the Beacons and Hepu Dorne."

Jerith scoffed, but playfully. "That's going a little too far, don't you think?"

Muzz owned that it probably was, and they sat down and spent a good hour sorting through his recollections.

Sometimes Muzz prompted him with questions like "Do you miss oatcakes?" or "What do you think Sammy's doing right now?" One of them was "Do you remember that revolt the Highers were plotting?"

Jerith held his head. "Of course I do. Martrell blabbed the whole thing to you."

"Sort of... And remember how I showed up at your meeting? You scolded me for that."

Jerith groaned. "You scared me silly with all your traipsing around the Cave."

He shook his head. "That Highers plot was so crazy."

"Yes, and they're still working on it. They're about to start much trouble."

"And you know this because..."

"Because Thea has an amazing device called an Infrareader that connects with Mrs. Whitford in the Cave. Those tiny red lights you sometimes see? They're used for eavesdropping."

Jerith's mouth turned into an O, and his eyes darted over the ceiling. "Wangling Whitford!"

Muzz giggled at his ursp. "Don't worry, those snoopers have bigger cubes to melt than us."

"Meaning..."

"Meaning they're using the Infrareader to figure out how to stop the Highers from staging their attack. I had a chance to listen in on some of their plotting just the other day — Chell and Tendra bickering about where to strike first."

"Ha! That was happening *before* the Walkabout."

"Well, it's still going on and, from out here looking in, it's obvious they don't know what they're getting into. The cave guards have been ordered to capture insubordinates so they can be *culled*, and Framp and friends can hardly wait."

Jerith clasped his hands together, his face tense. "What can we do about it?"

Muzz hesitated, checked outside the door, closed it, and whispered, "There's another, bigger plan that could trump the whole thing."

"What plan is that?" Jerith's voice hummed with curiosity.

"Since you're you again I guess I can tell you."

Muzz stood up and started pacing. "It's much complicated, and it's secret." She gave a big shrug. "I hardly know where to begin." She faced him square on. "Uh... I think I'm going on a journey soon and, if I do, I'm not sure when I'll be back."

"Chilblains! Just when I remember who we are, you're going away?"

"I've promised to try something so weird I can hardly explain it, but it involves a kind of time travel that's almost plausible. If it works, the world I come back to could be an improvement on the one we have now, but far different."

Jerith had confusion written all over his face. "Whose idea is this?"

Muzz plunked back down. "Mrs. Whitford's and the Hepu Thea's. Trust me, their predicted outcome is not impossible. At least not the way they've framed it."

It was Jerith's turn to pace. Muzz gave him a long look. *How handsome he is.* She thought of his nurse. *Does he still have a crush on her?* She decided not to ask.

"Tell me this," he said. "What if their plan doesn't work, and the insurrection goes forward. All of the Highers could be punished, banished, or worse."

"Of course, you're right! Mrs. Whitford and Thea have so much confidence in their scheme that they seem to have overlooked that. But if it doesn't work, precious time will have been lost. There could be battles and arrests."

Jerith punched one hand with the other fist. "I don't like this," he said flatly. "Too many risks."

"Yes, and one is that I may lose track of you. I'd miss you much."

Jerith paused, studied her. "Really? I mean *really* miss me? Even with all this froose?" He grimaced at one of his a peach-fuzz covered arms.

Muzz blushed again, lowered her eyes.

Jerith said, "Something about how quiet you are makes me much hopeful." There was such a husky edge to his voice that Muzz felt shivery around her heart.

She looked him straight in the eye. "Jerith, I never knew how much I cared about you until the you I knew vanished. I love having you back."

Jerith's eyes lit up and he walked to her, held out his hands, pulled her to her feet. A huge, unexpected wave of excitement enveloped her. He leaned toward her. She lifted her face and felt their lips touch.

It was a long gentle kiss. *A greeting and a farewell in one.* Muzz felt her heart beat fast. When it ended, they stood holding hands, facing each other.

"If for any reason we get separated by all this, I'll find you, Jerith, no matter where you are."

"D'you promise, Funny One?"

Muzz gave a solemn nod. "I promise, okay?"

Jerith squeezed her hands and looked her in the eye. "Better than okay."

CHAPTER TWENTY-TWO

On her way back to The Retreat with Alok, Muzz's mind kept see-sawing between worries about the Highers and images of Jerith. After they kissed, they simply held each other for a long time that she wanted never to forget. *Will I ever see him again?*

"You're quiet," Alok remarked as they started up the hill. "Are you okay?"

"So-so. Did you get to speak with your father?"

"I did. He says he's almost sure we'll be together when we return to *now* no matter how the dream travel unwinds. He really wants me to go."

"More than you want to yourself?" Alok shrugged and Muzz flashed him a smile. "I hope he's right. I wish there was time for me to meet him."

Alok whirled to gaze at her with excited eyes. "He says you two *did* meet."

"What?"

"He says when you were really small, he returned to the Cave one last time to see our mother. He loved her much, still does. He hitchhiked on the copterjet that went for Thea."

"Of course! She must be the 'disappearing female' they mentioned at my trial."

"You should ask her. Anyway, when my father returned that time, Mrs. Whitford wouldn't let him see our mother. She was married to *your* father by then, and Mrs. Whitford didn't think she'd be able to handle knowing my father and I were still alive. I think she was right, don't you?"

"Being the only Hepu in the Cave who knew about the outside world? That would have been huge. And knowing you two were still alive? What would *that* have been like?"

"Dismal. Crazy-making."

"Right." Muzz was back in the Cave in her mind, seeing the tinge of sadness in her mother's face. "But how did your father manage to meet me?"

"Mrs. Whitford — or, rather 'Great Grandma Whitford' — went looking for you and brought you to her grottoette. He says he had a card you liked and he gave it to you."

"A card? The card with the crimson bird! I have it with me."

"How amazing. How odd."

Muzz pulled it from the hem of her shawl, and handed it to Alok.

He read it. "Beachy! A Christmas card. And isn't 'Millie' Mrs. Whitford's name?"

"Mildred Whitford...? I guess it is. Maybe she wrote it for him and you. I always thought *my* father gave it to me. But if it was *your* father, he seemed much kind! He asked me to go somewhere with him."

"Back here, I'll bet."

Muzz stood still and thought hard. "Funny... I think that's my first memory."

Alok patted her shoulder, smiled and shook his head.

Late that afternoon Thea, Alok and Muzz huddled by their Infrareader peering at Mrs. Whitford who was peering back at them.

"So who lives — or *lived* — in the Klamath Mountains?" Alok was asking.

Muzz felt her insides stir with excitement.

"A woman named Betty Casadesus. A writer," said Thea. "Mother, will you please talk about her? You see, kids, I only met her in a dream."

"And I *more* than met her." Mrs. Whitford leaned in close. "When I was a little girl, I went to visit her often. She lived on a woodsy ranch and had silver hair by then — thick, straight, shoulder-length silver hair. In winter a fire crackled in her hearth, and she had two Labs — one yellow and one black, and a toy called a Frisbee that I used to throw for them. I'm your great grandmother, and she was my great grandmother, which makes her your great, great, great, great grandmother."

"Four greats?" asked Alok.

"Icebergs!" said Muzz. "And you reached her in a dream, Thea?"

"I did. Betty's mind must have been open and calm because one night I slipped right in. I almost floated in, if that makes any sense."

Muzz was not sure it did.

"When she spied me in that dream, I tried to speak. I wanted to tell her about our life on this cold, gray snowball earth. But all I could do was float through her dreamscape."

Alok lay on the rug and stared at the ceiling. "So she was dreaming and you were dreaming, and you dreamt your way into her dream?"

"Something like that, yes."

Alok gasped. "Isn't that a little scary?"

Thea shrugged. "It would be if it could be done by a harmful person, but dream travel requires a steady, benevolent mind."

She shook her head. "None of this is easy to explain, but I think I got through to her. Sometimes I feel her thinking about my face, my froose, our darkened world."

He furrowed his brow. "Are you implying that her world coexists with ours?"

"Maybe. Again, I'm not sure. Dreams so often elude explanation."

"This is really difficult to grasp. But please go on," he said.

"Well, here's the most exciting part: She can't forget that dream. She wonders what this world could be."

There was a silence during which Muzz noticed everyone's breathing. She took a deep breath. "So how do *we* figure in?"

Thea tapped a finger of her right hand on the palm of her left. "Okay, you need to know that not only are all of us are related, but we're all clairrevant."

Alok hid his face in the crook of one arm. "*She's* clairrevant too?"

Thea nodded. "She's the one who passed along the gene that makes all of us that way."

Mrs. Whitford said, "Sometimes she used to talk about exciting 'Technicolor' dreams. Some of them inspired the stories she was writing, and the poems."

"Where are they now?" asked Muzz. *I need something interesting to read.*

"Ha! Probably buried under all that ice," said Alok, shaking his head.

"Could be." Mrs. Whitford's voice sounded wistful.

Alok's foot bounced nervously. "Okay. So there's this window of time. And you've made a float-through, Grandma Thea. And in some way or other, even though she lived long ago, we sort of co-exist... Plus, she's clairrevant too. What else should we know about this dream assignment you want to give us?"

Thea held up a small, bright orange pill. "Stir this into the equation. It's a tablet that makes dreams more vivid."

"What is it?" Alok cupped his hand and Thea dropped the tablet in.

"It's a vitamin B supplement. It can bolster dream intensity."

Alok scrunched his nose. "A *vitamin?*"

"Is it dangerous?" asked Muzz.

Alok grinned. "No, it's just ordinary. People take vitamins when they think their food might be missing something they need."

"Nevertheless, taken before sleep, B vitamins are known to increase dream intensity," said Mrs. Whitford.

There was a pause. Thea studied first Alok, then Muzz. "I need you both to think this over carefully, and decide whether or not you can give it your all. Serious doubts could affect the outcome."

"Hmmm, I don't know," said Alok, shaking his head, his forehead furrowed in a frown. "We still have a couple of days, don't we. Before I answer you, may I sleep on it?"

"Of course." Thea turned to Muzz. "What about you, Muzz? Where are you in all this?"

"Well, Grandma, do I need to *believe* for it to work?"

"No, but you need an open mind," said Thea.

"Then I'm ready to try it, but only on one condition."

Mrs. Whitford sat up straight, all alertness and surprise. "What is it, Muzz?"

"We need to help the Highers first. Before they come to harm."

"But if dream travel works, what they're up to won't—"

"Matter?" asked Muzz.

Mrs. Whitford nodded. "Exactly."

Muzz said, "The key word there is 'if'... Because if it *doesn't* work, well, it's a much big risk. I'm sure you see that. The cave guards are *bursting* to cull 'wrongdoers.' That could happen soon."

There was a long silence while everyone including Muzz considered what she had said. She thought, *I still surprise myself sometimes.*

Thea shook her head. "Doesn't my float-through of Betty's dream mean—"

Mrs. Whitford said, "We should listen to Muzz, Thea. Nothing about our plan is certain."

"Yes, we need to listen to her," said Alok.

"But we're nearly out of time," said Thea. There was another silence.

Mrs. Whitford said, "I think Muzz has an excellent point. Right now things in the Cave are too chancy. Time is running out for the Highers. We need to convince them to put their scheme on hold. But how?"

"How about this?" asked Alok. "Can't we do what I first thought you wanted us to do? If diving can support our troops, why can't we send a group of divers down there to calm the Highers?"

Thea shook her head. "That would take at least a week to organize."

They all thought some more.

"I know!" said Muzz. "Why not teach *them* to dive, Great Grandma!"

Mrs. Whitford's brows shot up. "Possibly. We could try it. But there's no telling how fast that would turn things around."

"But you'll try?" asked Muzz. "You could invite them all to visit you, and get their attention by letting them know you know about their scheme."

Alok laughed. "*That'll* grab their attention."

"Maybe you two are on to something!" Mrs. Whitford checked the time. "Lightdown is three hours away. I'll send for Chell and have him spread the word that I have a treat for the Highers tonight directly after supper."

"Just like that time on your birthday," said Muzz.

"Exactly. I'd better ply them with lots of sweets or they'll be too disappointed to listen."

"Can we watch?" asked Alok.

Three hours later Thea, Alok, and Muzz secretly watched on the Infrareader screen as Chell and the other Highers crammed into Mrs. Whitford's grottoette that night for sugar cookies and a serious talk. When Muzz spied Chell, Tendra, and the others coming in, she gasped and covered her mouth. Luckily, Thea had the sound turned so low that their secret was safe.

The Highers had tough questions for Mrs. Whitford. Some of them including Tendra showed genuine interest, but it was Chell who ruled the day. "Why should we work on ourselves when they're the ones at fault?" he wanted to know. And nothing budged him.

After the Highers had returned to their family grottoettes without learning, Muzz complained, "Chell acted like a total know-it-all."

"We mustn't be too hard on him," said Mrs. Whitford. "After all, this is the first time he's heard any of this."

"Diving's so difficult to describe. Like the flavor of a strawberry, or something," said Alok.

"If only Chell knew enough to have a taste!" said Muzz.

"At least he's asking questions," said Thea. After a short wait she asked, "So! What do we do now?"

Everyone looked at Muzz. "Okay, we tried and it didn't work. I don't like it, but I guess I'm ready to travel." *Uh-oh! Did I actually say that?*

"Good, Muzz!" Thea turned to Alok. "What about you?"

"I have more questions for Great Grandma."

"Ask away."

"Well, say we get inside Betty's dream. Then what?"

Mrs. Whitford dropped her head, pondered, raised it, took a deep breath. "My great grandmother Betty was a teacher, a writer and — most important for us — an imaginer. She could imagine what would happen if the train we spoke of shot over that cliff. And she knew about the research going on back then. Many divers did. So if we can catch her attention, I mean *really* catch it, she'll write a book about us that will change people."

"Betty delved?" Muzz could see Alok weighing all the factors.

"She did."

"Did she teach you, Great Grandma?" asked Muzz.

"No, she had a friend who knew how to teach, and he taught me."

Alok folded his arms and frowned. "Okay, but even if she's a diver, even if we travel right into the middle of one of her dreams, won't she just wake up and say 'What a weird dream *that* was' and go about her day?"

Thea said, "She might, of course. That's a chance we have to take. But I think I grabbed her attention. I think a second dream — one that shows more about the Cave and more about us — will jolt her into action."

"So suppose your plan works, Grandma: We reach Betty; she 'gets' it; she writes a book. How could one story written generations ago make any difference?"

Muzz spoke up. "Don't you see, Alok? People weren't doing all they could. They didn't harness enough sun or wind."

"And they didn't harness *themselves*," said Thea.

"Which was essential," said Mrs. Whitford. "Because people can't do the right thing when they feel the wrong way."

Conversation stopped while they thought that over.

Muzz felt her heart warm to the thrill of adventure. "So when do we start?"

But Alok hung his head. "I'm sorry, everyone — really sorry. But there's a huge puddle of doubt in me that won't evaporate. If this time travel can really work, having me along could sabotage the whole thing."

Mrs. Whitford nodded. "That's too bad, Alok, but thanks for being honest. Having an open mind really is essential for our success. And not to worry. We'll figure this out. Maybe Muzz can go alone."

"Can I?" *Am I brave enough?*

"Muzz is brave enough," said Thea.

Muzz gave Thea a penetrating glance. *Is she reading my mind?* Muzz asked, "Is there anything else I need to know?"

"Just that I may go with you," Thea told her. She reached out and patted Muzz gently on the cheek. "Relax, eat well, if you go walking don't overdo it, get a good night's sleep tonight. Let's meet tomorrow a little before midnight. You'll need to wear comfy clothes and take care not to fall asleep during the day tomorrow, all right? For the best results, you need to be sleepy when the time comes."

CHAPTER TWENTY-THREE

On the way back to their cabins, Alok hugged her, offered to take walks with her, apologized again for backing out. "It's just that I'm filled with doubt to the point where I might drag everything down. You understand, don't you?"

Muzz more than understood, and told him so. *What if I'm too open-minded for my own good?* she thought as they parted.

She turned to watch him, her mind bouncing every which way. *What am I getting myself into? Who knows what will happen if this works or where we'll end up? And can I really want this dream travel to succeed when it may separate me from Jerith forever? And what was I thinking, promising him anything?*

Buried under a heap of worries, she knew she had to dig her way out. A walk in the garden helped only while she was actually sniffing roses, and diving calmed her some, but nowhere near enough. At supper she had trouble swallowing her food, could not hold a conversation even with Deb, and saw Thea eyeing her with concern, which made her try to eat more, which gave her a tummy ache. After supper, as people began shuffling out, Alok came over and whispered, "You need to do something about your jitters."

"I will," Muzz told him. She jumped up and went straight to Thea, who was carrying her dishes to the kitchen.

"Thea, I need to talk."

"Of course. How about walking to town with me. I have a letter to post." Soon the two females were striding side by side toward Bubbletown, Thea looking as beautiful to Muzz as ever including her froose.

"Do you sometimes want to lose your froose, Thea? Jerith does. That's why I'm asking."

Thea thought that over, smiled. "I guess I don't care much. Or maybe it's more than that; maybe I see my froose as some sort of badge. The badge of the 'disappearing female.'"

"So that *was* you?" asked Muzz, and Thea nodded. Muzz felt too stirred up to take the conversation further, and they walked in silence to the edge of town. A picnic table was nestled in a stretch of green where the Bubble's artificial sunset filtered through a stand of maples. "Let's stop here," Thea suggested, and they sat facing one another at a shady part of the table.

"You're out of sorts, Muzz. I know this is a huge responsibility for your young shoulders to carry. That's why I was hoping Alok would go along." Thea thought for a moment and added, "You should know, Muzz, that it was always *you* Great Grandma and I thought we needed for the dream travel's success. Anyone else who comes along, myself included, will be there mostly for support."

"Why me?"

"Great Grandma says you look and sound a lot like Betty, and even think like her. You're both much sensitive."

"How odd."

"Yes, it is odd. But we have a hunch that your being so much alike will help: something about sharing so many genes, Great Grandma says."

Muzz went wide-eyed, slowly shook her head. "Do you see it that way?"

"I'm not sure, Muzz, and neither is she. But we need to pull in every little strand that might help."

Thea's soft, kind tone, and the tenderness in her eyes prompted Muzz to sigh and droop across the table. She started to weep uncontrollably, looked up, found Thea's sympathetic gaze, crumpled and wept again. *This is about Jerith,* she thought inside. Thea gave her a handkerchief and, after her sobs wound down, spoke again.

"You're worried about Jerith," was all she said.

Muzz wiped away the tears. "I'm afraid I love him."

Thea's eyes went sad. "I think you do," she said. "Love is a wonderful feeling, but in your case a sorrowful one, and for good reason with everything so up in the air and no telling where it will all land."

Thea reached across the table and gently patted Muzz's head, which made her sob or sniff, or both.

Muzz nodded and sniffed. "I told Jerith I'd be going on a journey, and I didn't know when I'd be back. I promised to find him." She gulped. "It was a false promise, wasn't it? One I can't really keep."

"In the sense that we don't exactly know the outcome, yes, but in another sense, no. You see, there's good reason to believe that even if the world changes much, for example even if there are far more people on earth after the dream travel, we'll be among them, and our family, and even our friends, will still be together."

"How much do you think the world will change?"

"There's no way of knowing." From where she sat Thea faced the hill. She let her eyes scan the ridge that formed the Bubble's bowl. Then she focused on Muzz with a hopeful smile. "There was a theory back in Betty's day that even the drop of a leaf or the flight of a butterfly could have a powerful effect — cause a storm to break a heat wave, inspire someone to write a symphony, help a violinist play better than she ever had before. According to that theory, there's no telling the results of any single event or act. So... what if Betty dreams a dream, writes a book, and some people read it? What if they change even slightly? Maybe they won't dive in larger numbers, but they'll at least be able to picture us. What if that helps them care about us a little more? In several generations there's no telling where that might lead."

"Then you're right. This dream travel *is* a huge responsibility."

Thea pursed her lips, shook her head. "Yes, and still, the responsibility doesn't rest all that much on you, Muzz, do you see? The leaf's fall and the butterfly's flight are only a small, whispered beginning. The rest unfurls of its own accord. Either people will come together, or they won't. Either the train will stop in time, or it won't. Or maybe it will slow down enough to make *some* difference. There's no way of telling, just a way of trying."

Muzz did not know which was more soothing — Thea's words or her tone of voice — but she did feel soothed. "Is there any way to make sure I find Jerith again?"

Thea said, "You have a card you carry around, don't you — one that Great Grandma wrote."

Muzz caught her breath. "Sometimes I can't believe how much you know about me. How did you know that?"

"The knowing just happens, usually with someone I'm close to. I realize it's strange. But... I have an idea — a way to help you find Jerith again — that might work." She reached out. "Hand me the card, will you?"

Muzz took it from the hem of her shawl and handed it to Thea.

"I'm going to write something on it and include today's date. Tomorrow night when we go to sleep and dream, I want you to hold it tight. In fact, we'll string it around your wrist. When you see the message, no matter where you wake up, you'll want to do what it tells you."

She took out a pen, wrote on the card, and gave it back to Muzz. All it said was, *Remember to ask Grandma about Jerith*, and the day's date.

"Oh, my!" said Muzz when she read it. "Do you think that'll work?"

Thea grinned. "I hope so and, yes, I do think so. Our names may have changed, especially yours because it's a Hepu name. And when we return to the present, let's hope there's no reason for anyone to live in a cave or be covered with froose."

"What will my name be?"

Thea laughed. "I won't hazard a guess about that. But if you have the card strung round your arm, it should travel right along with you to 2010 and back to now. If I'm right, I'll still be your grandmother, and I'll know enough to explain what this note means. Let's hope so, anyway."

"Where do you think we'll be, then, Jerith and I?"

"You'll just have to see. Someplace nice, I hope, and someplace better."

When Thea and Muzz returned from town, a red light was blinking on the Infrareader. "Maybe Great Grandma has more ideas about dream travel. Stay and hear what she has to say."

But when they contacted Mrs. Whitford, she said, "Oh, Thea, I'm so glad I reached you. The Beacons raided the Highers' family grottoettes and found that plan of Jeeklo's in among Chell's things. A little before lightdown a posse of cave guards arrested Jeeklo and Chell."

"Oh, no! Where have they taken them?" asked Thea.

"Somewhere in the Forbidden Tunnel. At least that's what Tendra thinks. Now get this: When she came back to tell me the bad news, she said the rest of the Highers had changed their minds. They want to learn to dive.

Thea nodded. "This must have put a real scare into them."

"And me," said Mrs. Whitford. "But not enough to stop me. Starting tomorrow, I'm going to teach them a few at a time so we don't draw any attention."

"Poor Chell!" Muzz exclaimed.

Thea had been standing so that Mrs. Whitford could not see Muzz, but now she nodded and moved to one side.

"Muzz, dear, you heard all this? You must be so worried. Everyone here is, too."

"What's going to happen to Chell and Jeeklo?" It bothered Muzz that her voice broke when she asked that.

"It's still too early to tell."

There was a knock on Mrs. Whitford's door and without turning anything off, she covered the screen with her lovely painting by the person named Monet, which blocked Muzz and Thea's view. They heard muffled female voices. Thea switched to the overview, and there stood Muzz's mother.

She was slumped as if the wind had been knocked out of her, her head hair was hanging in drab clumps, and her face looked haggard. *Poor mother!*

The only word Muzz caught was 'cull." Pronouncing it made her mother wring her hands.

Mrs. Whitford gave her a long hug, asked her something. She closed her eyes and shook her head and, as quickly as she had come, vanished into the tunnel again.

Mrs. Whitford returned to the Infrareader shaking her head. "There's talk of culling, Muzz, just as you predicted," said Mrs. Whitford. "And your mother had a horrible dream that Chell was culled. But I doubt it will happen. There's a lot of resistance. This time your father has joined forces with Jeeklo's. Both of them are refusing to take the arrests lying down, and a large group of adults supports their demand to free the two young males."

On the following morning, after too little real sleep, Muzz returned to Thea's room for an update. Most of the next day in the Cave had happened by then. Many of the Highers had already become divers and Tendra, their new leader, had postponed their revolt indefinitely.

"Great Grandma and I think the time travel is more urgent than ever because of all this," Thea told her.

Muzz knew they were right. Everything seemed to be happening at once, and there was no way she could think of to slow it all down. She nibbled at her meals, took long silent walks, punched a hole in her card and looped a string through, made sure it would stay on her wrist, thought deeply about Chell, her mother and the oppressive mood in the Cave, consoled herself a little by making bread with Alok in the afternoon.

Watching the bread rise and then punching it flat again felt somehow reassuring. So did sprinkling it with cinnamon. The dough smelled so good, and the baking bread even better, and by evening she was eating some, and had more or less accepted what she was about to do.

CHAPTER TWENTY-FOUR

Even so, midnight rolled around too soon for her. But there she was, her card fastened to her wrist, knocking on Thea's door. *Maybe for the last time.*

Thea let Muzz in with a finger on her lips. When they were well inside the room, she whispered, "It's better that no one else knows about this. No use getting people's hopes up — or their fears — in case it doesn't work. And if it does, well..." She shrugged as if to say there was no telling where that would lead.

When they reached the Infrareader, Mrs. Whitford was peering through, her eyes brimming with excitement. "Muzz, dearest," she whispered, "I'm so glad to see you. I'm more proud of you than you can imagine. Actually of both of you."

Thea cast Muzz a bright smile and squeezed her hand. "It's for certain. I'm coming with you. Here, take your vitamin B." She gave Muzz an orange pill and a glass of water, and downed her own right when Muzz took hers. Muzz had a little trouble swallowing. *Nerves,* she thought. *Calm them.* She got the vitamin down.

Thea's face took on a serious expression. "You need to know, Muzz, that I'm coming because there may be some snags and, if so, I want to be there to help."

Something clicked inside Muzz. She was surprised at how coolly she accepted Thea's comment. She knew right then that what she had started by shouting "no!" and running more than a year before was just about complete. She was all determination. *Either this will work or it won't. Either I'll be back here, or I won't. If I do my part as best I can, that's all I can do. And for now, that's all that matters.*

"Tell me what you mean by 'snags.'" Muzz lowered herself to a cushion and calmly waited to hear.

"Well, we need to be asleep when Betty is. That's the first thing. And then we can't control whether we're all dreaming simultaneously or not. So that's an issue. Our dreams need to overlap long enough for all three of us to get in sync. Does that make sense?"

Muzz thought that over and said it did.

"But there's another thing I faced the first time: When I floated into Betty's dream, for some reason I was almost caught in there. I had trouble getting out."

"I see," said Muzz. *But I'm still calm.* "What do you think happened?"

Thea considered that. "I think she liked me. Yes. I think she liked me so much that she didn't want to let me go. I felt as if she was trying to hold onto me."

Muzz grinned. "Can you blame her for that?"

"Ha! Whatever the reason, I had to force my way out. I'm thinking if something like that happens again, it'll be better to have two of us there to help free each other."

Muzz nodded. Her face felt open and clear. "I get what you're saying... and I'm much glad you're coming with me. I'm ready whenever you are." *It's as if nothing can stop us. I hope I'm right.*

"Good," Thea told her and turned to Mrs. Whitford on the screen. "Bye-bye, Mother. We're off to 2010."

Using both hands, Mrs. Whitford blew about a dozen kisses, which they returned. "Bon voyage!" she cried just before Thea switched off the screen.

Thea took a deep breath and turned to Muzz. "I'm proud of you, too," she said. She and Muzz gave each other one last powerful hug. "Let's go!"

Soon after that, they were lying side by side in a couple of beds in a room down the hall from Thea's, both of them waiting to fall asleep. The room they were in was small and completely dark. For some reason, Thea had asked Alok to sleep in the room next to them, and Muzz could hear him snoring softly.

She closed her eyes and waited. Her bed was comfortable, a window was slightly open to let in fresh air, and Thea had switched on some music so soft that Muzz had to strain to hear it. It was some kind of chanting, and she listened and listened to it, thinking she might never doze off. And then...

I am floating, floating, I don't know where or how. But I am going, going, and I am not alone. Someone has my hand — Thea's gentle touch. I look up and see her exquisite eyes, and we are floating somewhere together, holding hands.

Where are we now? Is it a sunlit place with trees all around? No, the sun has set. The moon is rising over a mountaintop and shines into a room where soft music sends another female to sleep, a woman.

I strain to hear the music, all three of us do, and then — floating, floating — our dreams begin to braid together.

As one we zoom high above a coast to a place with dunes, crashing surf, pastel colored rooftops. I understand the name of the place. Mon... Mon... Monterey. Betty's dreaming herself into a new home. Yes, this is Betty. She doesn't know our names. She doesn't quite know we are with her. Her dream home beside the ocean is nestled in a stretch of beige dunes. She goes inside, walks upstairs, and we go with her. There are three of us, a braid of three.

Upstairs Betty finds a large, well-equipped room — a studio for making music, pictures, stories, poems — all her favorites. She looks around, checks work spaces and equipment, seems to think it is 'all there.' Satisfied, she floats downstairs again and we float with her.

And then, there it is! Beneath the staircase waits a small, irresistible door. Betty opens it, and it reveals some sort of tunnel or trough in the dunes, very deep and narrow, with a thin ribbon of pale blue sky overhead. She and I walk through the deep, narrow trough in the sand. Thea has let go of my hand. Rooms begin to form on either side sculpted in the sand. I float alone into the third room and wait there for Betty in my best wraparound, my beads, my shawl. When she looks inside and sees me, she is startled. I walk to her and join her. I see how much we look alike. She seems to trust me; we exchange thoughts without words. We pass many more rooms with creatures in them, female Hepus wearing breeding beads and their favorite wraparounds — Mother, Tendra, Martrell, and many others are here. 'Creatures' is Betty's word. She is amazed and, somehow, so am I. But we keep on walking past room after room. She turns to me with a wordless query. Her eyes ask, "Who's in charge here?"

I grasp her hand and we float-walk together further along the trough, which is slowly becoming a tunnel. At the furthest end in the furthest room, we find Thea waiting. I know right away she is the leader, so I stop at the door and Betty goes in. I see that Thea also cannot speak. It is a mystery why none of us can speak. Thea stands behind a tall, dark object — an Infrareader — something Betty does not recognize. Betty glances all around.

I am inside Betty now, gazing through her eyes at Thea. She moves closer and Thea holds her hands out in a gesture of welcome. Betty moves close enough to see into Thea's fathomless, special eyes. Thea cannot speak, but her hands, her face, her whole self plead for something.

"Please help us" is the thought they convey. Betty moves close enough to see the froose on Thea's face. She reaches out to touch it, so surprised that she almost wakes up and...

Where am I now? Floating over a sleeping Betty. Bobbing, caught like a balloon on a string. "Help, please help," I whisper, and hands reach for me. Thea's hands. "She's not letting us go." But Thea is insistent, pulling, tugging to break the string. "There!" she says and...

"Hey, Zoey? Zoe! You're making weird little noises."

Zoey blinked, reached out, felt the warmth and softness of sand.

She groaned, turned toward the voice, and rubbed her eyes. "Where are we?"

Her brother Alex, sitting on the blanket beside her, doubled up with laughter. "Exactly where we were when you fell asleep. At the beach, and not just any beach." He threw out his arms. "Look! Now do you remember where we are?"

Zoey blinked at the stretch of sand with foamy waves. She heard the muted thud as they rolled in, and something else. Someone calling in another language. *We're not in London anymore.* She stretched, groaned, grimaced at Alex, inhaled the fresh salt air. "Barcelona, you pain in the bum! We're on a beach near Barcelona, aren't we? Something... de Mar."

"Sant Pol de Mar." Alex folded his arms with a mock-stern flourish. "And what day is it?"

Zoey closed her eyes, pointed her nose toward the sky, said nothing.

"Come on, say what day it is," he insisted.

Zoey made a face and sighed. "January 4th," she said flatly.

"And what's tomorrow?"

"You sound like Mrs. Bainwright from the second form, you jolterhead."

Alex puffed himself up and batted his eyelashes at the near empty beach around them. "Tell me, children, what spiffy celebration will we be attending tomorrow evening?"

Suddenly Zoey felt into it. "The Fiesta de Los Reyes... the Three Kings! Hooray!" She held out her hand and patted the sun-warmed sand at the edge of the blanket. "What a great day. It smells divine here." She yawned. "And I can't believe how warm the sun is. I mean, it's *winter.*"

Alex laughed. "Of course you're speaking from inside a blanket sandwich."

It was true. She had spread her blanket on a sunny patch of beach, and Zoey saw that while she was sleeping Alex had covered her with his. She gripped it, drew it around her neck for added warmth, closed her eyes again, and mumbled, "Beachy."

"Beachy? Do you realize you just said 'beachy'?"

Zoey shook her head and laughed. "Did I say that? I meant 'peachy'. I must have drifted off again. Peachy." She stretched and blinked at Alex. "Before you woke me up, I was having a really interesting, peculiar dream."

Alex was staring at one of her arms. "What's that on your wrist?" he wanted to know.

Zoey looked where he was pointing. Sure enough, something was dangling from her wrist. She pulled it off, examined it, scrunched up her face. It was an old card she had found once and kept. But how or why she had it with her, she did not know.

Alex held out his hand. "Let me see that, then."

She shrugged, sat up and gave it to him, sighed sharply. "I really don't know how it got here. I thought it was at home in my junk drawer, or lost or something. I think I kept it for the pretty bird. Wait! You slipped it on my arm while I was sleeping, didn't you!"

"No way. You must have packed it and brought it with you."

Zoey touched her head and shook it. "Hmmm..." She lay back down, turned toward Alex, and propped herself on her elbow to observe him better. "Read it to me, will you?"

"Okay, let's see. Odd... it's some card Great Grandma Whitford sent years ago. It says, 'Wish you were here. Merry Christmas to all you dear ones. Love, Millie.'" He grinned fondly. "Millie's a cute, old-fashioned name, isn't it?" Alex tossed the card next to his flip-flops on the sand.

"The card. Give it back," Zoey told him.

But Alex was in no hurry. He picked the card up again and examined it in a deliberate, teasing sort of way. Then he frowned. "What's this?"

He crossed his legs, read in an official sounding voice. "There's a note on it that says, 'Remember to ask Grandma about Jerith.' Jerith? What's *that* supposed to mean?"

Zoey felt an odd stirring and a faint glimmer of something she could not quite recall. "Here, give it to me. C'mon, you're so annoying. Let me see it." She swiped the card from his hand and read it herself. Then she tossed it on her towel and shook her head. "Jerith... Jerith? I haven't a clue."

Alex chuckled. "Oh yes, you do. It says, 'Ask Grandma.'" He grinned at her and shrugged. "So do it. Next time you see her, ask."

Zoey took the card and reread the note. "Oh, wait, *this* is weird," she said. "It's dated yesterday, see? January 3, 2103."

She sat up and held it out to Alex, who took it. She dropped her hand. "Oh, I get it. I'm sure now." She pointed at him. "You did do this to trick me, didn't you! I mean, we haven't seen Grandma for over a week. She couldn't possibly have written this. You did it. You did it to mess with my mind."

But Alex was on his feet, hardly listening. A news report in Spanish blared from a distant radio. *Hope it's nothing serious*, she told herself.

Alex smiled faintly and looked around. "Spain!" he sighed, sweeping his hands as if to scoop up the whole beach and hold it.

He turned to her. "Now, Ms. Zoey, are you going to stop accusing me of nonsense long enough to take a walk up the beach, or what?"

Zoey studied the wide, curved sweep of sand, the hill beyond it. She blinked at a nearby family — the only others on the beach — chattering so fast in Spanish that she could hardly catch a word. The pretty dark-haired mother was laughing while her husband and two small sons buried all but her smiling face. Their winter clothes were caked with sand.

It dawned on her that Alex might be telling the truth about the card, so she tucked it into her daypack. *I'll ask Grandma when we get back to London. She must have written the wrong date. That's all.*

She stood and brushed off some sand. "Sure. I'll walk if there's time. What time is it anyway?"

"Relax, will you? Sheldon isn't due for over three hours. There's plenty of time to take a walk, get some food to stave off starvation, hop the train back to the hotel, shower and dress. All before he arrives. And that's if his plane's on time."

Alex folded his blanket and stowed it, and so did Zoey. She threaded her arms through the loops of her daypack and slung it on her back. He did the same. *Yes,* she thought, *there will be some perfectly good explanation for Grandma's note having that strange name and impossible date.*

Zoey turned her attention to more pleasurable thoughts. The beach was lovely, the pale winter sun a delight, her other half brother due to arrive in just a few hours. Barcelona was one of the nicest places she could think of. The parade of the Kings would take place the following night. Somehow at that moment, despite its many troubles, the world and all it held really did strike her as peachy.

———

19114332R00098

Made in the USA
Lexington, KY
06 December 2012